Also available from Cole M░░░░░
and Carina Press

The Criminal Intentions Serial
The Blossom + Bite Series
The Crash Into Me Series
The Undue Arrogance/Cocky Series
Over and Over Again
Pinups

Writing as Xen

Shatterproof
From the Ashes
The Whites of Their Eyes
Sweet Vermouth
Cracks

Some content in *Just Like That* may be triggering for some readers, due to depiction of trauma or other topics that may be difficult to read. Content warnings for this story include the following:

- A main character dealing with the death of a spouse, including grief, guilt and PTSD flashbacks.

- A main character with chronic anxiety, including graphic depictions of panic attacks and anxiety reactions with physical responses.

- A main character with a dead parent.

- Graphic depictions of nightmares involving drowning.

- Brief mention of suicidal ideation.

- A subplot that seems to depict the tragic death of two queer characters.

- Use of derogatory Japanese slurs toward mixed-race people, by a character and directed at himself.

- Penetrative cis male/cis male sex without a condom, and including exchange of bodily fluids.

- A relationship that includes multiple uneven power-exchange dynamics, including May/December, mild hints of D/s kink with breathplay and senior/junior employee.

- Depiction of bullying between high school age boys, including brawling and extreme methods of harassment, specifically recollection of urinating in a sports drink.

- Depiction of neglectful parents and their impact on the students.

- A moment in which both main characters recklessly endanger themselves for the sake of their relationship and each other, with the threat of drowning involved. (It's their TSTL moment for the drama, y'all. Just let it be what it is.)

As always, if you feel you can't handle these subjects, I'd rather you put the book down and walk away than hurt yourself.

And as always...

Take care of yourselves, loves.

JUST LIKE THAT

COLE MCCADE

carina
press

carina
press®

Recycling programs
for this product may
not exist in your area.

ISBN-13: 978-1-335-14645-8

Just Like That

This edition published by arrangement with Harlequin Books S.A.

For questions and comments about the quality of this book, please contact us at
CustomerService@Harlequin.com.

Carina Press
22 Adelaide St. West, 40th Floor
Toronto, Ontario M5H 4E3, Canada
www.CarinaPress.com

Printed in U.S.A.

I haven't met you yet.

But this is for you.

JUST LIKE THAT

Chapter One

Albin Academy was on fire.

Summer Hemlock saw the plume of smoke before he saw the school itself—just a thick coil of black puffing up into the cloud-locked sky, spiraling above the forest of thin, wispy paper birches that segregated Albin from the rest of the town. He ground his rental car to a halt at the foot of the hill and clambered out, staring up the winding lane... then over his shoulder, at the clustered handful of shingle-roofed houses and stores that barely qualified as a town.

No sign of alarm from the Omen police department. No fire trucks lighting up and screaming out into the streets.

With a groan, Summer *thunk*ed his forehead against the top of the Acura's door.

Business as usual at the boarding school, then.

He guessed seven years away hadn't changed a thing.

He climbed back into the Acura and sent it coasting forward once more, struggling with the gear shift on the steep hill and the narrow lane that crawled its way up the slope. Thin fingers of branches kissed their tips across the road to create a tunneled archway, a throat that spilled him from the lane and into the academy's front courtyard.

He remembered, as a boy, walking up this lane every morning as the only local who attended the academy, the thick layer of mist that seemed a staple of Massachusetts mornings coming up to his shoulders, making his uniform cling to him damply. He'd always been a little scared, on those walks. Something about the fog, the thin black trees, the *silence* of it, where he could hear his own lonely footsteps on the pavement and imagine them echoed back by some strange ghost in the woods.

Maybe the ghost of Isabella of the Lake, the drowned girl who haunted the rowing pond behind the school.

Or maybe just his imagination, chasing him with all the fears he hadn't been able to face.

At the moment, though, he was driven less by fear and more by resigned curiosity as he forced the Acura to make the steep ascent. By the time he pulled into the courtyard, the plume of smoke had turned into a brooding cloud hovering over the school, wreathing its pointed spires in ominous black. Most if it seemed to be coming from one upstairs window in the front west tower, the pane pulled up to let the smoke escape.

The entire courtyard was crowded with teenage boys, all of them lounging about in loosely knotted groups. They wore ennui like cologne, draping it around them as casually as their expensively tailored uniforms—and utterly uninterested in both the burning school, and the harried-looking teachers trying to shepherd them away from it.

Maybe Summer was a little weird.

Because the chaos of it was a familiar, bittersweet ache of homecoming, and it made him smile.

He stole an empty parking slot, cut the engine, and slipped out to weave through the crowd, holding his breath against the stink of chemical fumes on the biting early spring air. As he pulled the front door open, a severe-looking man in a navy blue suit—someone new, Summer thought, no one he recognized—reached for his arm.

Without even thinking, Summer stepped back out of pure instinctive habit, pulling out of arm's reach and edging past the man.

Until he was forced to stop, as the man stepped in front of him, blocking the door.

"Excuse me, sir." The man looked at him coldly through half-rim glasses. "Visitors are not allowed at the moment. In case you can't see, we're in the middle of an emergency."

Summer smiled, not quite meeting the man's eyes. It made him uncomfortable, always, this feeling like people were crawling inside his skin with a single stare—but most never noticed that he was looking right over their shoulders, instead. "It's okay," he said. "I work here. And I'm used to Dr. Liu's explosions. I'm just gonna grab a fire extinguisher and help."

The man just blinked at him, cocking his head with a quizzical frown.

So Summer stole his opportunity and slipped inside, just

barely managing to squeeze past the suit-clad man without touching.

He barely had a moment to register the disorienting feeling of familiarity—as if he'd traveled back in time, back to that rawboned thin pale boy he'd been, walking into the eerily quiet, high-ceilinged entry chamber of dark paneled wood and tall windows with his shoulders hunched and head bowed—before he vaulted up one side of the double stairway, taking the steps two at a time, and dashed for the northwest wing. The smell of bitterly acidic smoke led him on, beckoning him through vaulted corridors where the air grew thicker and thicker, until the murk fogged everything gray and stung his eyes.

Coughing, he pulled the collar of his button-down up over his mouth, breathing through the cloth and squinting. Just up ahead, he could barely make out a few shapes moving in the hallway—but a familiar voice rang down the hall, low and dry and authoritative, this thing of velvet and grit and cool autumn nights.

"Extinguisher first, then sand," the voice ordered. "Dr. Liu, if you insist on getting in the way, at least make yourself useful and remove anything *else* flammable from the vicinity of the blaze. Quickly, now. Keep your mouths covered."

Summer's entire body tingled, prickled, as if his skin had drawn too tight. That voice—that voice brought back too many memories. Afternoons in his psychology elective class, staring down at his textbook and doodling in his notebook and refusing to look up, to look *at* anyone, while that voice washed over him for an hour. Summer knew that voice almost better than the face attached to it, every inflection and cadence, the way it could command silence with a quiet word more effectively than any shout.

And how sometimes it seemed more expressive than the cold, withdrawn expression of the man he remembered, standing tall and stern in front of a class of boys who were all just a little bit afraid of him.

Summer had never been afraid, not really.

But he hadn't had the courage to whisper to himself what he'd really felt, when he'd been a hopeless boy who'd done everything he could to be invisible.

Heart beating harder, he followed the sound of that voice to the open doorway of a smoke-filled room, the entire chemistry lab a haze of gray and black and crackling orange; from what he could tell a table was...on fire? Or at least the substance inside a blackened beaker was on fire, belching out a seemingly never-ending, impossible billow of smoke and flame.

Several smaller fires burned throughout the room; it looked as though sparks had jumped to catch on notebooks, papers, books. Several indistinct shapes alternately sprayed the conflagration with fire extinguishers and doused it with little hand buckets of sand from the emergency kit in the corner of the room, everyone working clumsily one-handed while they held wet paper towels over their noses and mouths with the other.

And standing tall over them all—several teachers and older students, it looked like—was the one man Summer had returned to Omen to see.

Professor Iseya.

He stood head and shoulders above the rest, his broad-shouldered, leanly angular frame as proud as a battle standard, elegant in a trim white button-down tucked into dark gray slacks, suspenders striping in neat black lines down his chest. Behind slim glasses, his pale, sharply angled gray eyes flicked swiftly over the room, set in a narrow, graceful face that had only weathered with age into an ivory mask of quiet, aloof beauty.

The sleek slick of his ink-black hair was pulled back from his face as always—but as always, he could never quite keep the soft strands inside their tie, and several wisped free to frame his face, lay against his long, smooth neck, pour down his shoulders and back. He held a damp paper towel over his mouth, neatly folded into a square, and spoke through it to direct the frazzled-looking group with consummate calm, taking complete control of the situation.

And complete control of Summer, as Iseya's gaze abruptly snapped to him, locking on him from across the room. "Why have you not evacuated?" Iseya demanded coldly, his words precise, inflected with a softly cultured accent. "Please vacate the premises until we've contained the blaze."

Summer dropped his eyes immediately—habit, staring down at his feet. "Oh, um—I came to help," he mumbled through the collar of his shirt.

A pause, then, "You're not a student. Who are you?"

That shouldn't sting.

But then it had been seven years, he'd only been in two of Iseya's classes...and he'd changed, since he'd left Omen.

At least, he hoped he had.

That was why he'd run away, after all. To shake off the

boy he'd been; to find himself in a big city like Baltimore, and maybe, just maybe…

Learn not to be so afraid.

But he almost couldn't bring himself to speak, while the silence demanded an answer. "I'm not a student *anymore*," he corrected, almost under his breath. "It's…it's me. Summer. Summer Hemlock. Your new TA." He made himself look up, even if he didn't raise his head, peeking at Iseya through the wreathing of smoke that made the man look like some strange and ghostly figure, this ethereal spirit swirled in mist and darkness. "Hi, Professor Iseya. Hi."

Fox Iseya narrowed his eyes at the young man in the doorway.

He had nearly forgotten his new TA would be arriving today—or, more truthfully, he had put it out of his mind, when he was not particularly looking forward to training and shepherding an inept and inexperienced fresh university graduate in handling the fractious, contentious group of spoiled degenerates that made up the majority of Albin's student body. He only needed a TA to ensure his replacement would be properly trained when he retired. Otherwise, having a second presence in the classroom was little more than an unwanted but unfortunately necessary nuisance.

The nuisance he had been expecting, however, was not the man standing awkwardly in the doorway, face half-obscured by the collar of his shirt.

The Summer Hemlock he remembered had been a gangly teenager, so pale he was nearly translucent, all angles and elbows everywhere. Fox recalled seeing more of the top of his head than anything else, a shaggy mop of black falling to hide blue eyes and a fresh, open face; he'd always huddled in his desk with his head bowed, and mumbled inaudible things when called on in class.

The young man in front of him almost mirrored that posture…but that was where the resemblance ended.

Summer was tall and athletic now, a lithe runner's build outlined against his dress shirt and low-slung jeans; pale skin had darkened to a glowing, sunny tan that stood out vibrant even in the smoke-filled murk of the room. The lank mess of his hair had been tamed into a stylishly bed-headed tousle, perhaps in need of a trim but framing his face and rather strong jaw attractively. Too-wide, nervous blue eyes had deepened, shaded by firmly decisive brows.

Considering that Fox guided his students through to senior graduation and rarely ever saw them again, it was rather bizarre to contrast the boy he had taught with the man who had apparently come to take Fox's place, when he retired next year.

But right now, he didn't have time to think about that.

Not when Dr. Liu was currently racking up exponential increases in charges for property damage.

Fox flicked two fingers, beckoning. "Sand. Join the chain. Let's do our best to keep this contained."

Summer's head came up sharply, and he looked at Fox for a single wide-eyed moment—and that drove home that sense of bizarrely unfamiliar familiarity, when Fox recalled quite clearly that direct eye contact could turn the boy into a stammering wreck, cringing and retreating. That moment of locked gazes lasted for only a second, before Summer nodded quickly and averted his eyes.

"Of course, sir—yes."

Summer strode forward swiftly on long legs, and skirted around Fox to pick up a bucket and scoop up sand from the massive black trash bin that had been repurposed specifically to deal with Dr. Liu's regrettably frequent "accidents." The man was a nightmare and a half, and Fox supposed they could consider themselves lucky it had been two months since the last time the good doctor had practically burned the school down.

But they were running out of empty classrooms to repurpose for chemistry lessons while previously damaged rooms were repaired, and Fox intended to have *words* at the next faculty meeting.

Honestly, he didn't understand how Dr. Liu still had a job.

And he quite firmly directed the chemistry teacher out of the way once more, as he returned to marshalling the emergency response group to put out the secondary fires that had erupted from jumping embers and ample fuel throughout the room. Fortunately this was rather a practiced habit, at this point—and within twenty minutes the blaze was contained, the last of it smothered beneath sand and fire extinguisher foam. They had, regrettably, learned years ago that Liu frequently worked with substances that only burned hotter when doused with water.

At Albin, the students weren't the only ones who often had to learn from experience.

Yet throughout the suppression efforts, Fox repeatedly

found his gaze straying toward Summer. His apparent shyness had vanished the moment he dove into the fray, joining the others rather energetically and hauling bucket after bucket of sand to chase down one sparking blaze after the other before it could get out of control.

By the time the clouds of smoke began to thin, Summer was a mess—his once-white shirt smeared with soot and ash, streaks of it along his cheeks and jaw, underscoring one eye in a rakish dash like face paint. But he was laughing, as he helped an older student shovel sodden, charred remnants of notebooks into a trash bag.

But the moment Fox called, "Mr. Hemlock," Summer went stiff, every bit of ease bleeding out of his body to leave his back rigid and his shoulders tight.

Hm.

Interesting.

Summer glanced over his shoulder, looking toward Fox but not quite *at* him. "Yes, Professor Iseya?"

"Leave the cleanup to Dr. Liu. It's the least he can do to compensate for his crimes."

"Hey!" came from the corner Liu had sequestered himself in. Fox ignored him, crooking a finger at Summer.

"If you've brought your possessions, fetch them. You can use my suite to clean up and change. We have matters to discuss."

Summer ducked his head, scrubbing his hands against his jeans. Beneath the smears of soot streaking pronounced cheekbones, tanned skin turned a decided shade of pink. He nodded quietly, obediently.

"Yes, Professor Iseya."

Fox frowned. There was something...*off* about Summer's furtive behavior, something more than just a reticence he clearly hadn't shaken over seven years away from Omen and Albin Academy.

It didn't matter.

Summer's demons were Summer's demons, and Fox wasn't staying at the school long enough to figure them out.

Fox waited only long enough for Summer to retrieve his suitcase from his car, then retreated to his private suite in the southwest tower. While he let Summer have the run of the bathroom, Fox wiped off his face, washed his hands, and changed into a clean shirt, slacks, and waistcoat, then settled in the easy chair in the living room to wait; to keep himself busy he flipped to his last page marker in the absolutely abysmal Jordan Peterson book he was forcing himself to read for a class exercise.

Pop psychology, all of it, based in flawed and inhumane principles, but it provided an interesting exercise in logical fallacies and poor application of outdated psychological principles; examples he could use to demonstrate poor reasoning to students as a caution against falling into the same traps. He underlined another passage riddled with subjective bias in red, and jotted down a few notes on his legal pad, idly listening as the shower shut off with a faint squeak and an ending of the quiet, rain-like sounds of water striking tile.

A few moments later Summer emerged, steaming and still dripping, a pale gray T-shirt clinging damply to his chest and slim waist, a fresh pair of jeans slouching on narrow hips. He scrubbed a towel through his messy wet hair and peeked at Fox from under the tangle of it in that *way* he had, offering a sheepish smile.

"Sorry," he said. "Not really up to dress code, but technically I'm not checking in for work just yet."

"I hardly think you need to worry about work attire in my living room." Fox pointed his pen at the plush easy chair adjacent to the sofa. "Sit."

Like an obedient puppy, Summer dropped down into the chair, resting his hands on his knees. "Thank you for accepting my application."

"Your qualifications met the requirements, and as a former student you're familiar with the school, the curriculum, and the standards of my classes." Fox crossed his legs, tapping his pen against his lower lip, studying Summer thoughtfully. "However, I don't think you're suited to teach."

"Wh-what?" Summer's gaze flew up quickly, then darted away. "Then why did you accept me as your assistant?"

"No one else applied." Fox arched a brow. "Look me in the eye."

Immediately, Summer bowed his head, staring fixedly at his knees. "Why?"

"You cannot, can you?"

"Does it matter?" Summer threw back, biting his lip and turning his face to the side.

"It matters." Fox set his pen, notepad, and atrocious tome aside to lean forward, resting his hands on his knees and lacing his fingers together. The longer he watched Summer, the more uncomfortable the young man seemed to grow, sinking down into his shoulders and curling his fingers slowly until they dug up the denim of his jeans in little divots. "Do you recall why most parents send their sons to Albin Academy, Mr. Hemlock?"

"Because…" Barely a murmur. "Because they're rich and horrible and don't want to deal with their problem children themselves, so they ship them off where no one can see them?"

"That is a more crass explanation of our function here, yes," Fox said dryly. "The point is that these boys have no respect for authority—and while we are not their parents or their disciplinarians, we do at least have to maintain the appropriate seniority and boundaries to keep them out of trouble. They will push those boundaries at every turn, and considering you haven't changed a bit from when *you* were a student… I don't think you're capable of dealing with that."

"That's not fair!" Summer protested. "I'm not a kid anymore. You don't know me. You've spent all of five minutes talking to me."

"One can generally make an accurate psychological assessment in less."

"Well, your assessment of me is wrong." Summer's jaw tightened. "I can do this job. And since you accepted me, you can at least give me a chance before telling me how much I suck."

So there was something of a backbone there, Fox thought—and wondered just what it was that had made Summer so shy, so withdrawn. Leaning back, he steepled his fingers. "You interviewed with Principal Chambers, did you not?"

"Y-yeah." Summer nodded.

"And what did he tell you?"

"That no one else wanted the job." Summer smiled faintly. He had a soft, sad mouth that seemed ill-used to smiling, yet was haunted by a perpetual ghost of warmth nonetheless. "And that my mother must be happy to have me back home."

"Are you?"

"Am I what?"

"Happy to be here."

"I…" There—an almost imperceptible flinch. "She needed me here. She's not young anymore, and it'll be better for her if I'm close by to help."

That, Fox thought, was not an answer. It was a reason, but not an answer to the actual question he had asked. He pressed his lips together, tapping his fingertips to his knuckles.

"I have a proposition for you," he said. "We can call it a training exercise, or a psychological experiment—whichever suits you."

"Am I a TA or a test subject?"

"Both, perhaps." Fox tucked a loose lock of hair behind his ear. Irritating mess; he always meant to cut it, and yet… He let his gaze drift to the mantle. The butsudan resting there, its deep-polished rosewood glinting in the afternoon light drifting through the windows, its doors currently closed and its contents private…as they should be. Tearing his gaze away, he made himself focus on Summer. "Once per day, I expect you to do something outside your comfort zone. Challenge yourself to take on a role as a leader, or mentor. Challenge yourself to approach this job with confidence, rather than asking permission to do what you must do. If you cannot learn to be bold, Mr. Hemlock, at the very least learn to fake it in the necessary environments so that your knees knocking together do not drown out the lesson you are trying to deliver."

Summer's lips twitched faintly. "Pavlovian conditioning is a little 101 level, sir. Are you trying to make me assert my own authority?"

"I'm not trying to *make* you do anything," Fox replied. "My only goal is to see if you can take the steps needed to face down a classroom of unruly, disrespectful children on your own. Do I need to hold your hand in that, or do you feel capable of attempting it under your own impetus?"

Summer plucked at his jeans. "The children don't scare me."

"Oh? Then what does?"

No answer. Simply a heavy silence, fraught with meaning, and yet—for all his understanding of psychology, of psychiatry, of the small markers that gave away intent and thought and emotion… Fox couldn't quite read what that meaning might be. Not when the Summer he had known as a boy was necessarily a stranger to him, with the appropriate distance between teacher and student; not when the Summer he saw now was a new person, shaped by years of experiences Fox as yet had no insight into, and technically stood on almost equal footing as his peer and assistant.

And if he were honest with himself…no matter how he tried, no matter what clinical understanding he possessed…

He somehow always felt at one remove from other peo-

ple's feelings, observing them and yet never quite understanding them, the soul of his own emotions locked away.

Summer took a deep, slow breath, his shoulders rising
and falling. "Every day? Does that include today?"

"You don't technically start work until Monday, so you
may take the weekend to consider, if you'd like," Fox said.
"Or you may start today. But that is still not an answer as
to what frightens you."

"Okay," Summer said shakily, rising to his feet with
wooden motions. "Okay then. I'll show you what scares
me."

He stepped rigidly across the living room, navigating
the low polished coffee table with an awkward bump of
his shins against the wood. Fox watched, brow raised, as
Summer drew closer to the couch—but startlement prickled down his arms in a rush like goosebumps and fine hairs
raising as Summer bent over him, bracing one hand to the
back of the sofa.

Before the young man captured Fox's chin, his jaw, in
roughened fingertips.

Tipped his face up.

And kissed him.

Chapter Two

Summer had no idea what he was doing.

He hadn't meant to kiss Professor Iseya. He'd just—he—after sitting there listening to Iseya list Summer's faults and remind Summer that he hadn't changed at all, something had risen up inside him. Something irritated, that whited out his thoughts and smothered his common sense until he wasn't really *choosing* to do anything; just reacting to provocation. If he wanted to look at it from a psychology perspective, Iseya had pricked at Summer's id.

Until it had bitten back.

But Freud had been a hack, and dissection of the psyche couldn't explain why Summer was bent over Professor Iseya with his mouth pressed hot against the man's and the taste of him on his lips.

Iseya's mouth was a stern thing of cruel sensuality, made

for whispering cold-edged, cutting words of emotionless logic with articulated precision, every curve and dip of his lips defined as if they'd been shaped by the razor of his tongue...but for just a moment, those lips went soft. Slack. A moment that shot through Summer with a wilding heat; a moment that charged him with a vibrant rush and made his entire body go so hot he felt as though he burned with every harsh draught of smoke he'd inhaled just minutes before.

He'd thought about this more times than he cared to admit, as a boy. Back when he'd been fascinated by the older man's frosty demeanor; by the glint of eyes a silver as pale and inscrutable as the forest's mist; by the controlled elegance in his minimalistic movements; by the quiet hint of command in his every gesture. When Summer had been a teenager, Professor Iseya had been a fantasy, out of reach, unreal.

Yet he was very much real, now.

Summer wasn't a boy anymore.

And the man whose mouth went fiery and firm against his own was very much not the icy caricature of his dreams.

That softening, that parting of Iseya's lips promised heat, promised more—and with a low sound Summer slanted his mouth against Iseya's, only for firm lips to lock and hold him, the lash of a rough tongue to whip him, his fingers curling and tingling with the sudden rush of warmth as Iseya's teeth grazed his mouth, teased him, left him shivering.

Until a hand pressed against his throat, seizing his breaths and stopping his heart.

He froze as long, firm fingers wrapped against his neck,

a heated palm pressing down on his pulse just hard enough for him to feel it; just hard enough to make his next breath come shallow and tight. His knees trembled, an odd, weakening sensation seeming to cut the strength from his limbs and leave his gut liquid-hot and tight as slowly, Iseya pushed him back. That one hand held him in complete thrall, controlling his every movement and keeping him trapped in place in silent command as Iseya parted their lips from each other.

Frigid eyes as pale as cracked ice fixed on Summer, piercing him. For all the breathless heat that had lived in that stolen moment…those eyes were cold enough to smother it, frostbite in every slowly spoken word.

"I," Iseya said softly, "would thank you not to be inappropriate, Mr. Hemlock. And if I am what frightens you… you have every reason to fear."

For just a half-second longer, Summer's focus remained on those lips—their redness, their fullness. On the pressure of that hand against his throat. On the confusing and aching feeling it roused inside him, taut and shaking and thrilling with something not quite fear at all.

Before it hit him just what he was *doing*, when he had never been so reckless or so forward in his *life*.

He flinched back, breaking free from Iseya's grip. The man regarded him coolly, utterly calm and unreadable, yet for the few breaths that Summer held his eyes he couldn't help but imagine judgment there.

Judgment…

And rejection.

Because Summer hadn't been back in Omen for a day

before he'd crossed a line, and proven he was still the same awkward, utterly hopeless boy he'd always been.

"S-sorry," he whispered, though it barely came out on a dry croak, his throat closing. "*Sorry*."

Iseya said nothing—and Summer didn't know what else *to* say.

He just knew he couldn't stay here, not when he felt as though his every shortcoming and failure, his every maladjustment and cowardice, were laid bare for that cutting silver gaze to dissect before discarding him as worthless.

And so "*S-sorry*," he stumbled over, one more time.

Before he bowed his head. Clenched his fists.

And ran.

He didn't stop until he was outside, and shut inside the safety of his rental car with at least the barrier of metal walls to hide him.

Clenching his hands against the steering wheel, Summer groaned and *thunk*ed his forehead against the leather of the upper curve—and then again and again, just for good measure.

What the hell, Summer.

What the hell, what the hell, what the hell.

His pulse was on fire, his entire body prickling as if a sunburn had crisped his skin to paper and left him feeling like he was going to split right out of it. He'd...he'd *kissed* Professor Iseya. Like he was still that same shy fumbling boy with a completely impossible crush, he'd kissed the man without so much as an if-you-please, and probably just fucked himself out of a job.

One more *thud* against the steering wheel, hard enough to make his temples throb.

Dammit.

He couldn't go back in there. Not today. He'd left his suitcase at Iseya's, but he'd wait until the man was in class Monday to get a janitor to let him in to retrieve it. Whether or not he'd be unpacking it in his faculty suite or looking for somewhere else to stay?

Would probably depend on if Iseya had him fired or not.

He'd deserve it if he did.

Welp.

At least if he was unemployed, he'd have more time to help his mother fix up a few things around the house.

And wouldn't have to worry about having an anxiety attack in front of two dozen staring, snickering boys.

Summer backed the Acura out of its parking slot and did a U-turn in the now-empty courtyard, the students already back inside and in class like nothing had ever happened, despite the fresh scorch marks on the upstairs wall and window frame. The drive down the high hill felt less ominous than the approach—every foot of space between himself and that mortifying moment of impulse letting him breathe a little easier, put it behind himself, tuck it away as something to be dealt with later.

The town at the bottom of the hill was still the same—cobbled roadways and colonial style homes, only the more modern shops, street lighting, and sidewalk bus stops reminding Omen of what century it was. Summer had always managed to find a way not to come back, even on holiday and summer breaks, instead flying his mother out to Baltimore when he wanted to see her; Omen had some-how always felt like its name, this ominous trap that would ensnare him in a life, a future, a *self* he'd never wanted to hold on to.

But he still remembered the way home—and he couldn't help but smile, as he pulled up outside his mother's house. The sunny little cottage hadn't changed, either, still over-grown with flowers everywhere. Daffodils nodded their sunny heads, while hollyhocks clustered around lavender and flowering azalea bushes; jasmine climbed the walls, dripping blooms whose fragrance nearly drowned him when he stepped out of the car, chasing away the last sting-ing scent of smoke in his nose. Little glass wind chimes and baubles hung in every tree and from every eave, catching the meager gray light and turning it into winking shards of color.

He'd barely made it past the wooden gate, stepping under the arch of the flowering bower overhead, before the front door opened and his mother came tumbling out. Small, round, Lily Hemlock was a compact bundle of energy swirled about by gauzy scarves, trailing her in a flutter of color as she nearly launched herself into him.

"*Summer.*"

He caught her with an *oof*, rocking back on his heels be-fore righting himself and wrapping her up in a tight hug. "Hi, Mom."

"I was wondering when you'd get in. You didn't call, you just—"

"Sorry. I stopped by the school first." He grinned wryly. "It's burning again."

"Oh, it's always burning. The fire chief doesn't even bother unless they actually call anymore."

She pulled back, gripping his arms and looking up at him with a measuring gaze, blue eyes bright against the dark twist of her hair; when had those jet-black locks started to fade to iron gray?

When had she become so *frail*, the bones of her hands pressing into his skin?

But her presence was still larger than life, as she gave him a once-over and clucked her tongue primly. "Look at you. Have you been eating? You're too thin."

He laughed, taking her arm and nudging her toward the door. "I'm twice the size I was in high school."

"And you were too thin in high school, too. Too thin times two is still too thin." Suddenly *she* was the one tugging *him*, and he let himself be marshalled along without protest. "Come. Sit. I've just finished baking."

Summer only smiled, as his mother practically dragged him inside. The house was as warm and open inside as it was the outside, all weathered, unvarnished wood everywhere and sprigs of herbs strung up along the walls and ceiling, the aromas of her latest concoctions making the entire house smell earthy and clean. Familiar. Safe.

And as she ushered him to a place at the kitchen table, he was finally able to *breathe* again.

Even if he had no appetite for the orange crème muffins she piled on a plate in front of him; he still wasn't going to tell her that, not when she watched him like a hawk.

"Go on," she said. "I know they're your favorite."

"And you made them just because I was coming home?"

He chuckled and picked off a bite of one steaming muffin, plucking it between his fingers. "Today's really not special, Mom. Within a week you'll be sick of having me underfoot."

"I could never." She dropped herself down into a chair opposite him, propping her chin in her hands and watching him fondly. "And knowing you, you'll probably still never be here what with living up at that school."

"It's mandatory. I've got to do my part as dorm monitor." He made himself swallow a bite; even if he'd loved his mother's orange crème muffins since he was old enough to talk, right now it tasted overly sweet, cloying, lodging in his still-tight throat. "Though I may just end up moving in with you and looking for a new job. I...uh... I kind of screwed up."

Her eyes sharpened. "Now how did you manage that when you've not even started yet?"

"...nothing. I didn't do anything."

"So you managed to screw up by not doing anything?" Her brows lifted mildly. "That's unlike you. Usually when you screw up, you're at least trying."

"Funny."

"Darling, what did you *do?*"

He winced. "...*IkissedProfessorIseya,*" he mumbled under his breath.

"Try that one more time, dear. With air."

"Oh *God.*" Summer let the muffin plunk back to the plate and dropped his face into his hands. "I kissed him. Professor Iseya. I just...kissed him."

His mother gasped. "*Fox* Iseya? Oh dear."

"...I don't think 'oh dear' really covers it."

She made an odd sound, before pressing her fingers to her mouth—but that didn't stop her lips from twitching at the corners. "Oh—oh, darling, I still remember you doodling his initials in your notebooks. And learning how to read those—what were those letters?"

"...hiragana..."

"...yes, that. Just so you could write his name the proper way."

"Oh my God, Mom, *stop.*" He pressed his burning cheeks into his palms, closed his eyes, and told his churning stomach to calm the hell down. "I was seventeen."

"And it was *adorable.*" She chuckled fondly. "But whatever possessed you to kiss him today?"

"He pissed me off."

"One, language. Two, *that* is highly unexpected, coming from you. My mild-mannered boy." She patted his hand, and he cracked one eye open on her warm, indulgent smile. "Three, most people don't kiss people when they're angry."

"Yeah, well, I'm weird. We've always known that." He sighed, dropping his hands and folding his arms on the table. "He didn't even give me a chance. He just told me I haven't changed and I'm not fit to teach a class, which makes me wonder why he even agreed to work with me. Then he challenged me to like...assert my authority or something just once every day, if I want to prove myself. So... I kissed him."

She clucked her tongue. "Well, that *is* certainly quite assertive."

"I can tell you're trying not to laugh." Groaning, he

dropped his head and thudded his brow against his forearm, burying his face in his arms. "Go on. Get it out."

"I wouldn't laugh at you, darling." Her small, warm hand rested to the top of his head, weaving into his hair... and it struck him with a quiet ache just how *weightless* her hands were, as if her bones had turned hollow as a bird's. "I take it, though, it didn't go over well."

"How did you guess?"

"Because it's Fox. Not because of you." His mother sighed gently and tucked his hair back with a lingering touch. "You were too young to know him before his wife died. We were actually fast friends, he and I, before he shut everyone out and isolated himself."

Professor Iseya's...wife? Summer lifted his head sharply, staring at his mother, his heart thumping in erratic sick-lurch rhythm. "He was married?"

"For some time when he was close to your age, yes." She smiled, blue eyes dark, soft. "He was really the kindest, sweetest man...but when he lost Michiko, well..." She shook her head. "Loss and grief can change people."

"When did this happen?"

"When you were...about four or five, I would say. Terrible tragedy, truly. She fell asleep behind the wheel one night on her way home from her job in Medford, and lost control of her car on the bridge over the Mystic. Her car sank right to the bottom of the river." His mother bowed her head, lines seaming her round, soft features. "Fox was never the same after that."

"I...oh." Guilt plunged through Summer in a hard strike,

sinking deep as a spear into his flesh. He knit his brows. "Why haven't I ever heard about this?"

"You were quite young, dear, and it was grown-up business. And over time, the whole town learned to stop speaking about it out of respect for Fox. I don't think the man's ever stopped grieving."

Or he never allowed himself to grieve in the first place, Summer thought with dawning realization.

And just like that, far too many things fell into place.

When he'd been a student at Albin, all he'd seen was Professor Iseya—aloof, untouchable, mysterious, his icy armor all the more fascinating for the secrets it promised. As a boy it had been too easy to daydream about being the one to tease past that armor to discover everything hidden inside; to be the *special one* the cold, somewhat frightening professor defrosted for. There'd been a touch of the forbidden, too, when Iseya had been nearly forty by the time Summer graduated, and that stern, subtly domineering demeanor had inspired a few whispered thoughts of just what he might *do* to Summer in private when Summer was young, vulnerable, inexperienced.

But those had been childish fantasies, entirely inappropriate and impossible, and suddenly that frigid exterior took on a wholly different meaning when seen through older eyes.

When it was the defensive shield of a man in pain, struggling to find a way to function in his everyday life, fighting his pride to keep from putting his grief on display for all the world to see.

Yet if Summer had been four or five years old when Iseya's wife had died…then Iseya had been shut inside himself for twenty years, now.

And maybe Summer was reading too much into it, thinking a few psychology and education courses gave him any insight into the workings of a distant man's mind...

But he wondered if Iseya even knew how to find his way out, anymore.

Or if he was trapped inside himself.

And completely alone.

Summer sighed, rubbing his fingers to his temples. "I'm an asshole."

"*Language.*"

"I'm twenty-five."

"And I'm still your mother, and this is still my house." She reached across the table and curled her thin, papery fingers around his wrist; her skin was cooler than he remembered, and brought back that pang, that quiet unspoken fear, the entire reason he'd been willing to take a job in the town he'd once been so desperate to escape. "You didn't know, Summer. Now you do. It's up to you what you do with that information."

"Yeah...yeah. I know." He smiled and caught her hand, squeezing it in his own. "I've got to think for a bit, but... I think I know what I need to do, in the end."

"What's that, dear?"

"I," he said, holding her hand just a little tighter, as if he could give her his warmth to hold and keep, "am going to do something brave."

And he couldn't think of anything that would take more courage than walking up to Fox Iseya...

And apologizing to him flat out.

★ ★ ★

Fox sat on the shore of Whitemist Lake and watched the sun rise over the spires of the school.

The mist always made sunrise at Albin Academy a strange and silvered thing, when the thick blanketing layer of fog rose almost to the treetops and captured the sun to glow strange and ethereal about the edges. The mornings tasted cool as rain, and every blade of grass around him clung on to condensation like dewdrops, soaking it into his slacks. At times like this he often felt as if the threshold between one world and the next had somehow blurred. And if he looked hard enough, stared deep into the clouds weaving tendrils through and about the trees...

He might somehow see through to the other side.

But this morning there was nothing to see but his reflection, as he looked down into the water and watched the ripples spread while, one at a time, he plucked up clover flowers from the grassy shore and tossed them in. If he followed with the legend of Isabella of the Lake, he was supposed to weave the clovers into a crown for her to wear, down in the watery deeps.

Yet this morning, his mind wasn't on Isabella.

It was on Summer Hemlock, and yesterday afternoon's bizarre encounter.

Whatever had possessed such a shy, timid young man to actually kiss him—*him*, of all people?

And why, for just a moment, had something sparked inside him when he had neither needed nor wanted such things for nearly twenty years?

You are a case study in denial, Fox.

That was what the grief counselor had told him, a decade ago.

Then again, she'd also told him he was a pain in the ass, considering most psychotherapeutic methods didn't work on someone who knew them by heart.

He plucked up another clover flower, its stem cool and crisp against his fingers as he began tying a delicate knot—only to still at the faint sound of footsteps at his back, rustling in the grass. Probably one of the boys; they liked to make wishes in the lake, throwing flower crowns down to Isabella and asking her for better grades on their midterms or for one of the students at the public school one town over to go out with them. Fox prepared himself to shut away behind the mantle of authority and excuse himself, drawing silence around him like a cloak.

Until a soft "Hey" murmured at his back, and Summer Hemlock sank down to the grass at his side.

Fox stiffened, eyeing Summer sidelong—but as always, Summer wasn't looking at him. He never looked at anyone, and not for the first time Fox wondered just what had ingrained that particular behavior. That fear. For Fox direct eye contact had other implications, ones few around him understood...

But Summer seemed to be carrying some weight on his shoulders, that bowed his head and kept his eyes downcast.

Summer settled with one leg drawn up, draping his arm over it and leaning back on his other hand. He still wore the same close-fit T-shirt and jeans as yesterday, albeit as rumpled as his hair, and an odd, quiet little smile played about his lips even if it hardly reflected in pensive blue eyes that looked out across the lake as if he, too, could see something in the mist.

Fox looked away, letting the clover flower fall to the grass and leaning on his hands. "Mr. Hemlock," he greeted. "I presume, since you've not changed your clothing, that you returned to fetch your personal effects."

"No," Summer answered quietly. "I came to say I'm sorry."

Fox arched a brow. "For…?"

"You know what." That smile strengthened, strangely cynical and self-mocking. "But you're going to make me say it, aren't you?" Summer turned his head toward Fox, almost but not quite meeting his eyes. "I'm sorry for kissing you yesterday. I'm sorry for not asking first. I'm sorry for crossing your boundaries. And I'm sorry for running away."

"I hardly expected you to be so forthright."

"One brave thing per day, right?" Summer let out a breathless, shaky laugh. For all that he had grown into an athletic young man, there was a softness about him, a gentleness, that made every laugh, every gesture a thing of uncertain sweetness. "This was my brave thing. Apologizing to you. I'll figure out what tomorrow's is. And Monday's… if I still have a job."

Fox realized he'd been watching Summer—the way his lashes lowered to shade the oddly deep blue hue of his eyes, the nervous curl of square, strong fingers—and diverted his gaze to the lake, pressing his lips together. "Why would you not have a job?"

"Because what I did was an asshole move?"

"And I don't have the authority to fire you. I'm tenured, not all-powerful." With a sigh, Fox relented and added, "...but I hadn't intended to discipline you in the first place. It was an impulsive kiss. Not the end of the world. And I should likely apologize as well, for needling at your nervous tendencies and subjecting you to anxiety-inducing scrutiny. Not that I understand why *that*, of all things, was the choice you made to show your courage."

Summer let out a sudden low laugh; like his voice, it was a quiet thing that always seemed just a touch breathless, whispering deep in his throat. "I guess I wasn't as obvious back then as I thought."

"Obvious...?"

"I was in love with you when I was a student, Professor Iseya."

Fox blinked. His chest tightened. "You most certainly were *not*."

"I thought I was. At least, with who I thought you were. I know now that's not actually who you are...so I guess you're right that I wasn't." Another laugh, startled and hesitant. "God, this 'being brave' thing sucks. I can't believe I just blurted that out to you, and you're still sitting there with that same empty expression like I just told you it's going to rain."

"You're speaking of feelings you had as a child. They have no bearing on now, or on our professional relationship as adults. Am I supposed to react any other way?"

"No...no, I guess not." Summer's laughter faded into a sigh, and he glanced at Fox—for just a moment really looking at him, Summer's dark eyes half-lidded, messy hair framing his gaze in black tendrils. "But I do still find you attractive. And you made me angry. So I kissed you to make you stop saying those things about me. I still shouldn't have done it."

Fox opened his mouth.

Then closed it again.

Then scowled, a *most* disquieting feeling of uncertainty settling in the pit of his stomach, light and strange. "This has to be one of the most bizarre conversations I've ever had."

"Me too." Summer tilted his head back, looking up at the sky, lips curling. "But this is me, Professor Iseya. And I guess you need to know that if we're going to work together. I'm a walking bundle of anxiety waiting to trip into a panic attack, but every once in a while I hit a break point and just...do what I have to do, and say what I have to say." His shoulders shook with silent laughter. "Don't worry. Once I leave I'll probably hyperventilate."

"I'd rather you didn't. Challenging you to be brave was never meant to upset your anxiety."

"Sometimes I want my anxiety to be upset. Sometimes I... I..." He trailed off, lips remaining parted, before he shook his head. "Nevermind. It doesn't matter. Do you want to just put this behind us?"

Fox watched Summer from the corner of his eye; the way the rising light fell over his profile—his straight, somewhat awkward nose, the stubborn set to his jaw, the softness of his mouth. In this moment he looked older than his mid-twenties; not in his fresh, clean-shaven face, perhaps, but something about the way he carried himself, some tiredness that spoke of long hours of thought, of introspection, of weary self-awareness that he carried with him heavily.

And Fox didn't quite know what possessed him, what it was about that soft quiet air about Summer, that made him ask, "…first… I'd like you to answer a question."

Summer was silent for some time. And it was in that moment that Fox realized Summer might actually refuse him; he didn't know when it became a foregone conclusion that people would simply do as he said, but…

When his only human contact was with children or other teachers who were intimidated by him, it became too easy to stop seeing others as…

Others.

As entities who existed outside the thin shallow projections by which he defined their presences, ghosts he could banish at will.

He couldn't banish Summer at will, he thought. Couldn't summon him at will. Couldn't compel him to speak.

And that made him a strange new thing.

Something with thin bright edges that cut at the cloud of distance surrounding Fox at all times, slicing narrow gashes that forced him to look into the harsh, raw reality of the world outside.

How strange, he thought.

How strange indeed, that the world suddenly became more real, more crisp, the colors sharper about the edges in the slow span of breaths it took to wait for Summer to answer.

"Maybe," Summer said after those long, waiting breaths, choosing the words carefully. "It depends on the question."

Very well, then.

"Why are you attracted to me?" Fox asked.

And Summer laughed.

He laughed, quick and startled, a short light thing that made Fox think of mayflies startled into taking flight. Wide blue eyes darted to him, then away—very firmly away, Summer turning his head to stare across the grass, toward the stark cliff edge that led down the other side of the slope, into dense forest. His mouth pressed to his up-raised shoulder, muffling his laughter into a muted sound, and the tips of his ears turned quite a shade of red against the dark backdrop of his tousled hair.

Fox blinked. "Did I say something funny?"

"*No*," Summer mumbled against his shirt. "I'm just embarrassed, I... Why would you ask me that?"

"Because I want to know," Fox said. "I would think that would be entirely self-explanatory."

"Oh *God*." With a groan, Summer closed his eyes, letting his head fall back limply on the toned arch of his neck, hanging between his shoulders, face tilted up to the sky. "I forgot how literal you are. You really haven't changed."

No, Fox thought, and wondered at the tight feeling like his ribs were pressing in too hard on his lungs. *I suppose I have not.*

"But that's one reason why I'm attracted to you." Summer opened his eyes, looking up at a morning sky that reflected in his eyes to give them a gray-blue sheen like glacial silt; a small smile touched his lips, warm and sweet. "Maybe I don't know the real you, but I know some real things *about* you. I like the way you talk. You're literal and while you hide a lot, you say what you mean when you do talk. If you don't want to say something you just won't, instead of deflecting or falling back on social niceties that are just a step away from lies. But even though you're so straightforward…there's all kinds of subtle nuance, too. Soft things between the lines. Sometimes even though you mean what you say…you mean something else, too."

Fox blinked again.

And again.

And had to look away from this strange young man with his equally strange smile, clearing his throat. "Perhaps you're only imagining what you're reading between my lines."

"It's possible. Projection is a thing." Even without looking at him…that smile was still in Summer's voice. "But it's not the only reason I'm attracted to you."

"I can't imagine more than one reason," Fox muttered.

"I can imagine a thousand. Only I don't have to imagine, because they're as real as the color of your eyes and the way you wear your hair." Summer laughed. "I don't know how I'm not hyperventilating right now, but I guess I hit 'fuck it' mode and can freak out later. Why do you think I *wouldn't* be attracted to you?"

"I…"

It was almost instinct for Fox to *want* to deflect around that, and yet somehow Summer's quiet faith in his honesty, his straightforwardness, made him at least want to be somewhat truthful.

"I consider myself a non-entity on that front," he said. "If romance is a playing field, I benched myself long ago.

Most do not pay attention to players who are not actively on the field."

"You're bad at sports analogies," Summer teased softly, and Fox scowled.

"I have little interest in the sports ball."

"...'the sports ball.'" That prompted a soft snicker, barely repressed. "And there's another reason. You're funny without meaning to be. But just because you've benched yourself doesn't mean you aren't still someone's favorite MVP."

"Now who is making terrible sports analogies?"

"I don't watch the sports ball either." Summer shrugged one shoulder ruefully. "Swimming turned out to be my thing."

Fox arched a brow, risking a glance back at Summer. The way he'd tanned and filled out, building into compact athletic musculature with a sort of flowing, liquid grace to it rather than thick-honed bulk...he could see it. Summer cutting through the water in smooth, fluid strokes.

He should not be picturing this.

"So is that how you finally hit puberty?" he shot back. "Swimming?"

"There it is. The defensive barbs because I managed to fluster you when you're supposed to be made of stone." Summer was still looking up at the sky, but his lips curled sweetly, almost slyly. "Keep insulting me, Professor Iseya. It just means I get under your skin a little. Although that's kind of regressing, don't you think? Child psychology. I thought we universally agreed as a field to stop telling children when a little boy pulls your pigtails and kicks dirt in your face, it means he likes you."

"*I don't like you!*" Narrowing his eyes, Fox growled, tearing his gaze away and glaring at the water.

What was even happening here?

How was this shy, anxious young man sitting here with that smile on his lips, needling at Fox and leaving Fox completely uncertain of how to handle this at all?

Yet that smile never wavered, even as Summer lowered his eyes from the sky, looking at Fox with a strange and quiet frankness, a soft ache in his voice when he said, "I know."

That...should not sting.

A sudden sharp pang, as if an arrow had been fired straight from Summer's bleeding heart to Fox's own.

With a soft hiss, he clenched his jaw and looked anywhere *but* at Summer. At the mist slowly beginning to burn away from the surface of the lake, hovering like the last remnants of ghosts that refused to let go with the dawn.

"This," he bit off, "is the most absolutely *ludicrous* conversation. What makes you think I'm even attracted to men?"

"Hope," Summer answered simply, softly, and yet *everything* was in that one word.

Hellfire.

Fox closed his eyes, breathing in and out slowly, if only so he could keep his tone even and calm. He wasn't accustomed to this—to feeling out of sorts, shaken out of place, his stone foundations cracked and no longer holding him so steady.

Being around Summer was like seeing the sun after decades buried in a subterranean cave.

And the light hurt his eyes, when all he wanted was the quiet and comforting dark.

"You don't want me, Summer," he said firmly. "I'm quite old, used-up, and I don't even know how to be with someone anymore."

"I don't think that's true," Summer murmured.

"Isn't it?"

Silence, before Summer said slowly, "Maybe I'm wrong... I'm probably wrong. Or maybe you were a good enough teacher that I can figure some things out. But either way, I think you shut yourself away while you needed to...but your protective walls turned into a cage when you didn't need them anymore, and now you can't find your way out."

Shut yourself away while you needed to.

The simple memory of just *why* he'd shut himself away cut deep, digging down to a tiny pain that lived at his heart. He'd made it tiny deliberately, so he could compact it down into a thing so small it could fit in the palm of his hand, all of that agony crushed down into nothing so that he could never touch too much of it at any one time, its surface area barely the size of a fingerprint.

And then he'd tucked it away, burying it down where he couldn't reach it.

But those simple words threatened to expose it, even if it meant cutting him open to do so.

No.

He stood, reminding himself to breathe—to breathe, and to wrap himself in his calm. He was nearly twice Summer's age, and quite accustomed to rebellious boys who thought they were intelligent enough to outsmart their teacher, put him on the spot, leave him floundering. Summer was just an older, larger version of that.

And Fox could not forget that he was the one in control here.

"Is that so?" he asked, looking down at Summer—the top of his head, the hard slopes his shoulders made as he leaned back on his hands. "If that's your analysis, you aren't fit to teach elementary school psychology."

"They don't teach psychology in elementary school." Summer chuckled, those firm shoulders shaking. "Insulting me already didn't work, Professor. Why do you think it's going to drive me back from the walls this time?"

Fox turned his nose up. "Is that your intent, then? To breach my walls?"

"Not breach them, no."

Summer tilted his head back again, then, but this time instead of looking at the sky…he looked up at Fox with his eyes full of that sky, the first morning clouds reflected against liquid blue.

"I'm not going to get inside unless you let me, Professor Iseya. But I can stand outside the walls and wait…and ask."

Fox stared.

He could not be serious.

One minute Summer had arrived to apologize for that egregious and utterly ridiculous *kiss*, and now he…seemed to be emboldened to some kind of *designs* on Fox?

All because Fox had not summarily dismissed him from his position?

Absurd.

He pressed his lips together and took a few steps away

from Summer, drifting along the lake's shore, putting more distance between them. Giving himself space—to think, to sort himself out, when he wasn't accustomed to this.

Wasn't accustomed to someone who took one look at his walls and saw not someone cold, not someone cruel, distant, detached, inhuman...

But simply that those walls were made not of stone, but of pain.

He did not like it.

His walls had served him quite well for some time, and they did not need to be broken down.

"Do you think Rapunzel was comfortable in her castle?" he asked. "Perhaps, since it was all she knew...it never even felt like a cage."

Summer let out a sunny little laugh. "Are we talking Grimm's Rapunzel or Disney's Rapunzel?"

"Does it matter?"

"Considering in one I end up losing my eyesight trying to reach you, and the other I just get hit in the face with a frying pan?" A wickedly amused sound rose from the back of Summer's throat. "Yes."

Fox wrinkled his nose. "Please do not project us into the roles of fictional lovers."

A soft rustle rose, denim moving against grass, the sounds of fabric against skin. It was an oddly intimate sound, one that made Fox remember the sound of flesh on sheets, the pad of soft footsteps in the dark, a quiet room where he never wanted the light to find him and wake him from a dream of being in love.

He couldn't breathe.

He couldn't breathe, and he couldn't seem to move even though everything inside him wanted to *run* as Summer drew closer, *closer*, until he was a warmth at Fox's back, this bright thing that kept trying to chase away the cold touch of ghosts, of yurei whose icy spirit-fingers wrapped around Fox's neck, choking off his air, but Fox didn't want to let them go. Didn't want to let in the breath they were strangling from him.

When if he remembered how to breathe, that one tiny swelling of his chest might just shatter him.

"What about real lovers, then?" Summer asked, husky, low, his breaths and his voice like a lick of flame on a frozen night.

Fox stared blankly straight ahead, curling one hand against his chest, against his shirt, clutching up a handful of the fabric. He couldn't turn around. Couldn't face that warmth.

Didn't Summer realize?

Didn't he realize if he burned away Fox's wall of frost...

There was nothing beneath, and he'd just melt and evaporate and wisp away?

"Why?" he whispered. "Why do you want something like that?"

"You told me to be bold." Soft, entreating, yet...so inadvertently seductive, too. Fox didn't think Summer realized just how seductive his sweetness was. "I can't think of anything bolder than asking the most terrifying man in Albin Academy to kiss me." Summer drew closer, the crackle of grass beneath his feet, his shoulder brushing Fox's in a sudden quiet shock-jump of sensation before it was gone as Summer stood at his side, looking out over the water as well with that strange, gently melancholy smile on his full red lips. "Once per day."

Fox watched him from the corner of his eye, brows knitting. "That's…a bizarre proposition."

"Is it?" Summer slipped his hands into the pockets of his jeans, his shirt drawing tight against leanly toned musculature, wrinkles seaming against the flex of his biceps. "It's motivation. If I'm bolder, if I prove to you I can do this job… I get rewarded with a kiss. With one caveat."

There. One caveat.

All Fox would need to end this ridiculous game.

"And what would that be?" he asked.

"Only if you really want to." Summer shook his head slightly, messy hair drifting across his eyes. "I couldn't stand it if you felt like you had to. Like you were obligated, or like…" He trailed off, eyes lidding, voice quieting. "…like I didn't really care what you want. I think… I kind of think 'no' is the most important word we know, and not enough people listen to it."

"You have to know that I would say no right in this instant, Mr. Hemlock," Fox said through his teeth. "Which makes your proposition quite pointless, as it is."

Summer lifted his head, then, once more looking at Fox directly. Considering how he avoided eye contact so pathologically, Fox…didn't understand why Summer seemed inclined to so often look at him so fully, so intently, when he claimed to be afraid of Fox, claimed to be so anxious he actually found Fox terrifying.

But perhaps that's what bravery was, Fox thought.

Summer was afraid of him...

And yet still looking at him.

Trying to *see* him.

And telling him, in his own way...

That for some bizarre reason, he found Fox to be worth facing down that fear.

He didn't understand.

And he didn't understand how intently Summer looked at him, those rich blue eyes subtly dilated, turning them smoky.

"Summer," he whispered. "Call me Summer."

Fox's eyes widened. His fingers clenched harder in his shirt.

Did Summer not...understand what using given names meant, to him?

Perhaps he was only half-Japanese, his mother a white American woman who gave him his gray eyes in a rare genetic fluke, but he still knew so much of so many things from his father, things passed down to him like traditions written in blood.

Given names could be used with fondness for children, for family, for close friends who might as well be family...

But in certain circumstances, someone's name could be a love word.

Intimate and shivering, rolling off the tongue.

He turned his back on Summer, on those eyes that pleaded with him to be that intimate, to be that close, curling his shoulders in and digging his fingers against his shirt as if he could claw down to his heart and grasp it to stop its erratic and sharp beating.

"*Mn.*"

"You said it once before," Summer said softly, and Fox caught his breath.

He had.

Letting it roll off his tongue, easy and fluid, but he'd tried not to taste it, tried to simply use it to capture Summer's attention, to impress on him that he wasn't someone Summer should ever want.

But he wondered, now.

Wondered now what he'd let slip past his lips without feeling its texture, its flavor.

He glanced over his shoulder. All he could see was Summer's profile, the tanned slopes and lines of him catching the sun until he glowed. Amber-soft and gentle, and Fox swallowed thickly.

"...Summer," he said again.

It tasted like sighs. Like the taste not of summer, but the spice of autumn leaves turning and falling and crackling under every step. It tasted like the color of the sky just as the sun touches the horizon at sunset.

And it felt like silk on his lips and tongue, passing over his skin in liquid, smooth caresses.

He didn't like it.

He didn't like how *close* it felt, when he still remembered the taste of Summer's lips against his own, that same crackle-bright hint of warmth and sharpness, while Summer's pulse throbbed and trembled underneath his palm.

"Yeah," Summer said, a low thrum turning his voice husky. "Just like that."

Closer he stepped. Closer still, until he was a wall of heat at Fox's back, this vibrant living thing trying to make Fox remember *he* was alive, too.

"Would it be so terrible?" Summer asked softly. "To kiss me just once per day. Operant conditioning works better with a reward."

"I…" Breathing was so hard, right now, and Fox didn't understand this feeling. "I refuse to answer that."

"Shouldn't it be easy to say no, then?"

He scowled. "You are baiting me."

"Maybe a little." Summer smiled sweetly, just a faint curve of his lips visible in the corner of Fox's eye. "It's not every day I get to make the man I was in love with for my entire childhood *blush*."

Fox caught a strangled sound in his throat.

He was most certainly not *blushing*.

His face simply felt warm because of the rising sunlight, the heat chasing the last of the mist from the pond, the trees.

"If you are attempting to pique my pride, *Mr. Hemlock*, it won't work."

"I'm not."

Then Fox felt something he hadn't felt in decades:

Fingers in his hair.

Just the lightest touch, catching one of the damnable tendrils that would never stay in the clip, lifting it and making him shudder and tense with the prickling feeling of the strands moving against his neck, kissing his skin, then pulling back to leave him strangely deprived of *touch*, as if the sensitized flesh was achingly aware that it wasn't in contact with…skin, warmth, *texture*.

"I'm just riding my bravery until it runs out." Summer stroked his thumb down the strands captured in his fingers, handling them delicately. "Think about it, Professor Iseya. I'll be ready for class tomorrow. Tell me then."

Then: the feather-soft sensation of his hair free-floating, falling, drifting down to lay against his neck and coil over his shoulder again.

The quiet fall of footsteps, whispering and sighing against the grass.

The wild pounding of Fox's heart, a drumbeat calling the day into existence.

He turned.

He turned, but Summer was already gone.

And already...

Already, the world was turning gray again.

Chapter Three

Summer barely made it to the suite he'd been assigned to before he nearly hyperventilated.

Holy fuck.

Holy *fuck*.

He dropped down onto the sofa in the blessedly empty— and ridiculously messy—living room and buried his face in his hands. His heart felt like it would *burst*, the walls worn thin as paper and ready to shatter.

He'd just—

And then he'd—

And *then* he'd—

What had come *over* him?

Just. He. God. *What*.

When he'd been a boy, the closest he'd ever gotten to Professor Iseya was when he'd scurried up to the desk to hand in assignments under that watchful, cutting eye, feeling as if judgment was hanging over his head like the Sword of Damocles, waiting to drop down and pierce him right through.

Back then Professor Iseya had been an inscrutable taskmaster, larger than life, greater than human.

But knowing what Summer knew now, *seeing* him, understanding what was behind that stony outer exterior...

He just saw Professor Iseya as a man.

And that man was far more enticing than any childish fantasy or ideal.

Enough to make Summer want to learn what was really behind that cold mask when before, he'd never truly realized it was a mask at all.

Especially when for just a moment, that stone had cracked.

Iseya had *responded* to him, even if it was with flustered confusion and irritation.

And that feeling...

That feeling had been addictive enough to make Summer bold.

Even if he'd been hyperventilating in the back of his mind, that heady sensation of seeing every minute reaction to him—from the way Iseya wouldn't quite look at him head-on to the soft, deliciously deep way he said Summer's name to that annoyed *blush*—had pushed him further and further toward a reckless edge.

If he wanted to break it down in psychological terms, he'd been riding the dopamine rush. Dopamine could override common sense, sometimes in ways that made people brave, sometimes in ways that made them careless, reckless, deeply unwise.

Summer wasn't sure which he was.

Nor was he sure his head wouldn't explode any moment now, either, when he had just—yes, okay, apologize for being a dick and kissing him, then act like a *bigger* dick as if he could somehow flirt through psychoanalysis? Mission *not* accomplished.

The only thing he was entirely sure of?

Was that he was terrified of hearing Iseya's answer in the morning, his entire body prickling like a live wire.

He already knew it would be a solid *no*.

That didn't stop him from hoping, even as he buried his face in his hands and breathed in quick shallow breaths through his fingers until he no longer felt like he was going to pass right out on the floor.

He tensed, though, as the sound of the front door latch echoed over the room, a click and a jiggle before the door creaked open. He peeked over his fingers. He hadn't quite processed when he'd been told who his roommate would be, but now he almost flinched as a tall, somewhat slouched figure stepped into the room, mumbling absently to himself and apparently ticking something off on his fingers one by one.

Dr. Liu.

Oh, *God*.

Summer was going to have to get a padlock for his room if he didn't want the things in it to end up on *fire*.

At least that explained the disaster of the suite.

He'd always imagined, as a kid, that the two-person suites the single teachers shared would be…bigger. More officious. But they were just homey little rooms with dark, worn, unvarnished hardwood floors to match the dark, worn, unvarnished hardwood walls, with a combined living and dining space, an open kitchen, two bedrooms linked by a bathroom with en suite access from both sides.

Everything had that feeling of old spaces, of haunted spaces, quiet and whispered; the kind of place that had lace curtains and ghosts and a fifth step between every floor that creaked when the shades walked on it at night. The window in Summer's room looked out over the cliff and onto a valley full of trees, bisected by a winding coil of river; if he remembered right, the other room had no window, running along the interior hall.

But the entire living room was filled with books.

Books, a little lab paraphernalia, science magazines, tossed on every surface—the dining table, the sofa, the coffee table, the easy chairs, even on the kitchen island separating it off from the rest of the space. They'd all been left open to one page or another, and bristled with Post-it notes in a rainbow of colors sticking out everywhere. At least a dozen of them had pens left in their open creases.

That wasn't as bad as the clothing thrown everywhere, though.

Shirts, jackets, pants, tossed over the backs of chairs or piled in a heap beneath the living room window, and Summer... Summer was pretty sure that was a pair of boxer-briefs stuffed into a potted plant next to the small flatscreen television.

Whomever had left Dr. Liu unsupervised clearly hadn't been thinking with their forebrain.

Liu himself stopped in the doorway, blinking at Summer owlishly through his oversized eyeglasses, his dark brown eyes narrowing as he leaned forward and peered at Summer through the untrimmed shag of his fluffy black hair. He was unshaven, scruffy, a mess of stubble dotting his cheeks and jaw, and that stubble made a scratchy sound as he scrubbed the backs of his knuckles against his chin.

"I know you," he said quizzically.

"Er...yeah. Hi." Summer dropped his hands from his face and offered a smile, a sheepish wave. "I'm Summer Hemlock, the new psych TA." He stood, navigating around the coffee table to offer his hand. "I used to be a student here."

"Oh, yes, I remember you." Liu looked down at Summer's hand with a confused stare, as if he didn't know what to do with it, then absently adjusted his glasses as he pushed the door closed behind him. "You've gotten very big."

"Not that big." Summer let his hand drop, then glanced around the suite. "Um...do you need help around here? It's a little..."

"A little what?" Liu blinked.

"Messy," Summer said.

"Oh." Another blink, and then Liu looked around the suite as if seeing it for the first time. "I hadn't noticed," he said.

Before shrugging, beelining for his bedroom, and disappearing inside, shutting the door with a firm *click* of the latch.

Summer stared after him, before smiling faintly.

You wouldn't, would you.

At least it was Liu. He wasn't sure he'd have been able to room with any of the other older teachers, when he'd likely revert back to the stammering boy he'd been and never come out of his room, too anxious to be around someone who was hard-coded in his brain as an authority figure.

Liu, though...

Liu was kind of like apples.

Harmless on the outside, mostly. Sweet, sometimes tart. But apples had sugar-cyanide compounds that could be digested into lethal hydrogen cyanide, and too many apples could kill someone.

Twenty-two.

Summer thought that's what the number was.

Twenty-two.

And just like apples, Dr. Liu was only dangerous in large doses.

Or when left unattended in the chem lab.

Summer could live with that.

It wasn't really any different from having Liu for a teacher, all those years ago—and he smiled to himself as he bent to start gathering up the clothing scattered on the floor.

Even when things changed, they stayed the same.

It took him well into the day to finish cleaning the apartment, including scrubbing the kitchen and bathroom from top to bottom; Liu needed a *keeper*, and apparently that was Summer's job now.

But halfway through digging out what looked like crusted *fire extinguisher foam* from the bathroom sink, a heavy *thump* sounded outside the suite's door, followed by a sharp rattle on the door.

He lifted his head, scrubbing the back of his forearm over his sweaty forehead, and listened—but there was no sign Liu had even heard, let alone that he was coming out of his room.

Summer peeled out of his yellow rubber gloves, pitched

them onto the sink, and stepped out to open the living room door.

No one there.

Empty hallway.

But his thick, bulky suitcase sat right there in front of the door.

The suitcase he'd left in Professor Iseya's suite, and had been too nervous to retrieve.

There was a note tacked to it now, though, folded on a piece of softly textured, semi-translucent paper. Summer tilted his head, frowning as he picked it up and flicked it open on a short note written in angular, slanting handwriting with a certain razor-like grace to it.

Simple black letters.

Two words, and nothing more.

Challenge accepted.

His chest seized. His fingers clenched, before he hastily unclenched them, smoothing the delicate paper.

What...?

Did...did Professor Iseya mean...?

His mouth dried. His chest *hurt*, and he thought...oh.

Oh.

Then, tomorrow...

Tomorrow, if he was brave enough...

Maybe, just maybe...

Professor Iseya might just kiss him.

Summer was a wreck for the rest of the day.

He finished cleaning the suite, rattling between one wall

and the next in a mess of nervous energy just to keep himself busy. If he didn't keep moving, he'd probably break down.

So he cleaned. He unpacked and put away his things. He shelved Liu's books on the low built-in shelves lining the walls of the living room, and just hoped he left them in some kind of order that would let Liu find what he was looking for when he came back to...*whatever* he was doing. He headed into town on a short drive to stock up on groceries, pick up a few necessities, and buy his own sheets and duvet to replace the institutional ones provided by the school, stripping bare white to instead pile his bed high in deep oceanic blue threaded through with star-shot silver, and enough pillows to bury himself in until he'd wedge himself in place and not be able to kick and toss and turn all night.

That didn't mean he didn't, by the time he wore himself out, showered, and threw himself into bed.

Sprawling on his back, walled in on either side by pillows and surrounded by the vaguely chemical scent of new bedding with its fabric dye still fresh, he stared up at the ceiling—wood beam rafters, when he was so used to the white stucco of dorm room after dorm room. He'd probably stayed at school at the University of Maryland longer than he needed to, just...

Trying to find his way.

Trying to figure out what he wanted to do.

No—trying to figure out who he wanted to *be*.

He should know, after all these years.

But all he'd ever known was what he didn't want.

He didn't want to be the quiet boy everyone had snickered at because he was *poor*, a local *townie*, his mother insisting on sending him to the boarding school because it was what his father had wanted, before he'd died. He'd been an administrator at Albin once, long ago—before even Professor Iseya's time. Albin was part of Roark Hemlock's legacy, and in some ways it was part of Summer's.

His father's name was on a plaque in the main hall, below a painted portrait.

That still didn't mean Summer ever felt like he'd belonged here.

Like he'd belonged anywhere in Omen, as if the small gray town had made him a small gray person and if he just got *out*, he'd be...he'd be...

He didn't know.

Bolder.

Happier.

Someone with a *purpose*, instead of someone who just coasted along day by day, trying to figure out how to fit in, how to get by, what he should be doing with this illusion of a life while he was busy trying to find a real one.

He hadn't found anything out in Baltimore except the realization he wasn't cut out for his original career choice in forensics; that he couldn't handle the blood, couldn't stare down the horrors of humanity without breaking down into a hyperventilating anxiety attack. So he'd transferred his psych credits into the only other MA track where they'd still count: education.

That didn't mean he wanted to teach.

Or that he knew what he wanted at all.

The only thing he'd brought home with him was a tan, a few more inches in height...

And, he guessed, a resurgence of that old crush, even if it felt like a wholly new thing.

It had to be a wholly new thing, when he was seeing Iseya with wholly new eyes.

He idly ran his fingertips over his stomach, touched the fingers of his other hand to his lips, remembered...

Professor Iseya's mouth.

That hand on his throat.

But more...

The way Iseya's breath had caught, wild and warm and quick, when Summer had captured just a few strands of that tumbling wispy black hair he'd always wanted to touch, to bury his fingers in, to tease down from its clip and wrap himself up in until he and Iseya were tangled together inextricably.

That moment.

That moment had told him he was very much interested in the man Iseya was now, rather than the legend he'd been back then.

Summer wasn't yet sure what to do with that.

But as he rolled over and buried his face in the pillows and hugged one close to his chest, he hoped...

He hoped tomorrow he would have the chance to find out.

Fox had never been on friendly terms with sleep.

Not when sleep brought memories.

Not when sleep brought dreams, horrible things of a lightless dark where there was no air and only the choking, frigid sensation of water pouring endlessly down his throat and into his lungs while he fought for eternities for breaths that would never come.

Not when sleep somehow never let him escape from the awareness that his bed was painfully empty, when he rolled over in the middle of the night to drape his arms against a warm body.

And there was no warm body there.

He stared out the window of his bedroom, in his private family suite that he should have given up long ago and yet the school administrators had allowed him to keep out of something too close to pity for his pride to accept. Hour by hour, inch by inch, the shafts of moonlight pouring through the window slid across his bed, marking minutes in cutouts of light and shadow, time moving forward while Fox himself didn't move at all.

His hand stretched across the bed, splayed against the sheets, resting in that empty space.

He didn't remember the shape that was supposed to fill it anymore, when he'd thought he always would.

When he'd thought that hole in his life would always be the same, an outline so precise, so perfect, it would always hold the imprint of *her*.

But that imprint was fuzzy around the edges, now. Time had eroded away the shape of that hole until it was less precise and somehow more just an impression, an idea, a vague concept without specifics, and he thought…

He thought he was betraying something, somehow.

Thought he was betraying himself.

His memories, the love he'd thought would be forever.

Simply by letting that empty space inside him go vague.

And simply by remembering the taste of another on his lips, a startling and new thing that wouldn't leave him over a day after Summer had caught Fox's chin in his hand and made him remember what it was like to breathe in tandem with someone else.

It should hurt more, he thought dimly.

It should hurt, should cut so deep he bled.

But it didn't.

It only left him frustrated, and wondering.

If he was more upset that he missed *her*...

Or more upset at the realization that he didn't.

But he didn't know what should take the place of that feeling, now.

Or who he was without it.

When he felt as though his entire *self* was just papier-mâché painted in a thin and crumbling layer over that empty hollow of grief.

Strip that away...

And what was left?

He didn't know.

And he was almost *angry* with that bright and beautiful blue-eyed boy...

...for forcing him to ask.

Chapter Four

Summer was up before his alarm.

And changed clothes six times before he headed out to meet Iseya for morning planning.

With the psych class as an elective, it only ran in three blocks after the lunch period; the mornings, per the rather tersely written schedule he'd been emailed a week or so back, were for lesson planning, grading papers, and discussion. Summer supposed they were also his own informal class periods—where he'd ask Iseya what he needed to know, learn what he needed to ask.

As if he had any idea what to ask.

Any idea what to even *say*, as he stood outside Iseya's office and tried to calm the flutters and the twists in his chest, his stomach, even in his legs. Swallowing, his mouth like nettles and sand, he scrubbed his hands against his thighs.

He'd settled on simple black slacks, dress shoes, a white dress shirt, though he couldn't *breathe* and he pulled the top two buttons loose until the collar no longer felt like it was choking him to death.

Just…go in.

He was *supposed* to be here.

Iseya wasn't going to tell him to get out.

He wasn't.

And that note in Summer's pocket…

He slipped his fingers into the pocket of his slacks and just touched the paper, feeling its somewhat brittle, strange texture against his fingertips.

Challenge accepted.

His heart gave a strange little flutter.

And he pushed the doorknob open, and stepped inside.

In years, Professor Iseya's office hadn't changed a bit.

Still the same orderly, sparse designs, dark furniture chosen to naturally complement the building's darkly weathered wood finish, minimal decorations save for small bits of terra-cotta pottery tucked here and there on shelves, tastefully spaced among rows and rows of neatly organized textbooks, reference books, literature on every aspect of psychology under the sun. Yet touches of green brightened the room, with delicate hanging basket planters suspended from the ceiling, overflowing with dangling, fragile tendrils of honeysuckle vines.

The honeysuckles were blooming now, even at this time of year—and their soft, alluring fragrance subtly wafted through the room, their curling petals and long stamens nearly dripping with it.

Summer remembered, once, coming to turn in an extra credit assignment he'd asked for to make up for missing a quiz after his mother had taken him out of school one day to spend the day in the woods with her, hunting bluebells and sunflowers and digging up medicinal herbs.

He'd caught Professor Iseya watering the honeysuckles, reaching up to spray them with a little bottle, handling them with those long, graceful fingers that touched them as if they would burst apart and scatter if he was the slightest bit too rough.

That moment, for young Summer, had been...

Magic.

And it brought a little of that magic back, to see that Iseya still kept his honeysuckles. That touch of softness, that sweetness, that hint into something more human than the cold façade he tried to project.

Even if, right now, Iseya might as well be made of stone, for all that he reacted to Summer's entrance.

He sat behind a long, smooth desk made of polished cherrywood that gleamed almost burgundy in the low hanging overhead light, glossed so deeply that it almost perfectly mirrored his reflection—from the stark silver of his eyes to the sharp edges of his glasses, from the streaks of gray in his tightly-bound hair to the deep, steely color of today's perfectly pressed button-down, a dark gray that only brought out the pale amber of his skin in a luminous glow.

The precision of his posture only accented the angular, broad strength of his shoulders, and the fact that at his height his chair was a little too small for him; any chair would be a little too small for him, Summer thought, when he was larger than life…

…and currently refusing to look up from the stack of student papers in front of him.

Summer tilted his head.

…*I know you know I'm standing right here.*

But Iseya only scratched off a quick-dashed mark in red ink.

And Summer smiled fondly, his heart squeezing in the best and worst ways.

"Good morning, Professor Iseya," he said, stepping in and closing the door behind him.

Iseya still didn't look up.

He just pointed his pen at the curving chair opposite his desk and bit off a terse, almost subvocal, "*Sit.*"

It was almost embarrassing, how quickly Summer scrambled to obey.

But then he always had had a weak spot for the natural sense of authority Iseya exuded, and it made Summer's breaths catch just a little to let himself give in to the urge to do exactly as Iseya said.

He sank down in the chair, shifting a bit uncomfortably, trying to find the right way to sit before he just gave up and leaned forward, resting his folded arms on the edge of the desk.

He wanted to *ask*.

Nearly vibrated with it.

But instead he made himself say, "Grading pa—"

His voice cracked. Squeaked.

And Iseya's gaze flicked up, sharp-edged blades of silver skewering Summer over the rims of his glasses.

Iseya said nothing.

Summer's cheeks went hot, and he cleared his throat, dropping his eyes to stare down at the desk. His own reflection stared back up at him, just a little too wide-eyed and timid, and he didn't think all of the red in his cheeks could be blamed on the cherrywood lacquer.

Right.

Try again.

"Grading papers?" he managed to ask in a rather stilted mumble, then closed his eyes, suppressing a groan.

Whatever confidence he'd had yesterday morning, standing by the lakeshore and watching how the sunlight dappled over Iseya's hair and shoulders...

It had clearly deserted him today.

His bones felt like water, and the only reason he didn't turn and bolt was because he didn't really think his body would hold him up if he tried to stand.

"If you have the slightest recollection of my classes at all," Iseya said crisply, his deep, rolling voice edged in glacial frost, "you'll recall I have no patience for obvious questions."

"Don't," Summer said. It came out faint, soft, but he made himself say it. That was something he'd been trying to learn to do since he'd escaped Omen: make himself *say* the things that needed to be said, even if his voice was small when he said them. "Don't talk to me like I'm one of your misbehaving students. Please. I'm supposed to be your peer, even if I have a lot to learn from you before I'm ready to teach."

"Is that what you want to be to me, then?" Iseya asked, deceptively soft when there was a core of flint to those precise words. "My peer?"

Summer drew his brows together. "I don't know if you're asking me that in a professional context or a personal context." He darted his tongue over his lips. "And I don't... know what your note meant. 'Challenge accepted.' I wasn't trying to challenge you—"

"Weren't you?" Iseya countered. Still so flat, so cool, almost mocking, and Summer deflated. "Isn't that the point of your little game? Not just to challenge yourself, but to challenge me? To prove that you can convince me to break down my walls for you, one day at a time, one kiss at a time?"

That stung—like brambles wrapped around his heart and digging in, that *stung*, and Summer flinched, lifting his gaze to find Iseya watching him with that same icy, impenetrable stare, almost accusing.

"Why are you being like this?" Summer blurted. "Are you...are you that upset that I want to see you as a person instead of this...this terrifying figurehead?"

"I am not *upset*," Iseya hissed, slamming the pen down atop the pages, the uncapped tip dipping to leave a deep red inkblot like blood spreading against white.

Summer just stared at him.

"You're acting like you are," he murmured, and bit his lip. "I'm...sorry. I'm sorry if you're still...hurting so much that it feels like I'm playing some kind of game with you.

Just…forget I ever asked. I didn't… I didn't mean to be disrespectful of…"

"Of *what?*" Brittle, sharp, Iseya's eyes flashing—heat slashing through that ice like a stab of lightning. "What do you think you know about me?"

Right now, looking at Iseya felt like…

Felt like pleading.

Pleading with him to just…stop, when Summer didn't have to be an expert to know that this…

This was the pain talking.

Not Iseya himself.

"I know that twenty years is a long time to grieve," Summer whispered, heart in his throat.

This wasn't how he'd wanted this to go. A simple wish, a silly game, an ache in the pit of his stomach, but somehow it had gone all wrong and he'd upset Iseya—but now that he'd started it, he had to finish it and say what had to be said to see this through.

He always said all the wrong things anyway.

He guessed that wasn't going to change.

"And a long time to define yourself as if that grief is all you are," he finished, the words driving through his tongue like iron nails.

Iseya faltered, physically recoiling as if Summer had slapped him. His gaze flickered strangely, before he looked away—and when he spoke his voice was softer, that lashing edge gone.

"If you think you will find anything else underneath that," he murmured, "you will be sorely disappointed."

Summer half-smiled, even though it hurt like someone

had pulled his rib cage open and plucked one curving bone out to fit it to the shape of his mouth. "Is that what you're afraid of? That you'll disappoint me?"

"What makes you think I'm afraid of you in any way, Mr. Hemlock?"

"The fact that you won't look at me directly unless you're angry with me," Summer pointed out. "Because I won't look at people, either...because then I'm afraid they'll see too much about how I feel."

Iseya made a soft *tch* sound under his breath, lifting his chin a touch haughtily—and yet still those silver eyes remained on the bookshelf, not on Summer. "Is that why you avoid eye contact? A mystery solved, I suppose."

"It's why *I* do. I'm wondering if it's why you do, too."

"It's considered rude to stare at people with prolonged eye contact in Japanese culture." Iseya thinned his lips. "Granted, I was not raised in Japanese culture outside my family home after my adolescent years, but I believe the common phrase is 'that's my story, and I'm sticking to it.'"

That startled a laugh out of Summer, quick but still enough to ease some of the tight feeling in his chest. "It's not like you to be that indirect."

"My father always told me I was too blunt. Perhaps I'm attempting to rectify that now." But with a sigh, Iseya closed his eyes, lightly adjusting his glasses with his middle finger pressed against the bridge. "We should be discussing today's lesson plan. Not being inappropriately confrontational with each other."

"Kissing is already a pretty inappropriate conversation

topic, so throwing in confrontation isn't really that much worse."

Iseya's jaw twitched.

His finger slipped on his glasses.

And slid underneath one lens, nearly poking him in the eye with one gracefully squared, neatly manicured fingertip.

Iseya swore softly, squinting his eye up and pulling his glasses off, shaking them free from the loose tendrils of hair drifting into his face and glowering at the lens. "*Why* do you keep returning the subject to kissing?"

"Because I'm not sure what you meant," Summer admitted. "You sent me that note, didn't you? 'Challenge accepted.' This."

He fumbled in his pocket, finding the folded slip of paper, setting it on the desk and unfolding it, smoothing his fingers over the crease. Some part of him wanted to touch Iseya so painfully bad...but when he couldn't, he touched that note, paper that had been handled by Iseya's fingers, as if the indirect contact could transfer.

And he looked up at Iseya once more, while Iseya stared down at the note with his eyes hard and haunted, as if it was some terrible ghost.

Summer swallowed against the lump in his throat. "But now you're angry that I'm challenging you at all, even if it's something for both of us. A reason for both of us to be brave. So I guess..." He took a shaky breath "I guess I'm asking if we're doing this. If you agree. If you *want* to kiss me, Professor Iseya. Even if it's just to see how Pavlovian I can be."

Narrowing his eyes, Iseya pointed the arm of his glasses sternly at Summer. "I was not entirely serious about framing it as an interesting psych experiment, and that will not make me more agreeable," he bit off, then sniffed, opening his desk drawer and fishing out a microfiber cloth. With brisk motions he wiped off the lens of his glasses, his richly full-lipped mouth firming to a thin line of dusky pink. "You are aware that this is highly unprofessional and may be frowned on by the school board?"

"Two adults engaging in consenting activity in private?" Summer smiled wryly. "It's the twenty-first century, Professor Iseya. I really don't think they're scared the kids will catch the gay. And I don't think you have to worry about losing a job you're planning to quit."

Iseya made an exasperated sound and tucked his glasses back on, hooking the arms over his ears delicately and then teasing his hair loose with a gesture so practiced and absent he didn't seem to realize he was doing it. The strands that spilled loose fell down to disappear past the edge of the desk; Summer knew from years of watching him that those loose tendrils trailed nearly to his waist, but…

But Summer had never seen Iseya with his hair down, even once.

And he'd always wondered how long those trailing, dark locks really were.

He watched them with fascination as they fell to settle against Iseya's chest, before a soft clucking of the professor's tongue brought his attention back, and he dragged his gaze back up to find those gray eyes watching him with a mixture of frustration and weariness.

"What is this abrupt change that comes over you around me?" Iseya asked, his brows knitting. "You were never in any way so forward or bold before. And it's not hard to see that you are entirely petrified of me, and yet still pushing yourself to these extremes in some bizarre attempt to connect with me."

"I guess I changed more over the years than I thought." Summer smiled faintly. "Or maybe I get brave when there's something I want. I told you, there's a point where my anxiety hits 'fuck it' levels." He shrugged with a helpless laugh. "I guess I go from zero to 'fuck' in seconds around you. If it makes you feel any better, the second I walked away from you yesterday I hyperventilated."

Iseya arched a brow. "Why would that make me feel better?"

"So you know your terrifying mystique and intimidating presence are still entirely effective." Summer grinned. "Just not enough to scare me off anymore."

"You're serious about this, aren't you?" Iseya shook his head slightly. "It's not just about a kiss. You...actually want *me*. Is that the entire reason you *took* this position?"

"It isn't even part of the reason," Summer admitted. "I came back because..." He stopped, then exhaled slowly, admitting, "Because it was the path of least resistance. My mother needs more help at home, and the job opened up, and whatever I was looking for in Baltimore... I didn't find it. So I came back here...and even if I don't know what I want anywhere else..." His heart gave a hard wild *thump*, a leap, rising up through him like it would pour out of his mouth on every word. "...I found out that I want you."

Iseya said nothing.

He only looked at Summer, frank and silent and unreadable, while Summer's heart came plunging back down from its leap to wobble in the center of his chest, hovering and trembling and waiting to combust. It took everything in him to not flinch, to not lower his eyes, to meet that penetrating stare even though his breaths were coming shorter and shorter and he felt *naked*, with Iseya's gaze locked on him so closely.

Naked, too exposed...

As if Iseya could see his quivering insides, and stroked his touch down them with a vulnerable and terrifying intimacy.

"What were you looking for in Baltimore?" Iseya asked softly.

Summer parted his lips, stopped, searched...

And realized he didn't have an answer.

Nothing concrete, anyway.

And the only answer he had was...

"Me," he said softly. "I... I was looking for me."

"And so you haven't found yourself yet?"

"No." Summer half-smiled, a pang tightening and twisting inside him. "But that doesn't mean I'm going to stop looking."

Iseya cocked his head to one side, still watching Summer with that searching gaze that could see all the way to the heart of him and yet that still seemed to see nothing at all.

Then one long finger crooked, angular and enticing, beckoning.

"Stand up," Iseya commanded coolly.

Summer blinked several times—and realized he'd already obeyed. It was like his body was hard-wired to follow Iseya's every order, that crooked finger pulling his strings until he was standing on numb, trembling legs with his palms sweating and his fingers clenched and his throat working tight.

"Why...?"

Iseya's chair scraped, as he pushed it back—the sound so loud in the quiet of the office, and suddenly Summer was drowning in the scent of honeysuckles and the warmth of the room and the feeling of nervous sweat licking and trickling down his neck with warm wet tongues as a sense of something anticipatory and hot shivered in the air.

Iseya rose to his full height—so tall his shadow fell over Summer, so tall he seemed to take up all the space in the room until it was impossible not to *feel* him.

He was about to get thrown out, he just knew it.

Thrown out, told to pack his bags...

And get out.

Find himself somewhere else, because Iseya didn't want him underfoot.

Until Iseya braced one large, long hand against the desk, fingers splayed.

Leaned forward.

Hooked a fingertip in the open throat of Summer's shirt.

Dragged him in—into his heat, into a scent like...*fuck,* Summer didn't know, but it was heady and wild and strange and cool and crawling down inside him until he felt it in his blood.

And *kissed* him.

82   *JOANNA FAE*

Chapter Five

Fox had absolutely zero damned clue what he was doing.

Clearly his capacity for balancing risk versus reward was malfunctioning.

Because the only thing on his mind, as he had watched Summer say so many infuriating things with that soft red mouth...

Was that he had wanted that mouth to *shut up*.

There were a number of ways he could have accomplished that.

Summer was a damned puppy in front of him, and likely would have snapped his mouth shut at one sharp word.

Fox could have simply dismissed him, refusing to meet with him until he had properly comported himself and remembered his place. *Both* their places.

Yet instead Fox had found himself fixating on that inso-

lent mouth, and remembering how firm it had been against
his own. How hot. How Summer's lips had gone slack the
moment Fox had taken control, and…

And somehow Fox wasn't in control anymore.

Somehow Fox was standing, drawn in toward that irritating mouth, pulling Summer into him, his knuckles just
barely brushing his throat and catching the rapid wild flutter and rush of his pulse beating against his skin.

Somehow Fox was leaning into him, tilting his head,
watching Summer's eyes widen and dilate, darkening,
cheeks flushing, lips parting on a gasp of realization that
was far too gratifying, to see this impulsive, sweet young
thing so responsive, so needy under Fox's touch.

And somehow…

Somehow Fox was kissing him.

Fox was *kissing* him, and Summer's mouth was hot and
eager and needy under his own, lips parting beneath his as
if begging, pleading, desperate.

As if Summer had never wanted anything more than he
wanted Fox's kiss.

And Fox didn't know how to feel about that.

Didn't know how to *feel* at all, this clumsy thing inside
his chest, and yet even if his slow-beating heart was a crude
and awkward thing of rough stone edges…

He knew what to do with those soft, yielding lips.

And he slanted his mouth against Summer's, capturing
that sweet tremor of his mouth to still its quivering and
command it to meet his own, to match, to mate, until their
lips were wet and slick and burning with each other, until

he tasted autumn leaves and wicked heat and the vibrating, low sound of Summer's breathless moan.

That moan shot through Fox, tingled against his lips, drew him until he wanted to taste it, slipped into that inviting well of sweetness, flicked and teased and tangled with Summer's tongue until the lovely boy submitted so utterly, sagging against the edge of the desk, fingers grappling at the wood as if it was the only thing holding him up.

This shouldn't feel so good.

This shouldn't feel like *anything*, let alone this heady, hungry compulsion that drew Fox to slip his fingers around Summer's throat once more, capturing him fully and utterly, that rapid frantic pulse against his palm, the heat and strength of flexing, straining tendons against his encircling fingers.

Summer *whimpered*.

And Fox's cock throbbed, a jolt so sudden it was almost painful, a thing he hadn't felt in so long that the sudden deep *pull* of longing spearing up into his gut and down into his thighs felt alien and strange and *wrong*.

What was he *doing*?

Desire sank its teeth in deeper, and yet the pain of that bite was more than he could bear.

He thrust back, taking in a sharp breath, letting Summer go quickly.

Summer remained frozen, looking at him in a half-daze, his lips parted, the wet red tip of his tongue just barely visible—the collar of his shirt disarrayed, his cheeks flushed, his eyes so dark they simmered nearly black, as deep as a midnight sky.

"I… I don't…" Summer stammered, his voice thick, husky,

burnt at the edges with a raspy, needy burr. "Professor... Iseya...?"

Fox couldn't look at Summer's face.

Not when that lost, utterly absorbed, entirely needy expression made Fox *want* things he had consigned himself to never wanting again.

He turned his back, fixing his gaze instead on the glow of morning coming through the venetian blinds, even if he didn't really see them. Didn't really see much of anything, when he was aching inside and his chest constricted so tight, everything inside seeming to cluster around his heart to crush it beneath the weight of all the things rushing within him.

"Earn that," he said tightly, and hated how unsteady his own voice sounded. "Do something brave to earn that, and perhaps I'll consider making this an everyday thing."

Summer would back out, he thought.

Summer would back out, let his anxiety take control, and retreat from the challenge.

And then this little farce would end, and Fox could return to normal.

But Summer only made a deep, inarticulate sound in the back of his throat, bordering on a growl—before he said breathlessly, "Fine. Give me the lesson plan."

A pause, as Fox's eyes widened and he glanced over his shoulder at the fierce way Summer's brows drew together, the determination in the glint of his eyes, the set of his shoulders.

"You want me to be brave?" Summer said. "Then I'll lead your next class."

★ ★ ★

Oh, Summer thought. *Oh.*

He thought, perhaps...

He had made a very large mistake.

He stood up in front of the classroom that had been the focal point of his life for his entire senior year. Still the same dark, peeling walls, still the same row of windows lined with potted plants and psychology textbooks along the back wall, still the same rows and rows of wooden desks that were the only ones in the school not scratched up and marked with pencil and pen graffiti.

Because everyone was too afraid of Professor Iseya to risk it.

But Summer wasn't Professor Iseya.

Summer was just Summer, and as he looked out over the sea of bored, disinterested faces, a few boys looking back at him with smirks as though sizing him up and wondering just how long it would take to break him...

He thought maybe he'd jumped in a little too fast, feet-first, and gotten in over his head.

Maybe he could blame hormones.

Because even over the hours he'd spent reviewing the lesson plan in Iseya's office while the professor quite pointedly ignored him without a single word or even a look...

He hadn't been able to stop thinking about that kiss.

That hand on his throat again—he would never stop thinking about that *hand on his throat*, the way Iseya seemed to need to naturally assert dominance and make Summer go weak with the inherent control in that touch. Such a light thing, a subtle thing...

But it had left him turned to an utter helpless doll, in Iseya's hands.

While Iseya had kissed him.

Iseya had kissed *him*.

Deep, slow, a thing of languid strokes and hot, firm lips that completely melted Summer, the teasing exploration of a tongue that knew exactly what it was doing as it slipped against every sensitive point in Summer's mouth.

If he had ever thought Iseya was cold…

That idea had been completely shattered, this morning.

He'd been completely shattered.

And willing to do anything to convince Iseya to do that again.

But he couldn't feel that heat, right now.

Not when he'd been trying to speak for the last thirty seconds, but all he could manage was an odd, thick sound as his tongue dried and gummed and stuck to the roof of his mouth.

Not when he could feel Iseya at his back, watching him with those cool, inscrutable eyes, not saying a single solitary word.

And not when every last one of these boys was the mirror of the ones who'd made him feel so small, so invisible, so unimportant and shriveled and worthless every day he'd spent surrounded by people his age who came from a different world—one where he didn't matter a single bit if he wasn't a trust fund baby, if he couldn't pay his tuition with his weekend allowance.

He'd known what he was to them.

The legacy, free tuition, sad thing who only got into

such an elite academy—hell, passing Iseya's psych classes had been his first AP college credit—because his father had *worked* here, instead of because his father had had money.

He wasn't that boy anymore, he told himself.

But his silent tongue and locked legs and shaking knees couldn't seem to remember that.

"I... I..." He cleared his throat, but it didn't really help; just made him feel like he was swallowing his fear in little spiky balls. His pulse jumped, his heart racketing up into an awful twitching rapid beat, fluttering like a cornered rabbit's breaths. "My...my name is Summer Hemlock—"

"For real?" came from the back of the class, followed by a chorus of sniggers. "That's not a real name."

"Maybe it's an anime name," someone else said. "Maybe he's a weeb. You a weeb, new guy?"

Laughter erupted. Summer darted his gaze left to right, searching for the speakers, but all he saw was grinning faces, glittering eyes, *contempt*.

He threw a helpless glance over his shoulder at Iseya, but Iseya was impassive, unmoving, just watching him with one brow slightly arched.

Waiting.

He was on his own.

He was supposed to control the class, and he was on his own if he was going to do this thing he'd said he was going to do.

He swung his gaze back to the class. "Y-yes. Yes, th-that's... that's my name, and I-I'm... I'm your new TA, and t-today we'll...we'll be going...over..."

His voice didn't want to work.

His voice didn't want to work, trailing off into a faintness that wasn't even a whisper, just this thready thing crawling out of his mouth and falling limply off his lips.

He couldn't feel his body, but he felt *everything* at the same time, every hair standing up in a fine prickle and panic running through him like water, this spike of awfulness bolting right down the center of his chest and screaming at him to *run*.

It didn't make sense.

It never made sense.

Rationally he knew there was nothing threatening him, right now.

Just a bunch of kids being little assholes, because that's what kids did.

But when his brain latched on to that little panic-rabbit breathing fast and swift and terrified in the center of his heart, nothing he *knew* could make its thumping stop.

"What was that?" one of the students jeered. "C'mon, Winter Crabapple or whatever. Rain. Storm. Hey, maybe I'll call you Stormy like Stormy Daniels. You wanna talk a little louder?"

Summer barely heard it.

Everything was receding away, falling down this long dark tunnel that made him feel like he was rising up into the sky, and the world was somewhere below, the noises distant and growing farther and farther away. Even his own body, far down below, like he was having an out-of-body experience and staring down at his own petrified face, the frozen grimace that was trying to be a smile, the way his fingers clutched the syllabus in his hands until the pages crumpled into deep creases.

And then the moment when he broke, and gave in to the voice in his head screaming that he was in danger and he needed to *run*.

He twisted on his heel, and suddenly the squeak of his dress shoes on the floor was too real, too loud, shrieking up that wind tunnel separating him from the world. Everything was blurry, his vision wavering and strange, but the door was close enough—close enough that it only took three steps before he was flinging it open, bursting out into the hall, skittering several clumsy steps before he just leaned over and grasped his knees and *breathed*.

Deep, harsh, he sucked in breaths as fast as he could, but he never seemed to get enough *air*, his head spinning and his heartbeat turning erratic and hot and twisted and heavy and he just—he just—

"If a single one of you," Iseya said from inside the classroom, his voice drifting out the door, "moves so much as a fingertip while I am absent, everyone has detention on grounds cleanup for a week. Be still. Be silent. And open your textbooks to chapter fourteen, Jungian psychology. There will be a pop quiz when I return."

Not a single peep rose.

Not even a groan.

No one disobeyed the tyrant.

Not even Summer.

But still he wasn't expecting the soft tread of footsteps behind him, the door pulling closed, latching.

And then strong arms around him.

Strong arms around him, coaxing him to straighten, pulling him into the heat and solidity of Iseya's body.

"Here," Iseya said softly, that frigid voice defrosting into a rumbling, gentle murmur of baritone. "Here. Hold on to me. You're all right."

As he spoke, Iseya drew Summer against his chest—and, numb with confusion, frozen with unreasoning paralytic terror, Summer went unresisting.

He didn't understand what was happening.

Only that Iseya's arms were firm and steady around him, wrapping him up, cradling him in quiet, steady strength. Suddenly the stone of Iseya wasn't forbidding, but instead… stable ground. Stable ground that made Summer's world stop spinning out of control, that held him in place and grounded him until he could stop feeling like the floor was dropping out from beneath him.

Because Iseya was holding him up.

And he let out a shaky sound, and buried his face in Iseya's chest.

He'd never been more aware of how tall Iseya was than now; Summer himself wasn't short, five foot eleven, but Iseya had at least four or five inches on him—and the professor rested his chin lightly to the top of Summer's head, making him feel enveloped, sheltered, wrapped up in a safe space that shut out all the senseless things that made his mind and body think he was in danger in the most mundane situations.

He hated his anxiety.

He hated it so, so damned much.

But he didn't hate this.

The warmth and firmness of Iseya's chest against his cheek, the breadth of his shoulders, the fresh-washed scent of his clothing and the soothing warmth of his body heat soaking into Summer. Long, strong hands against his back, fingers splayed, holding him, capturing him, gripping just enough to remind him he was solid and real and not this strange ghost disconnected from his panicking body.

He could breathe, now.

It still hurt, stitching his ribs strangely, every breath like ice water, but…

He could breathe.

There was *enough* air, and he no longer felt like he was about to pass out, his heart rate finally starting to slow down to normal levels and even out until its beats came in steady rhythm again.

But it skipped once more, startled and erratic, as Iseya said, "I'm sorry."

Barely a whisper, more felt ghosting against Summer's hair in warm breath, slithering down the curve of his ear, his neck, into his collar; felt rumbling in the chest beneath his clenched hands, his cheek.

He had to swallow multiple times before he could speak; before he could even find words, past the sluggish clouds that always seeped into his brain after an anxiety attack.

"Wh-why are you apologizing?" he managed to falter out weakly.

"Because I let myself get angry enough to goad you," Iseya said, and for a moment his arms tightened around Summer, a gentle grasp that gathered him in closer. "I know the markers of anxiety as well as I know any other condition. And I should not have agreed to let you do something so drastic that would trigger yours, when I knew you weren't ready to lead the class."

Summer bit his lip, hunching his shoulders. "I... I v-volunteered."

"You did," Iseya agreed. "But I am still your senior, and it was my responsibility to stop you."

"No...it wasn't." Summer had said he could do it, and he...he needed Iseya to trust that when Summer said he could do something, he meant it—and he would have to pace himself more in the future, make sure he could hold his commitments. But still... "But...thank you for caring."

Maybe...maybe it wasn't Iseya's responsibility, to know Summer's limits.

But...it *meant* something, that Iseya cared about pushing them.

Iseya said nothing, though.

But...

He didn't let Summer go.

And Summer wondered how long this would last, wondered how long he could hold on to it, when he'd wanted for so long to know how it would feel to rest against Iseya's chest and listen to the sound of his heart moving deep and strong inside his chest.

He closed his eyes and sank into that sound, letting it soothe him until he timed his breaths by it, and slowly it felt as though his heart moved into line with it, taking calm, taking strength.

And after several long minutes, Iseya asked, "Are you feeling better?"

"Yeah." Summer smiled wistfully. "I'm…sorry I made you angry. Guess I didn't earn that kiss after all."

"We shall call that one free." And Iseya actually chuckled— a soft-vibrating sound of sand and sugar and dark chocolate, a thing that seemed to stroke over Summer's skin, shaking him gently with the movement of Iseya's shoulders. "Are you really so very desperate for a kiss from me that you will step head-first into an anxiety attack?"

"Does that really piss you off so much that you'll actually let me make you angry?"

"It *confuses me*," Iseya said, a note of frustration in his voice. "I don't understand what makes you so persistent."

"Then you don't understand what I like about you."

How could Summer stand here in Iseya's arms, listening to the lulling rhythm of his heartbeat, and say these things so simply, so easily, as if they were intimate secrets between them…

But he couldn't even introduce himself to a class of teenage boys?

It didn't make sense.

But somehow, around Iseya…

Everything made sense.

Everything felt right, and calm…as if Iseya's steady calm was an aura that soothed the entire world around him, settling the ripples of the pond of life into calm stillness.

And Summer wanted to hold on to it for just a little while longer, before Iseya iced over again and pushed him away.

But Iseya only sighed, his chest rising and falling heavily underneath Summer's cheek. "Very well, you bizarrely impudent monster," he said flatly. "I will agree to your... utterly nonsensical terms and conditions."

Summer couldn't help a laugh—until it sank in what Iseya meant, and that laugh choked off in his throat as he lifted his head sharply, staring up into mercury-silver eyes.

Mercury-silver eyes that glimmered with something other than cold contempt or irritated disdain, though Summer couldn't quite tell what it might be.

Not warmth, maybe, not yet.

But perhaps...

Curiosity.

"You...mean it?" he asked breathlessly, his entire body alight with soft-touch prickles, tingles, little spark-feelings all over every inch of his skin, spark-feelings that turned into a *burn* where his body pressed against Iseya's, where Iseya's hands rested against his back. "One kiss for one brave thing each day?"

"*On one condition,*" Iseya said sternly, and pressed a finger to Summer's lips, stopping his question before it could start. That fingertip was subtly roughened, as if weathered by years of paper cuts and turning pages in soft slow reverence and the pressure of pens and pencils against it, its texture subtle and sensuous against Summer's mouth.

Summer swallowed thickly, waiting.

Waiting, and hoping that condition wouldn't dash his hope before it could flutter more than a few inches from his tightening chest.

"Pace yourself," Iseya said, eyes narrowing, mouth setting in that commanding line Summer was so familiar with—and that made his entire body turn melting-hot with that desire to obey. "You have a year to learn to lead a class. You don't have to give yourself an anxiety attack diving in on the first day. One *moderate* task that you feel is within your limits each day, but that is more than you would do unprompted. And *I* choose when and where we kiss. Are we understood?"

Summer's eyes widened.

Was...was Iseya using Summer's own desperate, needy wanting to get him to moderate and manage his anxiety?

He almost laughed.

Almost laughed, this bright thing inside him just growing brighter, because in its own way...

In its own way, it was terribly, wonderfully sweet.

And he didn't understand how Iseya could do things like this, and then wonder why Summer liked him.

"Understood," he promised—and kissed the fingertip pressed against his mouth, only to earn an absolutely *disgusted* look as Iseya drew his hand back sharply. Summer wrinkled his nose playfully. "That didn't count."

"It most certainly counted, and you're lucky I'm feeling lenient or I'd make you forfeit tomorrow's kiss for it." Iseya huffed, turning his face away, glaring down the hall—before reluctantly sliding gray eyes toward Summer from the corner of angled lids, watching him through the fringe of long, straight lashes that swept downward rather than curling. "You will tire of this game soon, Summer. You will tire of *me*. And then we can resume a relationship as professional colleagues, perhaps friends. Nothing more."

"I don't think that will happen." It ached, that Iseya saw so little in himself, and Summer's smile felt like a bittersweet thing of melancholy and warmth, as he tilted his head. "But if it does... I'd be happy to be your friend."

"Oh, do *stop*. You're like a puppy in human form." Iseya made a flustered, irritable sound, pressed a hand firmly against Summer's chest, and pushed him away. "And you are quite clearly fine now, so let's go back in before they destroy the classroom. I'll introduce you *properly*, and put the fear of you into those whelps."

"I... I don't really think that's possible."

Summer smiled, though, stepping back, straightening his clothing, breathing in deep. He could do this, he thought.

He could do this.

This job might not be what he wanted to do. It might just be another step in these holding patterns he always fell into, until he felt like an impostor walking into that room like he belonged there. But he'd committed to this—so if he was going to do it, he'd try his best to do it right.

And as long as Iseya had his back...

He'd be fine.

And he'd have tomorrow's kiss to look forward to, to always carry him through.

Chapter Six

Fox was beginning to think he'd been a little too on the nose, calling Summer a puppy.

Because it was starting to feel like he'd adopted one.

The first day of class had been somewhat uneventful, at least.

He'd tamed the class back into obedience, introduced Summer, and then let Summer take a back seat to work on grading papers and observing his teaching methods while Fox led the three afternoon sessions, repeating each time—and impressing *very* clearly on his unruly pupils that even if they might not fear Summer...

They wouldn't escape Fox's wrath if they kept trying to *fuck* with him.

It wasn't that he was protective of Summer.

Not at all.

He simply liked a quiet classroom, of course.

Of *course.*

And the classroom was almost painfully quiet after the last bell, once everyone had filed out and there was only Summer and Fox, and Summer gathering up the stacks of assignments he'd been given to grade against Fox's rubric by tomorrow.

They'd only looked at each other for long moments, and Fox...

For the first time in a very long time, found that he didn't know what to say.

Most of the time he simply didn't *want* to talk.

But he'd never quite found himself at a loss in just this way, before.

Summer had spoken, instead, offering a shy smile, watching him through the messy fringe of his hair, shadowing blue eyes until they glowed like descending twilight.

"See you in the morning?" he offered. "To...to check and make sure I graded things right."

"Ah," Fox said, and inclined his head. "Of course."

For some reason, that had made Summer light up, brilliant and sweet, his smile widening.

Before he nodded, and ducked out of the room like he was actually *eager* to wade through nearly a hundred papers on why Jung was, quite frankly, a woo-peddling asshole.

Then immediately ducked back in, biting his lower lip, faltering in that way he had that said he was nerving himself up to something; Fox could almost see it ticking over behind his eyes, that rising swell of bravery before he blurted, "Can I have your phone number?"

Fox leaned back in his desk chair, crossing his ankle over his knee and studying Summer, tapping a pen against his thigh. "Why?"

"Um. So I don't have to go to your room if I have a question?" Summer ventured, then ducked his head…but his mouth was twitching at the corners, struggling so clearly not to turn upward, while he watched Fox from beneath his lashes, the shadow of his brows, the fringe of his hair.

"Email suffices perfectly well," Fox pointed out.

"It could," Summer said, trailing off…

And Fox thudded his head back against his chair, closing his eyes for a moment.

Summer might as well be wagging his tail.

Grinding his teeth, slitting his eyes open, he held out his hand. "Phone."

Tumbling back into the room, Summer plunked the stack of papers in a skewed heap atop Fox's desk, then fumbled into his pocket, producing a slim Samsung that he almost dropped before he managed to swipe the screen, tap in his code, then thrust the phone at Fox with that annoyingly shy, boyishly sweet smile.

Fox eyed him over the rims of his glasses.

Where did he find the *energy*?

But, with a sigh, he pulled up Summer's address book and tapped his number in, saving it under *Iseya, Fox* before passing the phone back; their fingers brushed as Summer curled his hand around the Samsung, and for a moment they held, Summer staring at him with his lips parted, while Fox wondered distantly, idly, how anyone's fingertips could be so *warm*.

Then, clearing his throat, Summer pulled back, straightening and tapping quickly over the screen before giving a decisive little nod. "I sent you a text so you'll have mine."

Fox frowned, pressing his palm over the pocket of his slacks, searching—the shape of his iPhone wasn't there.

Hellfire.

Where *had* he left the thing?

And why hadn't he heard it vibrate?

He checked his other pocket, then leaned forward, patted his back pockets. Nothing. Muttering to himself, he pulled the central drawer of his desk open; nothing but legal pads and pencils neatly slotted in their cases, and a fresh gradebook waiting for the current one to run out of pages. He leaned over to check the side drawer, dragging it open and peering past the stacks of file folders; had he left it in his suite?

Summer watched him curiously. "You can't find your phone?"

"It is an accessory, not a necessity," Fox bit off, then clamped his lips shut if only because yes, he heard himself *quite* clearly, and knew exactly how old he sounded.

Too old for Summer to be watching him with that sort of quiet fondness, as if...as if...

He found even Fox's irritability endearing.

He didn't have to be so *obvious* about it.

"So...that means I don't have to wonder who's texting you at three in the morning and asking if you're up," Summer said, just a little too innocently.

"Anyone texting me at three in the morning would know very well that I am not up, and if they wake me they may forfeit their lives," Fox growled, before finally unearthing his phone from beneath last semester's third period gradebook. "*Ah.*"

He tapped the screen.

Nothing happened.

Pressed the power button.

Nothing.

Summer lightly drummed his fingertips against his own phone with a humming sound. "I think you have to charge it more than once a month, Professor Iseya," he lilted, and Fox glowered at him, dropping his phone on the desk and leaving it there, silent and dead.

"Silence, impudent whelp," he hissed.

And Summer just snickered, before clapping a hand over his mouth.

Hmph.

Disobedient and yet obedient at the same time.

Irritating, and just as much of a contradiction as Summer himself.

Thinning his lips, Fox folded his arms over his chest, staring at Summer flatly.

Years ago, Summer would have recoiled, shrinking into himself and scuttling away.

But now the incorrigible, irrepressible thing just smiled wider, a choked half-laugh muffled behind his hand and in the back of his throat.

"Are you *quite* finished?" Fox said flatly. "I'll see your text once I've charged my phone. That should be quite enough. And if you text me at three in the morning, I should hope it is actually important."

"Wanting to talk to you isn't important enough?" Summer asked, a husky little hitch in the words, and Fox let out an exasperated sound, thrusting his hand out and pointing firmly at the door.

"*Get out.*"

Summer just burst out laughing, a raspy-sweet sound with a touch of shivering depth to it.

Before he gathered up the papers once more, stacking his phone atop them and turning to stroll out, somehow once again managing to do exactly what he was told while still being *entirely* intolerable about it.

"Have a good night, Professor," sailed back over his shoulder, before he hooked the door with his foot and pulled it to in his wake.

Fox just glared after him, sinking down deeper into his chair with a grumble.

What an odd, *odd* young man.

It was quite annoying, how Fox couldn't ignore him.

And quite annoying how, the following morning, Summer was practically *vibrating* during office hours, restless and clumsy and dropping his pen, his near-empty cup of coffee, the textbook he was referencing to double-check Fox's lesson plan for the day. Always the constant glances from under his lashes, the blushing, the way he caught his lower lip in just one canine tooth so that it drew in on one side and only turned more lush, plush, reddened and enticing on the other.

Fox absolutely refused to look.

Just as he absolutely refused to look at the way, when he concentrated, Summer would catch the tip of his pen between his lips and chew at it delicately, his mouth working over it in soft caresses and the pen indenting his mouth in yielding, pillowy curves, the pressure and friction turning it redder and redder.

Fox wasn't watching.

He was grading an essay, damn it all to hell. He wasn't—

"*Stop that*," he hissed, and snapped a hand across the desk to pull the pen from between Summer's fingers, his lips, his teeth. "You'll damage your teeth."

Summer froze, fingers still poised in the shape of the pen, wide eyes flicking from the textbook to Fox. His button-down shirt was pale blue today, the perfect color against suntanned skin, and he was *far* too casual with the sleeves cuffed to his elbows to bare toned forearms, his collarbones stark ridges past the open V of the neck.

Honestly, had *no one* spoken to him about the dress code?

"Um," Summer said, eyes still a little too wide. "Sorry?"

"Simply don't do it again." Fox set the pen down very firmly between the open pages of the textbook. "It's quite distracting."

Summer winced, averting his eyes. "Sorry," he repeated. "I—"

He was cut off by a knock on the door. Summer glanced over his shoulder, while Fox lifted his head; through the frosted glass window inset in the door, he could just make out the shape of a student, marked by the typical navy blue of the uniform blazer.

"Enter," he said, schooling his face to impassivity.

The door creaked open tentatively. "Professor Iseya…?"

a cracking voice asked—either nervousness or puberty, he could never tell.

The boy who peeked around the door was tall, gangly, still growing into his limbs, still growing out of his pimples, his shock of reddish-brown hair always a mess; Fox recognized him as Craig Rockwell, from block two class period. He held his *Principles of Modern Psychology* textbook clutched tight against his chest, several pieces of bent and creased note paper crammed in between the pages.

Craig started to open his mouth—then stopped, staring at Summer. "Oh, um...if you're busy, I'll come back later."

"Have you forgotten already that Mr. Hemlock is my assistant, and here to assist *you* as well?" Fox bit off. Honestly, if he couldn't even pay attention to that... He arched a brow, toying his pen between his fingers. "What can I do for you, Mr. Rockwell?"

Craig cringed, going visibly pale, straightening his shoulders as if he'd been called to attention. "Um!" He cleared his throat, looking somewhere over Fox's head. "I...um, there's a part in the homework, in the chapter on developmental child psychology...um, they talk about toddlers, but like, there's variable age ranges? On Google? I'm not sure what the right age range is and that seems like it kinda matters to answer the question?"

Fox started to open his mouth—but Summer got there first, perking and twisting in his chair. "That's actually—"

He froze. So did Craig.

And both slid their eyes toward Fox, watching him with a sort of wary trepidation, before Summer broke into a sheepish smile, ducking his head.

Interesting.

Summer had utterly frozen in front of an entire class full of students, but faced with only one...

He'd immediately jumped to respond, confident enough in his answer to not even check with Fox first.

Fox lidded his eyes, watching them over the pen propped between his fingers, before flicking his fingers.

"Continue, Mr. Hemlock. Mr. Rockwell, please have a seat and allow Mr. Hemlock to assist you."

That bright smile lit Summer up again, and he flashed a grateful glance at Fox before beckoning to Craig. Craig looked more uncertain, gaze flicking between Fox and Summer, before he settled down gingerly in the second chair, propped his book open on the arm of it, and leaned toward Summer, underlining a passage with his fingertip.

"Here," he said slowly. "This is the part that confused me."

"Oh!" Summer perked. "Wow, we're still using the same textbook? I remember this. Look, if you flip back here it talks about age ranges as defined by psychiatric assessment standards versus like, child milestone development standards in pediatrics, so you'll find the range..."

He was already flipping back through the pages, while Craig leaned in curiously, eyes wide, following along.

Fox simply leaned back in his chair, lacing his fingers together against his stomach.

Interesting indeed.

Summer's effusiveness seemed to put Craig at ease in a way that Fox had never truly mastered; he wasn't one for *ease*, not really. He had to draw clear lines between himself and the students, and he simply…

Wasn't one for demonstrative emotions.

You weren't always like this, Fox.

His therapist's voice in his head again.

How long had it been since he'd made an appointment? Years. Maybe even a decade. At some point grief counseling had seemed pointless, when every day was unchanging, unending, and he had nothing more to report but another day of fulfilling his job, keeping himself closed away so that the children couldn't sense a moment of weakness and prey on it like the strange little things they were.

That was the odd thing about children.

So vulnerable. So sensitive. So easily broken.

So very carnivorous, with their underdeveloped brains and still growing sense of empathy.

They needed gentle handling, nurturing.

With iron gloves so they couldn't bite with their ferocious little teeth.

Fox had the iron part down.

But Summer…

Summer seemed to be the one who understood the nurturing in ways that Fox couldn't.

And it was quite curious to watch both how Summer smiled and bloomed with easy warmth as he explained concepts in simple terms, and how Craig's face cleared with comprehension and almost *pride* as he grasped onto them.

"Oh," Craig said. "Oh—that, I get it, so it's about measuring functional capacity. I think I can use that to answer the question. Thanks, Mr.…what was your name again?"

"Su—" Summer caught himself, flicked Fox an almost sheepish look, then half-smiled, eyes creasing, brightening. "Hemlock. It's Mr. Hemlock."

"Thanks, Mr. Hemlock." Craig gathered his things up, standing with the awkward, jerky motions of effusive youth; a quick look toward Fox, a nervous dip of his head, and he scurried out of the office, the door slamming closed behind him with an absolute lack of manners.

And leaving them alone.

Summer looked over his shoulder at the door, then back to Fox, before offering a rueful smile, hunching down into his shoulders a bit. "Sorry, I just... I kind of jumped in there a bit."

"I was actually quite surprised you did," Fox said. "You seem much less anxious in singular interactions."

Shrugging one shoulder, Summer said, "I mean...he's just one kid. It's a lot easier to talk one-on-one than it is to stand up in front of a bunch of them, all of them staring at me, while I'm actually trying to make them *listen*. I'm... I'm not someone who captures people's attention. I'm not someone who can impress people. So I just feel like they're staring at me and wondering what I'm doing up there, because I don't belong."

I'm not someone who captures people's attention.

And yet...

Somehow he seemed to have captured Fox's.

"What you're describing," Fox said, "is impostor syndrome. You're well aware of your technical qualifications to do the job, and yet you doubt them nonetheless because you fear others can see your personal failings and insecurities."

A ghost of a smile flitted across Summer's lips. "I know the textbook definition of impostor syndrome, Professor Iseya. But knowing it doesn't make it any easier to get past it."

"I am far too familiar with that unfortunate dichotomy."

"I guess you would be, huh." But before he could explain that cryptic statement, Summer looked away, clearing his throat softly and rubbing his hand to the back of his neck, a pink tinge seeping into tanned cheeks. "So...was that brave enough to earn my kiss for the day?"

Fox nearly choked on his next breath.

He didn't know why he thought, after a night's sleep and by the light of the next day, Summer might well have forgotten this little gambit.

Or realized, at least, that Fox was quite old, quite dull, and quite impossible to deal with in any sort of...*romantic* context.

Yet here he was, with that tiny smile still playing about his lips, nearly quivering with a sort of shy, sweet hope that seemed to radiate off him in a cloud of warmth.

Fox sighed, setting his pen down on the desk.

He had made an agreement.

And he did honor his agreements.

With an irritated sound in the back of his throat, he stood, crooking his finger. "Well, come here. I'm not kissing you across the damned desk again," he muttered.

Summer's head came up so sharply his hair actually flopped back from those wide, brightening blue eyes, before he tumbled out of the chair and stood as if coming to attention.

"Where—I—should I—"

Fox closed his eyes.

"Hellfire," he growled, stepped around the desk, hooked his arm around Summer's waist, and jerked him in to kiss him.

He didn't mean to be rough—but there was something *annoying* about Summer, something that got under his skin and frustrated Fox until he felt like he was punishing Summer with that kiss, abusing his mouth in hard, hot caresses that only barely waited to ask permission, waited for the low moan and the slack softness of Summer's mouth to invite him in before he invaded, searching deep as if he could find whatever it was that made Summer so persistent, so irritating, so…so…

Intoxicating.

There was something intoxicating about the way Summer's body molded to his; about the taut, lithe strength hidden beneath the crispness of his shirt, his slacks, those shoulders firm and tapering down to a narrow waist, slim hips. About the way Summer had to just barely rise up on his toes to reach, leaving him leaning harder still against Fox; about the way his hands caught at Fox's arms just above the elbows, snared in the sleeves of his shirt, held on tight.

He was so *warm*.

And so completely, sweetly submissive, as Fox caught Summer's lower lip between his teeth and pulled it into his mouth to taste him, to tease him, to suckle and bite and nibble until the flesh turned warmer still in his mouth, tender and giving to every bite while Summer let out soft, helpless, hungry sounds that did absolutely terrible things to Fox's constitution. His control.

His restraint, as he let his fingers fall to dig into Summer's hips, and pulled the aggravating young thing into him.

No room between them. No space for breath, for hesitation, for doubt when Summer gave himself over so willingly with a deep, husky moan—but suddenly he was shoving Fox back, pushing him with his body, challenging him with the pressure of flesh to flesh as he nudged Fox until his hips hit the desk and he slid back, settling atop the cherrywood, and Summer angled his hips between his knees—ah.

Ah.

Fox let his thighs spread, flanking Summer's hips.

And as Summer leaned into him, pressed flush…

Ah, *God*.

The heavy, hard ridge of arousal was unmistakable, and the answering heat in Iseya was undeniable, a raw hot burst of throbbing pressure rising against his slacks, sliding against Summer until they were chest to chest, hip to hip, cock to cock, and their tongues twined in slow, deep mimicry of the subtle rhythmic movements between them, suggestive and hot and oh-so-slick, oh-so-enticing.

And Summer's hands were on his waist, fingers strong and warm through his shirt, teasing against his skin in sensitive shudders as Summer's soft luscious mouth *begged* with its wetness, with its warmth, with the delicious low sounds that slid between them each time their lips came together, locked, parted again before twined tongues drew them back in to taste deeper and deeper still, breaths lost between them and everything in Fox *burning*.

This was hell.

This was hell, and he was combusting in this damnable flame, and he wanted to hate every minute of it—the betrayal of it, the riot of his body and this quiet buried starved need for contact, for affection, for *heat*, the guilt of his traitor heart that wanted so *much* it almost didn't care who even if the *who* wasn't *her*.

No—no, that was the even deeper curse of it.

He did care who.

He just didn't want to care that *who* was this young man who brought the same brightness as his name, this heat that illuminated everything beneath a wild and singing summer sun.

Gasping, Fox tore his mouth away from Summer's, threading his fingers into Summer's hair just to stop that needy, seeking mouth from following his; he didn't remember closing his eyes, didn't remember losing himself in the dark, but now he opened them, looking at Summer and that mouth turned into a bruise and a bloodstain and a bursting ripe fruit, glistening with Fox's own touch.

Summer looked…

He looked like everything Fox had forgotten how to feel, captured in the graceful line of his jaw and the flutter of his pulse making his throat move in quick-sharp tremors and the way he looked at Iseya with eyes that were midnight in the brightness of his day, full of all the secrets and promises and intimacies that midnight could bring.

Too much.

Summer was too much, and even if Fox's body *hurt* with how electrified he was, how hard, how hungry...

He let go, leaning back against the desk, letting his hands fall to brace himself as he turned his face away, staring off to the side at one of the hanging honeysuckle plants without really seeing it.

"That's all you've earned for today," he managed to say. His voice felt like a thick strange thing in his throat, sticking to its inner walls. "Enough."

Summer didn't move.

Not at first...until a hint of color intruded on Fox's peripheral vision. Just the lightest touch, a ticklish skim, tracing his temple, tucking a loose strand of his hair back past the frame of his glasses, and Summer let out a deep, contented sigh.

"Well," he said softly, warmth rolling into the throaty edge of his voice. "I think that answers the question of whether or not you like men."

Fox's heart skipped oddly.

Everything felt odd to him, as if he were an ancient and rusted machine whose circuits and pathways had gone dormant for so long that the first surge of sizzling lightning pouring through them was just a painful rush, electricity searing and burning and singeing fine and fragile things to ash because they just couldn't handle it anymore.

Fox just couldn't handle it anymore.

He didn't know how to feel these things, and more than his body...

His mind, his heart didn't know what to do.

"Don't be impertinent," he bit off, refusing to look back at Summer.

"I think you like me impertinent." A smile in that voice, gentle, deepening it. "I think I'm the only person in this school who isn't afraid of you."

Fox arched a brow, leaning farther away from Summer—his body heat, his allure, that firm pressure still caught between Fox's spread thighs. "Don't lie. You are *still* absolutely petrified of me."

"That's one way of putting it." Summer coiled that captured strand of hair around his finger, then let go, stepping back. Air rushed into the space where he'd been, cooling Fox's body, leaving him...annoyingly *bereft*. "Maybe I like that little thrill."

Sliding off the desk and rising to his feet, Fox did everything he could to comport himself with some semblance of dignity, smoothing his clothing and tucking that loose strand of hair back into the knot bound against the back of his head.

Lifting his head, he looked somewhere over Summer's head—because if he looked at Summer, those dark, hungry, *longing* eyes would draw him in, asking a question Fox just...

Couldn't answer.

So he only shrugged, turning away, stepping around the desk again. "There's a diagnosis for that."

"I don't need a diagnosis," Summer murmured. "Though I wouldn't mind another kiss."

Fox froze, shooting a look over his shoulder. "*One*, Mr. Hemlock. One per day, and that one is more than enough."

"Summer," he pleaded softly, his voice catching, that little hitch of his breath strangely arresting, *erotic*. "Call me Summer again."

"...finish reviewing the syllabus... *Summer*."

He shouldn't have said it.

Not when that small thing, that intimacy that was intimate only to him and yet that joined the quaking in the pit of his stomach, left him feeling more unsteady than he had in over a decade.

Squaring his shoulders, adjusting his suspenders, Fox continued, forcing his voice to remain stern. "And save your boldness for tomorrow. It's not even noon, and I've had quite enough of your impertinence for one day."

Summer didn't say anything for several moments— though Fox caught a faint hint of movement.

Movement, and then warmth...as Summer drew closer, almost pressing against his back.

Leaning in.

And whispering against his ear, as curls of warm breath shivered over Fox's skin and threaded like caressing fingers into his hair.

"Have you?" Summer rumbled.

Before his fingers grazed Fox's hair, touching, pressing... tucking something in between the strands. Fox tensed, a little shimmer of sensation rushing through him—but Summer was already pulling back, retreating.

"I need some air," Summer said. "But I'll be back in time for class."

Before he was gone, and Fox turned just in time to watch the door close.

And reached up to touch the delicate, cool honeysuckle blossom Summer had tucked into his hair, plucked from one of the trailing vines and left with its petals, its nectar-damp stamen, just barely touching against Fox's temple like a kiss.

Chapter Seven

If Professor Iseya was trying to kill Summer...

He might just get his wish before long.

Summer lay stretched on his stomach in bed and replayed this morning. That *kiss*. Iseya's long, strong thighs wrapped against his hips, the way he could feel Iseya's hardened cock pulsing against his own, arousal thick on the air between them and its scent dripping as heavily, as headily as the honeysuckles. The way Iseya had *tasted*, as their mouths had mated together until they were practically drinking each other dry. The quiet control in Iseya's every touch, making sure Summer knew his place—and that place was submitting to him with needy gasps, pliant and wanting.

And how Iseya had refused to even look at him or ac-knowledge him unless it involved classwork for the rest of the day, once Summer had come back from calming himself down and clearing his head.

With a groan, he dragged a pillow up, buried his face in the sheets, and then flumped the pillow right back down on top of his head.

Wanting Professor Fox Iseya was *murder*.

Lifting his head, blowing his hair from his eyes, Summer buried his arms under the pillow, settled his chin against the case, and stared at his headboard, the worn dark-stained wood nearly black in the deep evening darkness, the barest hint of moonlight through the windows gilding and outlining the edges.

How long would Iseya let this keep going on?

Two days, two kisses, and Summer was already a tangled-up wreck.

While Iseya, no matter how hotly he kissed Summer each time...

Fell back on cold detachment and distance the second it was over, as if it had never happened.

As if he really felt nothing, and no matter how his body might respond when he touched Summer, kissed him...

He'd never let Summer in beyond that, to scale those cold walls to find the warmth inside.

Maybe this really was just an experiment to Iseya, and in a few months he'd get tired of it once Summer proved he could be conditioned by Pavlovian methods far too easily, and it stopped being even remotely interesting.

Iseya was just...

Was just doing this to give him incentive to take those necessary small steps with his anxiety, anyway.

That…

That shouldn't hurt so much.

The pain was a small thing in the center of his chest, but it had the weight and gravitational mass of planets.

Sighing, Summer mooshed his face into the pillowcase again.

He was a *mess*.

And he needed to get some sleep. He'd spent half the evening cleaning up a disaster zone of potentially hazardous chemicals Dr. Liu had left in the kitchen sink like it didn't even matter, and the other half dozing off over reviewing student homework assignments on why Freudian principles no longer applied in modern psychology. In the morning he was supposed to try drafting his first lesson plan on his own, submitted for Iseya's approval, and—

—and he lifted his head sharply, heart giving an erratic thump, at the sounds of shouting echoing from down the hall.

He tumbled out of bed, not even bothering with shoes or a shirt over his pajama pants, and bolted out into the living room. He caught a glimpse of Liu's door creaking open and sleepy, confused eyes peeking out before Summer spilled out into the hall.

Just in time to catch two boys come tumbling out of their room, tangled up in a smashing, punching, slapping brawl with limbs flying everywhere and clothing ripping, just a flash of grit-toothed faces and angry eyes before they crashed to the floor, while all up and down the hall more doors opened, lights flicked on.

"Hey!" Summer threw himself at the mess of thrashing

arms and legs, thrusting himself between one boy and the other just in time for the knee that had been smashing toward one boy's face to hit Summer right in the ribs.

He grunted, flinching back as a dull burst of pain hit him, but managed not to fall.

While the boy who'd just kneed him froze, his snarling grimace turning into a look of abject terror as he took in exactly who he was looking at.

Summer guessed he did have some clout as a teacher, after all.

Straightening, sucking in a few wheezing breaths and pressing his hand over his aching side, he looked between the two boys; the other lay on the ground with his cheek purpling and swelling, one eye forced nearly shut, while the boy in front of Summer had a busted nose, blood trickling down onto his upper lip. Jay Corey and Eli Schumaker, if Summer remembered them right from second and third block class rosters.

"Don't move," he told Eli firmly; Eli didn't budge an inch save for to drop his leg, staring at Summer with his eyes so wide the whites showed all around, face petrified in a mask of fear and his half-clenched fists still upraised.

Summer bent to offer Jay his hand. "C'mon," he said. "Up."

Sniffling, Jay rubbed at his nose and then stared at his bloody fingers, before giving Summer his other hand. Summer pulled him up, drawing him to his feet until he found his balance; then Summer lifted his head, looking down the hall. Several other students peered out with wide-eyed curiosity; a few other teachers had emerged as well.

"Go back to your rooms," Summer called. "It's past curfew."

He knew the magic word.

And on *curfew* doors started slamming instantly, while a few of the other teachers moved down the halls, checking to make sure the boys complied.

Summer returned his attention to the two battered boys in front of him—who quite pointedly stood apart from each other, keeping Summer between them and not looking at each other.

Summer sighed, folding his arms over his chest. "Okay, what started this?"

Neither Jay nor Eli answered. Until Eli muttered half under his breath, "...punk piece of—"

"Eli," Summer cut off firmly, but Jay was already glaring at Eli.

"You started it," he growled, and Eli whipped back around, gesturing fiercely.

"The hell I did, I told you you could come if you wanted to—"

"—and I told you I won't if that asshole's there and you invited him anyway!"

"Hey." Summer frowned. "Who's the asshole?"

"Nobody," Eli mumbled sullenly, at the same time that Jay bit off,

"Theo fucking Rothfuss, that's who. We were supposed to go to the movies next weekend but *this* dick invited Theo."

"He's my friend!" Eli flared.

"He pissed in my fucking Gatorade!" Jay shot back, and Summer nearly choked.

"Okay. No more yelling in the middle of the hall," he said, and gently gripped each boy's upper arm, just enough of a touch to nudge them along. "Come on. We're going to head to the infirmary, and we're going to have a little talk—and then the two of you can work this out in detention, so that's solving the problem of your weekend plans right there."

Both boys groaned.

But they didn't resist, bowing their heads and letting themselves be shuffled along.

While Summer tried not to be painfully aware of the pair of intense silver eyes, watching him from one of the open doorways and seeming to track his every last step.

Long night.

Long, *long* damned night.

And Summer thought he might just collapse where he stood.

It had taken less time to get the boys cleaned up and bandaged by a very tired-looking Nurse Atherton than it had taken to get them to sit down and talk. But once Jay had opened up, sitting in the library with Summer and Eli where no one else could hear and judge, a story had come pouring out about one of the other seniors—Theodore, one of the bigger boys who liked to bully the others just because he could and because, in a social hierarchy defined by whose parents had the most power and money, Theodore was very close to king with a family entrenched in centuries of luxury hotel operations around the world.

He'd done worse things than urinate in Jay's drink.

Much worse things.

And as the litany had come out, Eli had shrunk smaller and smaller in his chair, refusing to look at Jay even while Jay was practically pleading with him not to be friends with someone who could hurt him so deeply.

All of it was, quite frankly, a hot mess.

And too complex to be dealing with in the middle of the night, but then messes didn't really wait until more convenient times.

What had followed was nearly an hour of quiet talking. Of trying to get both boys to see the nuance in the situation— that it was painful for Jay to see Eli ignore the way Theodore had hurt him, because to Jay that meant condoning it. But also trying to make Jay understand that to Eli, it felt like Jay trying to control who he could be friends with...and that for Eli, aligning himself with Theodore was likely a matter of self-protection to keep from becoming Theodore's next target.

That had sparked Eli's ego, set off a defensive mess of denials and accusations about Jay needing to be more honest about what he really wanted out of their friendship, and Summer having to intervene until Eli calmed down and admitted he didn't even really like Theo that much and he didn't want to lose Jay as a friend or roommate, just...

Much of it had been less about lecturing and more about nudging. Summer had figured that out a long time ago; people in conflict never liked to be told what they should do. Instead ask leading questions, offer answers if asked, but point them at each other and let them work it out until they were at least honest with each other, no matter the outcome.

And he thought, maybe, this outcome might actually be good.

He'd at least gotten them to *talk* about their feelings, which, with teenage boys?

Was a world-class feat of strength in and of itself.

They could work the rest out in their room. And in detention. Including that if they stuck together, they were strong enough to hopefully resist bullies like Theodore.

Summer sat alone in the library for long minutes after he'd sent the boys back to their room, pressing his face into his palms and just breathing. That had been...*intense*. And while he'd just reacted in the moment and thrown himself into doing what was necessary, now that he was coming out of it he was fucking exhausted, bone-weary...and had a throbbing bruise forming on his ribs.

He wasn't about to drag Nurse Atherton out of bed again.

He valued his life too much.

He'd stop by the infirmary in the morning, and for now just...try to sleep.

Maybe he'd stop by the guidance counselor's office, too. Let them know they needed to keep an eye out for some of the power dynamics in the school. There was only so much they could legally do with matters of liability, but...

When someone could urinate in another boy's drink and get away with it, there was something seriously wrong here—and the boys should feel like they could turn to someone who would be on their side, no matter what.

Tomorrow.

He'd worry about it tomorrow.

As he didn't think Iseya would appreciate him showing up completely wiped out, groggy, unable to focus, and manic on a double-shot espresso.

Scrubbing at his eyes, he pushed himself to his feet and stepped back out into the darkened, empty halls. When he'd been a boy, everyone had always found the school to be creepy at night, with the silhouettes of mist-shrouded trees through the windows, the shadows hiding in the rafters, the creaking floorboards and the looming haunts of strange crevices and fixtures. Summer had rarely had occasion to spend time at the school at night as a student, with living in town...

But the few times he had he'd found it comforting, not creepy.

A place where old things lived, silent and settling into their bones.

He ran his fingers along the wall as he walked, the texture of the wood under his fingertips, the coolness of it the same as the coolness of the floorboards under his bare soles. Head down, watching his toes and the deep wood grain, he tracked his progress back to his room in the raised edges of door frames, the turn of hallways, the indentations of recessed doors with numbers tacked on in brass worn down to the dullest of shines.

It almost felt like dreaming, being the only one in the halls, the only one ghosting through these passageways, like he was a haunt and everyone hid away behind their doors to keep his wandering, baleful eye from landing on them and pulling them into the dark.

He was so caught in this thought, in the quiet sleepy delight of it, that he didn't realize when his skimming fingertips skipped over the carved edge of a doorframe to land not on the door, but on empty air.

Until he touched skin, warm and firm and smooth.

Skin, and the tight-honed curve of a shoulder.

He jerked his hand back, pulse thumping faster through his veins, and lifted his head, stopping where he stood.

And found himself face to face with Fox Iseya, those silver eyes piercing into him like diamond spears, rooting him in place.

Iseya leaned in the doorway of his suite, arms folded over his bare chest, a pair of loose, dark gray linen pajama pants holding for dear life on to the sculpted, trim angles of tightly defined hips. He was the same smooth shade of pale gold all over, like sunlight pouring over white sand—his skin taut and weathered and drawn tight over firm shoulders, over the pronunciation of collarbones as sharp as an indrawn breath, over the hard-toned breadth of his chest, over the rolling fluid rows of muscle tapering down his abdomen to the dip of his navel and the sinful slope of his pelvis. The neatly pressed shirts and suspenders he wore tended to slim his figure, disguising the true bulk of him.

But like this, shirtless and radiating heat and towering over Summer with such forbidding intensity…

He was somehow even more intimidating.

And even more alluring.

Especially when his glasses were absent, leaving those angled, long-lashed, penetrating eyes fully unguarded.

And his hair was barely caught up in a knot, endless skeins of it spilling loose to pour down his back in a tangled mess tumbling to his thighs, several wispy locks drifting across his brow and coiling over his shoulders, clinging lovingly to the long, elegant slope of his throat.

Summer's mouth dried. His heart tried to stop, petrified in its place, as rooted as his feet were to the floor.

He tried to say something.

And all that came out was a broken, ragged, "Ulp."

Iseya arched one sharp, dark dash of a brow, inclining his head as though acknowledging something perfectly normal. "Summer," he said coolly.

Fuck.

Iseya shouldn't…be like that. Shirtless, radiating this wild animal sensuality at once dangerous and inviting, saying Summer's name in that voice. Looking at Summer with *those eyes*, when without the glasses chilling them…

Summer realized they weren't the glacial, pale ice he'd always thought.

They were molten silver, burning-hot and leaving his skin, his entire body feeling far too warm.

He struggled to pull himself together, told himself to *stop* when he was just tired and overreacting.

But he had to look away to find his voice again; to even be able to breathe, when he was caught up in the stifling, oppressive need to just…just…

Touch, and his fingers curled against his palm, holding fast to the tingling after-impression still left in his fingertips.

"Is…is everything okay?" he managed to straggle out. "I sent the boys back to their room, and I'll report everything to the principal in the morning."

"The boys returned to their room as they were told. Considering I doubt you did much to discipline them, they were remarkably obedient," Iseya lilted mockingly. "I was waiting for you."

Summer's breaths skipped as he darted a look at Iseya. "For me…? Wh-why?"

"Because it would appear that I was correct in anticipating your behavior." Iseya's gaze roved down Summer's body, drifting, yet every lingering look as palpable as a touch of liquid fire slipping over his skin, coaxing the breath from his lungs until his chest ached and burned. "You saw to the students…and not to yourself."

It took a moment to click, to realize where Iseya was looking.

The bruise over Summer's ribs.

He'd already gotten used to ignoring the pain, so tired that the throbbing was just a quiet counterpoint to his exhausted heartbeat.

He flushed, face and neck warming, and rubbed a hand over the back of his neck, craning to try to look down at his own chest. The mark over his ribs was starting to turn a dark, ugly purple in the shape of a kneecap.

Great.

"It's just a bruise," he mumbled. "I'll get it checked out in the morning. Wasn't worth bothering the nurse again."

Iseya clucked his tongue, then let out an exasperated sigh. "Inside," he ordered, then turned away sharply, his hair flicking out in a lash of dark wisps to lick against Summer's chest before drifting away as Iseya disappeared inside his suite.

Leaving Summer blinking after him, staring through the open doorway.

Iseya...wanted him to come inside?

He stood numbly out in the hallway for several seconds longer, then cleared his throat, glancing side to side. No one in the hallway. Not that it mattered, it wasn't like anyone would *think* anything seeing him going into Iseya's suite this late at night.

So why was Summer so flustered, his face so hot?

"You have ten seconds before I close the door in your face and lock it," drifted sharply from inside.

Summer scrambled over the threshold, and pushed the door firmly shut behind him.

And stood there like a giant dork, unmoving and staring around the suite.

He'd been here before, but Iseya's suite looked somehow different by night. The standard-issue furniture had been replaced by quiet things in dark wood, tastefully arranged for a combination of comfort and elegance; the dark wood flooring was, in places, covered over by large tatami mats in paler tan colors, pinned in place by low long lacquered tables and chairs and a sofa made of black wicker so delicate it was like spiderwebs, accented by pale gray cushions.

When he'd been in the room before Summer had incidentally registered the tall, double-doored cabinet against the far wall, its outer finish made of polished, darkly colored rosewood. It hadn't really sunk in as anything other than a liquor cabinet or a closed bookcase, but now its doors were open and he realized...

He'd been entirely wrong.

The interior of the cabinet had only two shelves, with the lower shelf protruding out further to form a ledge; the cabinet's backing had been papered over with a delicate watercolor painting of a landscape, loosely written kanji pouring down the side in a story or message Summer couldn't read. The top shelf was centered by a small golden statue of the Buddha, standing with his hand upraised and fingers parted, and flanked by two unlit white candles. On the bottom shelf was a bronze incense bowl, with two picture frames to either side. In one was a small scroll with more kanji, just a few simple characters and yet they seemed written with a sort of visual poetry that made every line of delicate black ink flow.

In the other was a photograph of a woman.

She was lovely in a delicate, willowy way, with a sort of haunting sadness to her high-cheekboned face and a way of looking to one side as if searching for some secret hidden just out of reach, her black hair swept up from her amber-gold face and knotted ornately behind her head.

Summer's throat tightened, as he realized...

Oh.

He felt like he shouldn't be here, all of a sudden.

Like he was intruding on something sacred.

And yet he drifted closer, drawn by that portrait of a woman, and wondered if somehow, somewhere, in some strange place...

She knew that she was still with Iseya even now.

Summer stopped in front of what he could only call a

shrine, looking up at the gleaming shape of the Buddha, then at the woman.

I'm sorry, he thought. *I'm... I'm sorry for wanting him so much.*

"I was never raised Buddhist," Iseya said softly at his back. "But she was. So out of respect for her memory, I placed her name in the butsudan to honor her and keep her."

Summer looked over his shoulder. Iseya stepped out of the bathroom with a clean towel draped over his arm, a bottle of alcohol and a tin of some sort propped in the crook of his elbow. His gaze trained over Summer's head, distant, before lowering to Summer, watching him inscrutably.

"I'm sorry," Summer said. "I shouldn't...have... I don't know."

"You didn't do anything wrong." Iseya sank down to sit on the low, delicate wicker sofa. "Come. Let me have a look at you."

Summer glanced back at the shrine again, and at the photo of Michiko Iseya.

Before pulling away, and settling to sit gingerly on the edge of the sofa, barely resting enough of his weight to dent the pillowy-soft cushion.

He didn't belong here.

But Iseya's touch jerked him roughly from his drifting thoughts, as an ice-cold, stinging-wet towel pressed over his bruise.

"This may burn a little," Iseya warned, half a second too late, and Summer yelped, squinting one eye up.

"A *little?*" He hissed under his breath; he didn't know

what was worse, the pressure against the tender flesh, or the fact that the bitter-smelling alcohol soaking the towel *burned*. "Nngh…why does it sting so much? It's a bruise; it didn't even break the skin!"

"What exactly do you think happens to your skin on impact bruising?" Iseya said crisply; his head was bowed, focusing on Summer's bruise, but he flicked a sharp glance up from under his brows. "Even if you don't bleed from open wounds, your skin still suffers abrasions and microfissures. Which is why you need sterilization in the first place."

Summer didn't know what to say.

Especially with Iseya so close, both of them…barely wearing anything at all, thin pajama pants and body heat and Iseya's arm brushing Summer's each time he adjusted to dab at his side a little more, and Iseya *touching* him and yet it was only clinical, only necessity, and that shouldn't *ache* so much but with that portrait looking over Summer's shoulder, it just reminded him…reminded him…

He'd never really had a chance, had he?

He closed his eyes, trying to put the thought out of his mind.

Trying not to think, period, when having Iseya's hands on him this way, being alone with him with this illusion of intimacy, hurt more than it should.

It was fine. He was fine. It was just…a boyhood infatuation that had flared to life again and led to him being rash, impulsive, over this strange kissing game.

He'd get over it.

He'd get over it, and respect Iseya's need to keep his distance; respect his grief, and the memory of his dead wife.

Maybe they could be friends.

And that was okay.

He sucked in a breath through his teeth, though, as the cold-burning alcohol was replaced by something warm and thick; he opened one eye to a slit and watched as Iseya spread a thick, translucent golden salve onto the bruise, long fingertips coated in a glistening sheen and gently stroking it into Summer's skin. A thick, heady smell rose between them, something like amber and musk with a tinge of vanilla. It felt nothing but slick at first, but slowly as it soaked in a deep burn spread into Summer's flesh, absorbing with a soothing, pleasant heat that eased away both the sting of the alcohol and the throbbing pain of the bruise.

"What is that...?" he asked softly.

"Nothing much different from sports cremes," Iseya murmured, voice distant, distracted. "A little menthol, a few things to cover the pungency of the smell."

"You made that...?"

"Ah." Iseya's lips quirked faintly. "At one point I suppose I had a bit of a passion for herbalism. But at this point I don't really keep my own plants anymore, other than in my office. If I need to make anything I get what I need from a local supplier."

Summer blinked, then couldn't help but laugh. "You mean my mother."

"I do see Lily now and then, yes."

It warmed Summer, to hear the tinge of affection that just barely touched Iseya's voice when he spoke of Summer's mother. To know that even if his mother worried about Iseya, his distance...

Iseya still felt something for their friendship.

"Mom asks me about you sometimes," he ventured tentatively. "I think she misses you. She said you were friends."

Iseya stilled, his hand pulling away from Summer's skin, holding in midair while his eyes widened briefly; he gave Summer an odd look, before bowing his head and focusing on the tin resting open on his thigh, dipping his fingers in and coating them once more. "I suppose at one time, we were."

Summer got the message.

Don't push it.

So he just cleared his throat and reminded himself to hold still as Iseya began rubbing more of the salve into the bruise, kneading it in with a gentleness that pulled at Summer in all those ways he was trying to ignore.

Instead he changed the subject, and murmured, "So I think I'm going to refer Jay and Eli to the guidance counselor. Theodore Rothfuss, too."

Iseya arched a brow. "You think that would be effective?"

"Yeah. I mean, I hope so." Summer leaned back on his hand to move his arm out of the way, giving Iseya easier access to the spreading branch of bruised flesh that reached around his side. "These kids get dumped here because their parents don't want to deal with them. And they act like they don't care, that they're glad to be somewhere without their parents hanging over their shoulders, but...they're turning to us for structure and guidance, and maybe they get that from the teachers, but..." He frowned. "They need some kind of nurturing, too. But I don't think any of these three would go to the guidance counselor on their own."

"Likely not," Iseya agreed mildly, then added, "...especially since we do not have one any longer."

Summer blinked, cocking his head. "We don't? What happened to Dr. Cartwright?"

"Resigned about two years after your graduation." Iseya's hand pressed flat to Summer's rib cage for a moment, smoothing over the bruise in one last long, slow stroke that made Summer's heart beat so hard surely Iseya must feel it under his palm, before that touch withdrew. "We've yet to find anyone to fill the position. Shocking that no one wants to exile themselves to a small, remote town to play both parental figure and therapist to some of the world's most spoiled children."

Summer smiled faintly, sadly. "The fact that people see them that way is probably exactly why they need someone."

Iseya lifted his head, watching Summer, his eyes half-closed and strange, glimmering in the darkened room; neither of them had turned on the light, working solely by shadows and moonlight, and those shadows seemed to dwell oddly in Iseya's gaze as he fitted the cap back onto the tin.

"You truly empathize with these boys, don't you?" he murmured. "Even though they're no different from the ones who made you feel so small as a student."

"I guess I never minded, even back then." Summer shrugged. "Because even back then I could tell they were acting out because they were hurting."

A faint wrinkle appeared between Iseya's brows. "You

are the strangest young man, Summer Hemlock. I confess you do surprise me, at times."

"In a good way or a bad way?"

"In a way that does not need to have a positive or negative value derived from it. It simply is."

Iseya rose, then, moving with fluid grace that made the tight sinew of his waist, back, and shoulders slink sinuously as he gathered the salve, alcohol, and towel once more.

"Are you feeling any better?" he asked neutrally, voice drifting back as he vanished into the bathroom again.

"Yeah." He really did, the pain just a dull afterthought instead of an active throbbing, and Summer stood, scrubbing his hands awkwardly against his thighs. "Thank you. Saved me a trip to the nurse in the morning, but… I'll get out of your hair."

An amused sound drifted from the bathroom, followed by, "…you're doing it again."

"Doing what…?"

"Self-effacing. Assuming your presence is undesirable." Iseya's tall, prowling frame melted into view again, settling to lean in the bathroom doorway with those unreadable eyes locked on Summer, arms once more folding over his chest as he slouched with a mixture of grace and ennui. "Some things really don't change."

"…it's the middle of the night and I'm in the middle of your suite when you should be sleeping, and you make it pretty clear you find anyone breathing in your presence irritating." Summer shrugged with a little laugh, which trailed off as he glanced over his shoulder at the cabinet and that little photo. "And... I...it just...it feels like I interrupted something private."

"Not quite."

Iseya pushed away from the doorframe, his lazy, loping strides *different* somehow, that commanding, calm power that always infused his movements changed into something stranger, more vibrant, yet more languid, this slinking sense of *presence* that Summer tried to ignore and yet...couldn't. Any more than he could ignore the way the moonlight gilded Iseya's features, and slipped over his hair; the way his long lashes glittered *just so* as he stopped in front of the cabinet and reached into a small folded paper satchel on the bottom shelf to retrieve a little conical stick of incense.

"It's more that you interrupted unhealthy habits," he murmured, gaze focused on his fingers as he set the incense in the bronze holder. "I don't even know why I do this anymore. She's not here. She hasn't been here for some time. And I feel as though by holding on to her memory, I've stayed frozen in some quiet place in the past, while the rest of the world has moved on without me...so I'm not really here, either."

He said it so quietly, so dispassionately, gaze locked not on the photo of his ex-wife but on the golden statue of the Buddha. As if he was trying to divorce himself of all emotion; to make such simple, heartfelt things into something clinical that he could pluck out of himself and toss aside as easily discarded words.

And it made Summer's heart ache, every word a tiny knife cutting in to leave him bleeding.

He stepped closer, risking drawing into Iseya's space,

risking moving to stand next to him, close enough for body heat to bring them into contact even if skin didn't quite touch skin. Voice thick in his throat, he looked up at the shrine, watching not Iseya, but the faint hint of Iseya's reflection in the mirror-bright polish of the rosewood.

"You're here, though," he said softly. "Maybe you don't feel like it, but you're here. You're here to me."

"What does that even mean, though?" Iseya asked—yet the words were so quiet he seemed to be speaking more to himself than to Summer. "What does it mean for me to be here without her?"

"I don't know." Summer glanced at Iseya from the corner of his eye. "But it sounds like you might be ready to find out."

Iseya said nothing, but for a moment those carefully shielded silver eyes seemed to crack, turning liquid, brows knitting, lips parting as he stared at the Buddha as if it might give him some sort of answer in the silence.

Before he bowed his head, his breaths shuddering audibly as he plucked a small lighter from inside the paper sack, and lit the tip of the incense cone with a brief flick of his thumb, a spark, a flicker of flame. The peak of the cone turned into a deep-glowing ember, and a soft, powdery scent rose like dragon's blood.

Iseya set the lighter down, silver eyes flicking upward to track the curl of incense smoke; Summer followed it as well, a strange heaviness settling on his shoulders, before looking back to Iseya as the man spoke.

"It's ritual, at this point. And I suppose I have to finish it, even if it feels meaningless." He turned his head just enough to catch Summer's eye, the faint red spark of the incense's cone reflecting in his eyes. "You...do not have to leave, if you do not wish to."

A little flutter ran through the pit of Summer's stomach. "What's the ritual?" he asked, barely able to find his voice above a whisper. "What are you doing?"

Iseya turned away from him, then, tilting his head back, looking up at the rising coil of thick, ribbon-like white smoke as it wisped toward the ceiling.

"Trying," he said, "to finally say goodbye."

Summer said nothing.

It didn't feel like words were needed, in this moment.

Just...that he *be here*, to answer that quiet unspoken need in Iseya's words.

You do not have to leave.

When Summer thought, just maybe...

Iseya might mean *stay.*

So he stayed.

He stayed, and he watched the incense burn down with Iseya, and let its scent drift into him as he wondered what this meant.

If it meant anything at all.

Maybe Iseya was ready to let go, to stop living his life locked away in grief...

But maybe all he needed for that was a friend, and Summer thought...

That was okay.

He just...

He just wanted Iseya to be okay, no matter what that meant.

Yet standing so close to Iseya, Summer couldn't help how their shoulders brushed, as they stood silent vigil. How their arms pressed together. How the backs of their hands touched.

And when his hand fell against Iseya's, he didn't pull away.

Neither did Iseya.

And for a few sweet moments, as they stood amidst winding serpentine coils of aromatic smoke and breathed and didn't say a word...

Their fingertips tangled, and held.

They stayed that way, wordless and yet Summer leaping inside, at once calm and ready to burst with fluttering warmth, until the incense burned down to a little dense pile of soft gray ash. Until the smoke stopped, and that cherry-red ember that was the only light between them burned out. Still they remained for long moments...until Iseya pulled away, and reached up to close the cabinet, settling the doors into place with a soft *thump* and a quiet sense of finality.

He rested there with his palms against the wood, looking up at it, before he turned a look over his shoulder, watching Summer over one upraised bicep, its curve pulled taut.

"I suppose," he said dryly, "since it's after midnight, you'll be wanting your kiss now. For being brave enough to intervene with the boys."

Summer pulled from his quiet trance, blinking at Iseya while his breaths swirled into a storm in his chest. Something about the way the man looked at him promised...

He didn't know.

He didn't know what to think of the way those heady, compelling gray eyes lingered on him, or the way they seemed to burn in the shadows.

Especially when he couldn't forget that ache that made a third presence in the room, either.

After a moment, he just smiled, shaking his head, stepped closer.

And leaned in to press his lips to Iseya's cheek, nosing lightly past a messy skein of his hair to press a lingering kiss to the crest of his cheekbone.

Iseya's skin was subtly weathered, just a hint of roughness and texture that came with age and daily shaving, something Summer wanted to savor against his skin, to absorb...but he made himself pull back, rather than invading further, holding on to his smile even though some part of him felt like breaking as he met Iseya's wide, startled eyes, that strange lost look Summer almost never saw, lips parted, cheeks flushed.

"That'll do," Summer murmured, then lifted his gaze to the shrine, their dim and reddened reflections. "Thank you for letting me be a part of this."

Then he stepped back, offering another small smile.

"Goodnight," he said, and walked away.

He'd made it to the door, pulling it open, ignoring the strange needy feeling trying to pull him back toward Iseya, trying to tell him not to walk away, whispering of some unanswered craving...when Iseya's voice drifted after him.

"*Summer.*"

His name, in that silk-sin voice, low, compelling. He felt it like rough fingertips down his spine, and turned back.

To find Fox Iseya standing almost right behind him, towering over him and looking at him with his mouth set tight, his eyes narrowed and dark.

Summer recoiled a step, one heel edging out into the hall. "Professor Iseya...?"

Iseya braced his hand to the doorframe above Summer's head, leaned down...and captured his mouth, stealing him for a kiss unlike any other Summer had ever tasted.

Where every other kiss had been hard, dominating, passionate, deep...

This one touched his lips gently, wonderingly, as if asking for the smallest taste of him; as if asking to know him through the softest of touches, to learn what could make him tremble with the slightest brush and what could make him sigh. As if this moment wasn't about the kiss, the act of it, the stimulation, the pleasure...

But about *him*.

Iseya was kissing *him*, as if he was worth kissing slowly just to savor it.

And God, did he savor it—the way Iseya stroked his mouth gently against Summer's, the way each touch made his mouth pulse so sweetly and coaxed his lips to part further and further until he breathed Iseya in and shivered as he felt every light tracery of friction, of taunting softness, ripple over his entire body as if he'd been swathed in silk and covered in its caress. Summer closed his eyes, leaning into it, unable to stop his moan, his wordless begging.

Begging for more.

Just the lightest tease of Iseya's tongue-tip, following the line of Summer's lips, delving inside...

And then it was over, as quietly as it began.

A soft graze of Iseya's teeth against his lower lip, before their mouths parted, the last touch Summer felt Iseya's whisper, breaths cooling the dampness on his lips and proximity turning every word into the ghosts of other kisses.

"You're now forfeit for any kisses for the next forty-eight hours," Iseya breathed, sultry and deep-rumbling. "*Goodnight.*"

Summer snapped his eyes open, heart nearly pounding out of his chest.

And only got half a glimpse of Iseya's slow, almost cunning smile—

Right before the door closed in his face.

Chapter Eight

Fox was beginning to think he might have been wrong about Summer.

Perhaps he'd made a snap judgment, based on his recollection of the boy Summer had been. Perhaps he had formed his first impression of the man Summer had become based not on who Summer actually was, but on Fox's own resentment that he had to train someone to take his place; had to take some vulnerable, wide-eyed young thing under his wing and let this other human into his world for longer than a single class period.

When if he was honest with himself...

Summer had been showing Fox who he was from the start.

From the way he had thrown himself in to help contain another of Dr. Liu's conflagrations without even thinking of his own safety, wanting to help...

...to the way he swallowed his own terror to kiss Fox,

kiss his *former teacher*, after not seeing him for seven years and knowing full well he would be immediately rejected.

The way he challenged himself at every turn despite the anxiety wrapped around him like black, choking tendrils.

The way he challenged Fox, too, and yet did so with the softest of touches that seemed to ask, *Show me.*

Show me where all the tender places are, so I won't bruise what hurts.

And the way he had continued to put himself forward for the last few days, even without the promised reward of a kiss to motivate him.

Technically, denying Summer his next kiss wasn't fair, considering that Fox had been the one to kiss him.

But Summer hadn't protested in the slightest, only showing up day after day to put the work in and give his all to trying to help Fox in the classroom.

Fox still didn't think he was ready to lead the class.

But as he watched Summer move through the rows of desks, bending to answer a question or give a little encouraging nudge to a struggling student, smiling and making the tense, nervous boys relax while they worked through their test prep worksheets...

Fox thought maybe, one day, he could be—when at first he'd thought it was a lost cause.

So why did that make him feel so empty?

As if something precious was slipping through his fingers, water pouring out of his hands no matter how he tried to stop it.

He leaned back in his desk chair, toying a pen between his fingers and watching as Summer paused at Eli Schumaker's desk, offering a warm smile that Eli answered a bit uncertainly, before stretching up to murmur something in Summer's ear. Summer listened with grave attention, his expression utterly focused, before nodding and murmuring something in return, cocking his head, messy hair falling in a dark shag across his eyes—eyes that, Fox noted, still subtly avoided direct eye contact, focusing somewhere else on Eli's face. Then he tapped something on Eli's worksheet, before stealing his pencil and scribbling something down. Then, at a nod from Eli, he grinned and straightened, moving away.

And pausing, lifting his head, catching Fox's eye.

Before smiling brilliantly, his eyes creasing and glittering with warmth, before turning away.

Fox huffed under his breath, scowling, looking away, pitching his pen onto the desk.

Summer really needed to stop being so *obvious*.

They didn't speak again, though, until the third period let out, and Fox settled to lean his hip against the edge of his deck, propping the papers he'd just collected against his thigh and stacking them neatly into place.

Summer settled down next to him, resting almost thigh to thigh, his strong, square hands gripping the desk to either side of his hips.

"You," he said sunnily, "have been watching me all day."

Fox tossed him a glower. "I'm your supervisor. It's my job to monitor your progress and your performance."

With a playful smile, Summer rolled his head toward Fox, resting his cheek against his upthrust shoulder, the taut muscle straining against the linen of his crisply ironed off-white button-down. "So that's the only reason?"

"*Why* are you so annoyingly confident around me?" Fox threw back. "I can make any other teacher in this school quiver in his boots with one look. And yet you, the most anxious, awkward person I have ever met, refuse to cower appropriately."

"It's simple," Summer said, before his voice dropped, low and soft and just a touch heated, hungry, husky. "I'm the only one who knows what you taste like."

Why, that damned— "Are you so certain of that?" Fox bit off, slitting his eyes.

Summer's smile vanished. A touch of hurt flashed in his eyes, before he looked away, quiet, expression going still and empty and carefully blank.

"No," he murmured. "I guess I'm not."

Hell and damnation.

Fox, you are an asshole.

He twisted to set his papers down on the desk, then shifted to settle closer to Summer, until their shoulders and arms pressed in close-held warmth and his thigh rested against the knuckles curled against the edge of the desk, Summer's hand hot through Fox's slacks.

"You are," Fox said. "You're the first one brave enough to even try."

Summer lifted his head, haunted eyes watching Fox with unspoken questions, before he murmured, "So anyone will do as long as they're brave enough to keep pushing at you?"

"...no." That...shouldn't hurt so much, or hit so close to home, when Fox had been wondering that himself. "Anyone else wouldn't get a second chance to keep pushing at me. You puzzle me in more ways than one, Summer...and one of those ways is that I cannot seem to tell you to, quite frankly, go fuck yourself and give up on this bizarre notion you have of wanting me."

Summer recoiled slightly, blinking, face blanking.

Before he snickered, covering his mouth and trying to hold it in but failing.

"I've never heard you say anything worse than 'damn' before," he said through his fingers, muffled. "And 'hell-fire.' Always *hellfire*, every time you get annoyed."

Fox rolled his eyes. "Please do not act like a child and remind me exactly why I should be against allowing someone your age to be so forward with me."

That just made Summer laugh more, eyes delighted and bright. "It's not my age that bothers you and you know it. It's that you can't scare me off."

"Not for lack of trying," Fox growled.

"You really only have to do one thing to make me give up, you know."

"And what, pray tell, would that be?"

Summer shrugged, the corners of his lips curling wistfully. "Just tell me no."

That was the crux of it, wasn't it?

Every time, Summer had given him ample opportunity to say no.

And every time, Iseya had growled and glared and gone stiff...

...and not even hinted at that one word that would end it all.

He made a soft sound in the back of his throat, and this

time he was the one to look away. "…I know that," he bit off, and Summer only chuckled.

"Good."

They said nothing else for several moments, just sitting in the quiet classroom, with its scents of old wood and chalk dust and old paper, worn pages.

Until Summer murmured, "Would it be okay if I used your office for an hour or two after last bell tomorrow?"

Fox lifted his brows. "For what?"

"Counseling," Summer admitted sheepishly. "Eli's agreed to talk to me, and I think it could help."

"That's not your job," Fox pointed out. "Be careful. I know you mean well, but at times overstepping boundaries with students can create problems no matter what your intent might be."

"Don't worry. Everything above board. I just…" He shook his head. "They need somebody, Fox."

He froze, then, his breaths drawing in sharp and fast, and darted a glance at Fox. "I…sorry. Professor Iseya."

But Fox just looked into those twilight-shot eyes, and let the feeling of his name on someone else's tongue settle over him.

Coming from Summer…

It was like the taste of warm caramel on a crisp cool apple, that tart-sweet feeling exploding over the tongue at that first burst of broken skin.

It shouldn't feel so *luscious* to hear someone else saying his name.

So intimate.

And he let his hand fall to rest next to Summer's on the

edge of the desk, their pinky fingers just touching. "You can say it," he murmured. "And you may use my office tomorrow."

Summer's gaze darted back and forth, searching, deep, his lips parting, red suffusing his cheeks, the tips of his ears. "Fox," he said again, and Fox's stone heart beat hard enough for its outer granite shell to crack.

"Just like that," he said, and leaned in toward Summer, drawn by the warmth of him, by the way he lingered over Fox's name like a prayer. "Say it just like that."

"*Fox*," Summer breathed, reverent, hot, as the tips of their noses touched.

And Summer closed the last distance between them to seal their lips together in a burning, molten lock.

Heat rushed over Fox as if it had been waiting to consume him, to ignite him, dragging him under in simmering sensations that stole his air and left his lungs seared, left his entire body aching. Summer shouldn't be able to do this to him with just the simple touch of sweet lips; with the slow needy way Summer teased at his mouth with hot sounds in the back of his throat, practically begging Fox to taste him, to seek inside him, to take control.

Against the desk, their pinky fingers overlapped, interlaced, curling together.

And Fox gave in, letting Summer's magnetism draw him into letting go of his tight control of himself.

Summer's sweetness was in every honeyed wet taste of his lips, in the slickness of his tongue, in the depths of his mouth. Absolutely indecent, in his wanton willingness, in the way he opened for Fox—the way he leaned into him, eager hands reaching up to cup Fox's face, teasing back into his hair, threatening to send it ripping free from its tie.

Fox nearly arched into the sensation of fingers against his scalp, letting out a little groan that melted between their lips, his body vibrating with Summer's warmth. And he couldn't help leaning into that lean, strong body, the soft sounds of their slacks and shirts sliding together as he pressed chest to chest with Summer, caught him about the waist, jerked him in close *just* to feel how Summer shivered and tensed and then melted so liquidly; bit his lower lip just to hear Summer's soft, erotically pained hiss, just to taste the bruising of his flesh.

God, Fox couldn't remember feeling this kind of heat in far too long. It had receded to just a memory, buried in the fog of time, but now it came flaring to life until he thought he would scorch apart from the inside out, and the only thing that could ease the burning, hurting tension inside him…

Was also the thing coiling him tighter and tighter, until this raw, unexpected burst of desire was almost too painful to endure.

It was like this flood had been building for decades, and now his walls could no longer contain it, that last bit of pressure sending him spilling his banks, crashing over everything that tried to restrain it, to tell him to calm down, to move slower, to remember they were in a public classroom and he wasn't meant to need this, to want this, to crave this so deeply that he nearly devoured Summer's mouth until the enticing young man actually *whimpered*, his tongue flicking and stroking with soft, helpless hunger against Fox's.

If his dam was going to break…

Then let it break.

He leaned harder against Summer—then tumbled him back, spilling him against the desk, pushing him down onto his back. Summer hit the desk with a startled sound, eyes widening for a moment, their lips breaking apart as Summer stared up at him with his chest rising and falling sharply, his hair tumbled against Fox's desk blotter, textbooks toppling aside and a pencil cup spilling over.

Fox didn't care.

He raked his gaze down that agile body spread beneath him, Summer's thighs parting around Fox's hips.

Slid his hands up Summer's arms, coaxed them over his head, pinned his wrists with gripping fingers that clasped tight to the sensation of Summer's pulse fluttering out of control against his fingertips.

And locked his body against Summer's, heat to heat, fitting them together in perfect contours as he bent to once more seize Summer's mouth for his own.

This—this was heady, perfect, enticing, Summer arching beneath him, willing and submissive and so very warm as he pressed his body eagerly to Fox's; as he opened himself entirely for him, letting Fox take and plunder and claim his mouth as if he could leave a permanent mark if he just kissed him hard enough, deep enough, hot enough, searching down inside Summer as if he could touch him in ways no one else ever had.

Did he want that, he asked himself?

Even as he slid his tongue in velvet-wet strokes along Summer's, leaning into the suggestion of it, the lasciviousness of it, the mimicry of the slow, shuddering movements of their bodies, the rushes of sensation spearing up inside him and making him throb, want, *need* something more than the sensuous grind of hips to hips…he asked himself.

Did he want Summer, and not just this wild reawakening of any feeling at all?

The answer seemed to lie in the rush of Summer's breaths, in the way he moved so wantonly beneath Fox, in the strong slink and flex and flow of his body, and Fox—

Fox froze, ice crystallizing in his gut, as someone rapped imperiously on the door, before a mockingly acerbic voice floated over the room.

"I assume this isn't part of the lesson plan."

Fox sighed, letting go of Summer's mouth to instead drop his forehead to Summer's shoulder, slumping in exasperation.

He knew that voice.

Insufferable authoritarian prick.

And he gathered his dignity around himself as he released Summer's wrists, straightening and smoothing over his suspenders and his shirt, lifting his chin as he stared down the man watching them from the door with one platinum blond eyebrow sardonically lifted, glacially blue eyes hard with disdain.

"Assistant Principal," Fox said flatly, and almost dared Lachlan Walden to say a single word.

While Summer went scrambling up, making distressed noises and clumsily fumbling his way off the desk, knocking over a stapler, a stack of Post-it notes, before he managed to find his feet. He was red all the way down to the collar of his shirt, his mouth bruised to a lush dark fullness as if he was wearing lipstick, his hair a mess.

He looked exactly like what he was.

Completely debauched, and Fox felt an unexpected flare of possessive irritation that Assistant Principal Walden was even allowed to see Summer that way.

Summer stood at rigid attention at Fox's side, clearing his throat. "M-Mr. Walden!"

His voice actually cracked.

The corner of Fox's mouth twitched.

He shouldn't find that so amusing.

Walden, however, clearly didn't. He stared at them over the rims of his glasses, his mouth a forbidding line as sharp-edged and stiff as his crisp navy blue three-piece suit.

"Are the two of you done?" he bit off.

Fox arched a brow. "Quite," he said firmly, only for Walden's eyes to narrow, locking on Fox rather sternly.

Fox only held his gaze and waited.

Walden had only been hired two months ago to bring some sort of order to the chaos the school frequently fell into, and was a good ten years Fox's junior.

He had a long way to go before he could outfreeze Fox, when Fox had been the resident ice queen of Albin Academy for decades.

After several moments, Walden let out an irritable sigh and adjusted his rimless glasses, then smoothed back the close, neatly-glossed sideswept part of his hair, transferring his gaze to Summer.

Who squeaked.

"I came," Lachlan said haughtily, "about your request to repurpose one of the empty reading rooms, Mr. Hemlock." He pursed his lips. "Are you licensed to act as a psychotherapist?"

Summer cringed, shoulders slumping, and he bowed his head, pure hangdog sheepishness as he peeked through his hair at Lachlan like a child caught with his hand in the cookie jar. "No, I...n-no."

"Then your request is denied," Lachlan retorted. "Stick to teaching. After-hours student counseling is for studying only." His mouth creased downward in a disapproving frown. "You could get us sued."

Then, without giving Summer or Fox a chance to respond...

He turned and swept out, gliding as if trailing a royal train in his wake and slamming the door quite firmly behind him.

Summer flinched when the door hit home hard enough to echo, then peeked one eye open at Fox. "...could I really get us sued?"

"No," Fox said, eyeing the door in disgust, before turning his gaze back to Summer. "And a license is not required to fulfill the role of a school guidance counselor. Your teaching certification is quite enough."

Summer sputtered, then trailed into a groan, slumping to lean against the desk. "So you were bluffing."

"And you," Fox pointed out, "fell for it, because you were embarrassed."

"...he, uh...caught us...um..." With another flustered sound, Summer scrubbed the heel of his palm against one eye, fingers weaving into his hair, and let out a nervous little sound that wasn't quite a laugh. "You know. I just...

I guess I'm still working my way toward being brave with people other than you."

With a sigh, Fox settled to sit next to him once more, just looking down at Summer—how he slouched, how his breaths came in little short pants that told Fox Summer was doing everything he could not to give in to the anxiety trying to rise through him, making his pulse flicker erratically until it stood out against his throat, making his eyes dilate long after any lingering desire could account for the expansion of the pupil.

You are such a mess, Fox thought fondly, and slipped his arm around Summer's shoulders.

"You will get there," he said, curling his hand against Summer's arm. "I firmly believe that."

Summer immediately turned into him—pressing into his side, burying his face in Fox's chest.

And Fox let him, just wrapping his other arm around him and drawing him in close.

"You do?" Summer mumbled against Fox's chest, breaths and lips moving warm through his shirt.

"I do," Fox agreed, and rested his chin to the top of Summer's head.

Summer said nothing, and just burrowed in closer to him, wrapping his arms in a tight lock around Fox's waist.

It wasn't so bad, staying like this—wrapped around Summer, sheltering him, listening as he slowly paced his breaths until they calmed down and he went softer, warmer, against Fox.

Right now...

Fox wasn't sure who was comforting whom.

When this only made his entire body ache with the awareness of how long he had been starved for such simple human contact that had nothing to do with attraction, with arousal...

And everything to do with just sharing *touch*.

"I could do it," Summer murmured, voice muffled and soft, breaking the silence. "Get my license as a therapist." Fox felt more than saw Summer's smile, moving against his ribs. "I spent half my credits in a forensic and behavioral psychology track in university, before I switched to education."

Fox blinked repeatedly. "You? In forensics?"

He recalled Summer mentioning it before, but trying to *picture* it...

Impossible.

A soundless laugh shook Summer's body against him, and he only burrowed his face deeper into Fox's chest. "Don't say it like that!" he said, before falling still again, adjusting to lean more into Fox, until it was half the edge of the desk holding him up, half Fox. "...though you're right. I couldn't do it. The...the blood, the horror...it was too much. I couldn't face that."

"Why did you sign up for that program in the first place?"

"...I thought I could help people," Summer admitted, gentle and heartfelt. "I thought I could bring people some peace by helping them find out who killed the people they loved. And I enjoyed the psych part of it, but..." He shuddered, tension rippling through the tight planes of muscle under Fox's palms. "Not the death. And I didn't know what else to do, so I switched to education…and ended up back here."

So bitter, Fox thought. As bitter as he had been warm when he spoke of wanting to help people with such a simple, honest desire.

"You didn't want to come back here?" he asked carefully.

"Not like this."

"Not like what?"

"…like me." Choked, low. "Soft and weak and still scared of everything. Scared of *me*."

Ah… Summer.

Fox couldn't stop himself from tightening his hold, spreading his palms over Summer's back, gathering him in until there was hardly breath or space between them, stroking his hands down Summer's spine as if he could impress his words on him in touch, in warmth that he didn't quite know how to express in words.

But he tried, murmuring, "I don't think there's anything wrong with being soft."

"One of my professors said that, too. Before I left Baltimore." Summer sighed. "Professor Khalaji. He quit teaching in the criminology program and went back to being a police detective, but…he remembered me, even though I dropped out. And he told me…" He stopped, turning his head to rest his cheek to Fox's chest, his eyes slipping open, just hints of deep blue glimmering through his lashes. "He told me that 'soft' isn't something many people are anymore, and that it's not a bad thing to be soft. Not a bad thing to protect that. So maybe…"

He lifted his head, then, looking at Fox eye to eye.

There was so much fear swimming in those depths, Fox thought. So much hesitation, uncertainty, this bright shooting star of a young man with no idea where he was shooting off *to*.

Yet still… Summer smiled.

And there was something so very beautiful in that.

In the way Summer could crumple under the worst pain, the worst fear, and still *smile*.

"Maybe I want to protect being soft," Summer whispered. "And I want to make it safe for other people to be soft, too."

He said it the same way he said Fox's name: quiet, pleading, entreating.

Asking, as he always asked…

For Fox to let him in, in so many subtle ways.

I don't know how, Fox thought, but still…still he reached up to brush Summer's messy tangle of hair back from his eyes, tracing his fingertips along one arching black brow.

"That feels like a loaded statement," he said, and Summer lidded his eyes, leaning into the touch.

"Maybe." He smiled sweetly. "You could be soft with me, if you wanted."

Fox quirked his lips. "I don't know if I have any softness left in me, Summer."

"I think you do," Summer said. "Or we wouldn't be like this right now."

Chapter Nine

Hope, Summer thought, was infinitely more painful than fear.

Fear was a dread certainty, most of the time, that whatever could go wrong...would. Fear was a consistent negative, a terrible dread, but at least something that could be relied on to persistently centralize around its source.

Hope, on the other hand...

Hope was sheer uncertainty, tossing him up and down and up and down as if his heart was on a trampoline and trailing his emotions behind it every time he went bounding high and then came crashing down low, each string of feelings dug into his heart with hooks that made every tiny thing pull too painfully hard.

And God, did everything about Fox pull at him *so* painfully hard.

The way the man looked every morning, so perfectly

sharp and cool and elegant in his white shirts, slacks, suspenders, glasses, his hair bound up so neatly.

The way his voice had subtly changed in how he spoke to Summer, even when correcting his mistakes in reviewing lesson plans and assignments—the barb of disapproval vanishing to instead leave something almost like mocking affection, completely removing the sting from any errors Summer made and even turning gentle as Fox guided him, question by question, step by step, to find the right path and learn how teaching worked.

The subtle approval in silver eyes as they tracked Summer throughout the classroom, while Summer found his place working one-on-one with the boys to help with their assignments and answer their questions—and how Fox let him answer them his own way, finding common ground with the students by explaining in layman's terms that he hoped would make more sense to them than the clinical terminology in the textbook or the more advanced concepts Fox never quite seemed to realize were above everyone's head, when that inscrutable mind was often so far off into one theory or another.

The fact that when they were alone, he could even call him *Fox* at all, and watch the way every time Summer said his name, Fox subtly colored, paused for a half-breath, darted a flickering and meaningful glance at him before looking away.

And the way every day Fox's kisses sank deeper, pushed Summer dizzyingly higher and higher still, left him electric with the thrill of wanting and the hope that…that…

That maybe this could be something *more*, when he didn't think...

Didn't think Fox would touch him so softly and comfort him so gently in those moments when he couldn't breathe and the panic-rabbit thumped its feet inside his chest and he wanted to scream for no reason at all, just because some wire had tweaked wrong in his brain and he'd built himself up into a mess.

If only most of the things he built himself up over weren't Fox himself, when he took every distracted, hard-eyed glance or preoccupied, annoyed twist of Fox's lips to heart like an arrow struck so deep, even though Summer logically *knew* they weren't for him.

And if he was honest with himself, it wasn't just Fox preying on his mind.

It was the way Jay and Eli wouldn't talk to each other in the halls anymore.

The way he'd noticed Theodore strutting, and almost herding Eli away from Jay during lunch periods and free periods after classes.

He thought Jay might be sleeping in one of the other boys' rooms, now.

And he couldn't do anything about it, because Assistant Principal Walden had forbidden him from acting in any role other than teaching and tutoring.

It ate at him, especially when he'd been slowly getting Eli in particular to warm up to him, to trust him...

And now he felt like he was breaking his promises.

He couldn't sleep, thinking about that—tossing, turning,

staring at the walls, the windows, the ceiling, for once not lying awake thinking about Fox's lips, his body...

Instead lying awake wondering if he'd just made a mess with promises he couldn't keep, and left that boy feeling like maybe he couldn't trust anyone to keep his word, now.

Couldn't trust anyone to be on his side.

Summer exhaled heavily, flopping onto his back and slamming his head against the pillow, staring up at the arcs of moonlight moving across the ceiling.

He was never going to get to sleep like this.

Back at the university he'd at least been able to wear himself out with swimming, until he was so exhausted he had no choice but to sleep.

Now that he thought about it...

There was the pool used for swim club, here at the school—almost large enough for competitive sports, housed in its own attached building so it could be used year-round.

Technically no one was allowed in the pool after dinner hours.

...but technically that rule only applied to students.

It was just a tiny deviation.

And Summer always tried to follow the rules, but...

Maybe just this one time, for the sake of being able to sleep, he'd break them.

Why not.

He smiled to himself, then slipped out of bed to change.

Fox did not like this newfound restless energy.

He preferred his thoughts calm. Quiet. Even if it came

at the cost of a certain emotional deadness, at the very least it let him maintain his focus and a certain peace of mind.

Not this…this…

Constant *agitation* that had him feeling ready to snap at any moment, on a hair trigger, constantly needing to be moving and not even sure *why* save for that his body did not seem to want to hold still. He would find himself tapping pins, jittering his foot against his knee when he crossed his legs, restlessly drumming his fingers, standing from his chair and then sitting down again.

Or, as he was now, prowling the school grounds, hoping that a walk beneath the trees and the open moonlight would at least settle his thoughts.

And get them off Summer damned Hemlock.

That young man was starting to border on an intrusive thought.

With every moment Fox's mind wasn't on classwork, on keeping those unruly monsters in line, on planning the next week's lessons and assignments…

It somehow drifted back to Summer.

And sometimes Fox found himself simply touching his lips, when they always seemed tender and sensitive lately with the pressure of daily kisses stolen between classes, against desks, against the wall in his office, in the secret crevice of a hallway with students passing by utterly oblivious beyond.

With staff meetings and so many other things to worry about, it always seemed every kiss was just a half-second's stolen moment, over too soon when one thing or another always interrupted.

And it was rather quite annoying Fox that each time a student or a phone call or an authoritative rap on the office door cut them off...

Fox found himself left unsatisfied, and craving *more*.

He let his drifting steps take him through the overgrowth around Whitemist Lake, the little burrs growing among the grass and flowers catching on his slacks as if trying to drag him back from the edge, the scent of the night clear and damp and at least settling his agitation somewhat, even if it couldn't calm his thoughts.

His reflection was a quiet murky thing in the depths, and he could only look at it for a moment before he had to turn away.

It made him think too much of drowning; of ghosts sinking away into the dark and the deep, like Isabella of the legend.

Like Michiko, dying alone and trapped in her vehicle, swallowed into the darkness of night, into the blackness of the river, deep down where the moon couldn't even reach her to light her way.

He hadn't even been there.

Not to save her, and not to die with her.

He'd failed her.

How, he couldn't quantify. If he stepped out of himself objectively, he knew he wasn't being even remotely rational.

But then feelings weren't rational.

Grief wasn't rational.

And neither was the struggling, floundering sense of

drowning in his own attempts to find him*self*, when he realized he was ready to stop grieving but didn't know how.

He tilted his head back, let the wind kiss his cheeks, looked up at the quiet sallow curve of a dim moon shrouded by clouds.

"Were you there with her, that night?" he whispered. "Can you tell me someone was with her, even when I wasn't?"

The moon didn't answer.

The moon would never answer, because it was only Fox projecting shallow, selfish needs to imagine that some quiet silver hand had reached down from the heavens and eased Michiko's pain in those last silent, airless moments.

No matter how many times he told himself that, though...

It still comforted him in small, aching ways.

Maybe he hoped, one day, when he died a day or a thousand days or fifty years from now...

There would be someone to hold his hand, too.

Someone more tangible than fingers of pale moonlight.

"Is this really what I want?" he asked. "To pull myself so far out of reach that one day I'll only know this empty coldness...where no one can take my hand at all?"

Just as the moon had not answered for Michiko...

It did not answer for him.

He'd known it wouldn't.

But he smiled, nonetheless.

And bent to pluck a single little daisy from among the rioting wildflowers, before tossing it out onto the water and watching it sink.

Maybe he wasn't quite ready to wish to Isabella for what he truly wanted, when he couldn't define that just yet himself.

But one small offering, perhaps.

Just that he wouldn't ruin whatever this strange bright feeling was, that he had every time Summer was near.

He turned away from the lake, heading up toward the main school building again—but paused as bright rectangles of light caught his attention, spilling across the grass from the swimming annex's high, narrow rows of windows.

Fox frowned, knitting his brows together.

No one should be in there at this time of night.

He knew quite well that sometimes the students snuck in to skinny-dip despite all the safety warnings, but...

Whenever he caught them at it, he stuck them with grounds duty for months.

This time would be no exception.

Tightening his jaw, he changed his path to find the footstones buried in the grass and leading up to the annex. When he pushed the door open, though...

He didn't expect to find not the students—

But Summer.

Summer cut through the glossy blue waters of the pool like a seal, sleek and strong and gleaming, the sheen of water pouring over him turning his tanned skin into burnished gold. He was tight and toned from head to toe, with long, graceful legs sculpted into smooth flexions of muscle that kicked powerfully, while hardened arms cut through the water smoothly and made his naked back bunch and coil with kinetic energy captured in sinew, transformed into propulsion, nearly writhing with naked sensuality. The water glided over him as if it loved him, and wanted to cling to him as closely as possible.

From the hot, almost furious yearning in the pit of his stomach, the tightening in his thighs, the pulling at his core...

Fox knew the feeling all too well.

Summer reached the end of his lap and stopped at the edge of the pool, settling to tread water with one hand gripping at the molded concrete rim and the other pushing his hair back out of his face; he wore swim trunks that were barely more than briefs, tiny shorts in a dark, satiny blue that clung obscenely to his hips and thighs, cupping his bottom and seeming to lick at his skin as he pulled himself out, water sheeting off him in caressing droplets and his entire body one perfect flux, a ripple of strength pouring from head to toe as he hauled himself out so effortlessly and twisted to sit on the edge with his feet dangling in the water.

He reached for the towel he'd left folded on the edge of the pool.

Then stopped, eyes widening as they locked on Fox.

"Oh," Summer said faintly. "Hi."

Fox realized he'd been staring.

Utterly transfixed, captured simply by the obsessive worship of every inch of Summer, devouring him with every look and so completely lost in taking him in that he hadn't even realized what he was doing, hadn't even thought to stop himself until he was already caught, frozen, going stiff.

Oh.

Well.

This was awkward.

He cleared his throat, gut tightening, tearing his gaze away from the way a single glistening runnel of water poured down Summer's cheek to catch on the stark, graceful line of his jaw, hanging there like a captured tear…only to fall, glimmering, down to catch on the temptingly strong lines of his throat. Instead Fox stared somewhere over his head, fixing on one of the life preservers mounted on white tile walls that shimmered with the ever-shifting reflections off the surface of the water.

"My apologies for intruding," he forced out, his jaw tight, refusing to unclench. "I had thought one of the students was breaking curfew, as well as the rules about pool hours."

Summer let out a quiet, embarrassed laugh. "I think I'm probably still breaking the rules, but I was hoping I wouldn't get caught and fired."

"I think if I haven't reported you for grossly inappropriate behavior yet, you're safe from this minor infraction."

"Or you just don't want to admit you keep making exceptions for me," Summer lilted softly. "You want to come in? It's actually not too cold."

Fox flinched.

He felt it inside as much as out in that instinctive recoiling of his body; the instinctive recoiling of his *thoughts*, a defensive barrier slamming down.

He was fine, usually, as long as he didn't think about it—about the cold airless depths. He could be near water, could walk over bridges and along ponds without a second thought, so long as the water didn't…

Didn't touch him.

Didn't wrap around him in its cold, sucking embrace and give him a taste of what it must have felt like.

Sometimes it came to him in his dreams.

Where he couldn't escape, until his body woke him in a cold, terrible sweat.

He had no choice about his dreams.

He at least had a choice not to torture himself while awake.

He folded his arms over his chest, and told himself he wasn't wrapping them around himself in a defensive wall.

"I don't swim," he said carefully. "I prefer to avoid immersion in water entirely, other than the necessities for a shower."

Summer had started to unfold the towel—but now stopped with the pale terrycloth clasped between his fingers, watching Fox discerningly. His guilelessness was disarming, Fox had started to realize over the passing days; it was so easy to get distracted by the frank openness in his eyes that one didn't realize that as much as Summer gave away his emotions…

He perceived a great deal, as well.

And had a way of looking at people as if he understood far too much about the aches inside them; the darkness and the pain, all the raw places that eventually hardened into sharp-edged armor keen enough to cut anyone who got too close.

Fox had grown accustomed to making himself unseen, in his own way.

And it was discomfiting to be looked at by someone who seemed to want to know every last agony that still haunted him, in those secret places where he could not let go.

He turned his face away, folding his arms over his chest, waiting for the unspoken thing that seemed to hover on Summer's lips. Likely some platitude, some useless bit of comfort that had lost meaning years ago when one of the first things Fox had learned was...

Words did not change anything.

Not for him.

The words of reassurance, of useless sympathy, only gave comfort to those who had lost nothing.

They were empty, to those who had lost...had lost...

Everything.

So he wasn't expecting when that low, quiet voice said, "You aren't the one who drowned, you know. I'm not sure you know that."

It struck with the precision of a sword-thrust, and the cruelty of a death blow—a sensation as though his heart had split in two, striking rough and deep as Fox whipped his head back to stare at Summer, at that seemingly innocent face that could utter such terrible and hateful barbs, poison disguised as sugar in soft words.

"*Excuse* you?" he threw back, and hated how for a moment his voice quivered—then halted, his throat closing sharply, unexpectedly, with a rush so hard and so wretched he thought he would scream. "You have no right—"

"You're right," Summer said. "I don't. I don't have any

right because I have no idea how you feel, and I have no idea what it's like to lose someone the way you did." He stood, unfolding his body with feline grace, steps silent on the concrete rimming the pool as he rounded the edge to draw closer to Fox. "I just know this hurts. It hurts seeing you living like you're already dead, when you're *not*." His mouth actually *trembled*, before firming as he stopped in front of Fox, looking up at him with something dark and determined sparking in nightshade eyes, in the set of his jaw. "I know she left you behind and it's terrifying, Fox. I know you feel like…like you're completely alone. But you're not. So you don't have to hold on to the loneliness, the fear…like if you let go of them, you'll have nothing left."

"I *won't!*" Fox flared, and he didn't know why it hurt to breathe but it was *abysmal*, this horrid pain inside his chest, this dull heavy thing like a pounding fist smashing against the tender meat of him with every cursed word. He glared at Summer, fingers clenching, digging hard into the fabric of his sleeves, the flesh of his elbows. "I wasn't even *there*, Summer. I wasn't there for her. She died *alone*, crushed under that water in the darkness, and I wasn't even there so she wouldn't have to be the only one."

"But you can't change that by giving up on living at all."

For all Fox's harshness, Summer was gentle, soft—and he rested one warm hand against Fox's chest, fingers splayed, the ridges of knuckles and tendons standing out against tanned skin, his warmth pressing…pressing…

Right over the raw, aching beat of Fox's heart.

"What's in the water that scares you, Fox?" Summer

whispered. "Because it's not her. You know she's not there. You *know*, even if you don't want to admit it."

Fox stared at him, a horrid, hollow feeling building behind his eyes, spreading throughout him until he felt like this thin shell filling up with so much pain.

As if he really was *her*.

Trapped in a sinking vessel, the air crushing out of him, beating against the walls of his own heart as the anguish rushed in to drown him.

As he forced himself to answer a question that he refused to even acknowledge himself, even if it had been there inside him for two decades, crouched and waiting and cold and dark and so very, very terrible.

"I... I'm afraid..." Every word a struggle, every sound a raw wound cutting his tongue, reaching down into his throat to pull it tighter and tighter like closing purse-strings into a choking clutch, and the only reason he could speak at all was because those yearning, sweet blue eyes begged him to, held him fast, kept him from collapsing into silence. "...I'm afraid I'll be tempted to join her. To just... let myself sink, and not come back up ever again."

"*Fox*," Summer whispered, and slipped his other hand into Fox's hair, steady fingers weaving in deep, strong and comforting and warm and so very sure, drawing him in until their brows touched and he could taste Summer's breaths on his lips. "But you don't really want that, do you?"

Fox took several heaving, rasping breaths; he felt like he was drowning *already*, drowning on dry land, but Summer was anchoring him, keeping him afloat.

"No," he choked, closing his eyes, shaking his head, rubbing temple to temple with Summer. "But I don't... Summer, I don't know *how* to live."

"You don't have to know how." Summer's smile was in his voice, in the soothing rumble of it, the sigh at the edges of it. "You just do."

Fox didn't know what to say. What this breaking was inside him, that felt at once like falling apart and like clawing free from his own rubble, but it was awful and yet...yet...

He didn't want to stop.

Didn't want to pull away, to let go of Summer when something about this felt so terrifyingly *good*, too.

So he stayed—stayed, and leaned into that touch, and unclenched one hand to rest it to Summer's chest, taut bare skin and the steady slow beat of a wild and beautiful heart underneath his palm.

"How do you know these things?" he whispered. "How can you even be so certain of yourself?"

"I'm not," Summer answered, before sweet lips brushed against Fox's cheek. "I just never stop hoping that no matter what's wrong...it'll get better."

Then he drew back, his body heat receding—but didn't let Fox go.

Instead he captured the hand Fox held against his chest, wrapping those strong, rough fingers around his, and when Fox opened his eyes, Summer cocked his head to one side, messy spears of wetly spiked hair falling across his brow as he smiled.

"Will you try something with me?" he asked. "Something brave."

Fox let out a broken, startled bark of laughter, brief before it strangled off again. "Are you trying to turn the tables on me?"

"Fair play." Summer stopped, then, but still pulled at Fox's hand, drawing him in close one hesitant step at a time. "Step in the shallow end with me. I'll hold your hand all the way. And if you can't stand it…it's okay. We'll get out, and we won't even talk about it if you don't want to."

Fox's breaths turned to ice, and he tore his gaze from Summer to stare at the pool, luminous pale blue and clear all the way down to the bottom—and yet suddenly it seemed a limitless ocean, bottomless, airless, the depths a thing of sucking darkness only waiting to capture him and drag him down.

"I… I…"

I can't, he started to say.

But why couldn't he?

How could Summer face down fears he couldn't control every day, wired into his brain by chemical reactions and triggers, and still smile…

…yet Fox wouldn't even try?

He ran his tongue over his lips; his breaths felt too cold against his damp mouth, as if the life and heat were already sucking out of him to leave him cold as a corpse, his fingertips numbing.

Stop it, he told himself. *You are having a panic reaction for no reason.*

"I do not…do not have appropriate attire," he started, and Summer chuckled, squeezing his hand reassuringly.

"Never went swimming in your underwear when you were a kid?" he asked, and Fox stared at him flatly.

"Can you picture me as a child?"

"We all were, once." Thoughtful eyes dipped over him, then, before Summer stepped closer and reached up to finger the top button of Fox's shirt, toying with it before gently slipping it open. "So yes, I can picture it. I bet you were short and chubby and happy and cute, and then one day puberty hit and you shot up and turned lean and tall, and didn't even know what to do with yourself when suddenly you had all this extra *you* and no idea where to put it."

Fox scowled. "That is annoyingly accurate."

"Yeah?" Summer only smiled, starting on the next button, tugging it open as slowly as he was teasing Fox out of himself. "Tell me about where you grew up, then. Tell me what it was like for you as a kid."

Fox hesitated.

He knew what Summer was doing.

Focusing his mind on his memories from before the trauma, the pain, the locked-in grief, giving him something to distract him from the thoughts threatening to paralyze his limbs and his lungs even while Summer gently, so gently, pushed him toward testing himself as he parted his shirt one button at a time.

He had simply never expected to be in the position to have such a therapeutic technique used on *him*.

Or for it to actually work, his mind wandering unbidden to the memory of dark green water, white sand, rocks cresting in strange formations silhouetted against a brilliant evening sky.

"I grew up in Miyako," he said softly. "At least until I was a teenager. You may have seen it on the news a few years ago, when a tsunami struck the town after a major earthquake… but before that, it was…calm. Always calm, the bright sun on water so deep a green it was like this…rippling layer of bottle glass. The rocks just past the shoreline—Joudogahama—always drew tourists, but I loved to splash in the shallows around them." He smiled faintly. "I'd scare the crabs, sending them scuttling away. My mother came to Japan from the States for work, met my father, fell in love…and I remember walking with them on the beach, with the sand breaking up in warm crumbles between my toes and the sound of the waves, while the lighthouse farther along the coast came alight with dusk."

Summer let out a soft, almost pleased sigh, as he reached the last button on Fox's shirt; Fox hadn't even realized he'd continued pulling them open, until Summer was tugging his button-down out of the waist of his slacks. "So you have good memories of water, too. Of the ocean."

"I…yes." Fox's brows knit, as he looked down at Summer; Summer just smiled at him with his eyes crinkled at the corners and soft. "Why did you ask?"

"Because I want to know you. Not just what I think I know about you from meeting you here."

Summer finished tugging the hem loose, the fabric pulling and sliding against Fox's skin, before those angular, strong hands slid over his shoulders, slipping beneath the shirt to draw it, one inch at a time, down his arms, catching and rasping lightly against his sleeveless undershirt.

As much as Summer lingered, as close as he was, his radiance like sunlight…there was no seduction in this, even when Summer's fingertips grazed over the outer edges of Fox's arms.

Yet even without seduction…

It was still so very intimate.

Comforting.

Soft words, soft touches between them, and Fox submitting to let Summer tease him out of his clothing one piece at a time while he spoke of memories long past.

"You are still very strange, Summer," he whispered, and Summer let out a sweet little laugh as he let Fox's shirt fall from his fingertips to crumple on the cement.

"I'm okay with being strange," he said. "When did you come to the States?"

"When I was fourteen." Fox didn't stop Summer, as Summer gathered up bunched handfuls of his undershirt next, lifting it up along his stomach, his ribs, rough knuckles grazing his bare skin. "My mother's job moved her back, and she brought us with her."

"That must have been a culture shock," Summer murmured, nudging at Fox's arms, and Fox lifted them over his head.

For a moment the world was white, as his undershirt lifted away, before Summer tugged it over his head and drew it down his arms.

Goosebumps prickled down his arms, but it wasn't from the cold.

It was from that intent gaze locked on him, taking him in as he was—naked in words, naked in flesh, simple and accepting.

He almost flinched from it, looking away as he answered, "My life has been a culture shock. In Japan I was too tall, too large, too obviously haafu…in America I was too foreign, and although I learned English in the home, somehow everyone here seemed to speak a different sort of English that I never quite understood."

"So you know how it feels." Summer's hands settled against his waist, rough palms against his waist, skin to heated skin, thumbs idly sweeping over the crests of his hipbones as Summer drew him closer. "Not to fit in."

"I do," Fox admitted—and didn't pull away, when their bodies pressed flush together, insulating heat between them and soaking into his flesh with the warmth of human contact that he would never confess to needing, craving, starved for simple affections more than he had ever been for sex, for love. "Even if I had a slightly different coping mechanism than you did."

Summer's laughter was a close and sweet thing, a vibration melting from skin to skin, as he leaned in and nuzzled at Fox's jaw. "I turned into a wallflower. You made everyone afraid of you so you wouldn't have to be afraid of *them*."

"Not quite." But Fox chuckled—chuckled, and leaned in, letting his cheek rest to Summer's hair. "I thought, if I could not understand the way they spoke…then I should learn the way they thought, so I could decipher their motives and intent even when their words weren't as honest as they should be."

"So you learned psychology as a defense mechanism, and it became a lifelong passion."

"Mm…something like that."

"It's not a bad reason."

Then Summer's fingers danced along the waist of Fox's slacks, found the button, flicked it open, before the long rasp of the zipper sounded between them, hoarse and almost ominous. Fox tilted his head, looking down at Summer, the set look of concentration on his face.

"I would almost think," he murmured, "that you were trying to seduce me, in this moment."

"Not right now," Summer teased, catching the pink tip of his tongue between his teeth, eyes lowering to the hands working so deftly between them. "But I can't promise I won't try later."

Then Fox's slacks went sheeting down his legs, falling to pool around his ankles, leaving only his black boxer-briefs clinging to his hips and thighs; he took a shaky breath and stepped out of them, toeing out of his shoes and socks at the same time until he stood in his bare feet on the cool concrete.

And when Summer took both his hands, drawing him backward…

His gut clenched tight, as he pulled out of the haze of warm memories and into the cold reality of what he meant to do.

He couldn't, he wouldn't—but he was following, trailing one slow numb step at a time, holding fast to Summer's hands and never looking away from that warm smile, those warmer eyes, the gentle encouragement there.

Promising that Summer believed he could do this.

Even if Fox didn't.

Even if Fox's breaths were coming shallow and thin, his

chest binding up horribly as each rapid wash of air came in and out without giving him enough oxygen, his head swimming as Summer guided him around the corner of the pool and toward the steps, the railing, leading down into the shallow end.

It was only three feet of water, if that.

It wouldn't even come up to Fox's waist.

He had nothing to be afraid of, he told himself.

Nothing.

But he felt sick to his stomach, as he watched Summer step backward into the pool—the water closing around his feet, his ankles, his calves, and he was so perfectly *calm* when Fox just wanted to snatch him back from that insidious, falsely innocuous horror before it could rise up, swallow him down, take him away—

His fingers tightened convulsively.

Stop.

He forced himself to breathe slowly, evenly, counting to three on each inhalation before counting to five on each exhalation.

It was an indoor swimming pool. Safe. Sheltered.

Summer was fine.

Fox was *fine.*

But still his breaths seized, as the first cold lapping edge of water touched the tips of his toes.

He closed his eyes, and told himself it was no different from stepping into the shower, the thin skim of water accumulated on the bottom of the bathtub, something so ordinary and commonplace he never even noticed it.

But the shower was never this *cold.*

And the shower never made his pulse turn into a roaring river, a rushing, a horrible thing screaming in his ears until he couldn't hear Summer, only knew he was saying *something* in soothing murmurs as his grip drew lightly on Fox's hands, pulled him down, guided him down the steps as the sucking embrace of the water rose up around his calves and thighs and hips like the wet fluid mouth of the dead.

He reached the bottom step, eyes still squeezed shut, and stood there, hating how his bones shook inside his flesh, hating how everything inside him rattled and roared in a clattering cacophony of fear, all the brittle bits of himself tossed around inside his trembling shell.

So *icy*, clinging to him, and he couldn't breathe, his chest caving in as he sucked desperately at the air, but the air was too thick and he couldn't open his eyes; if he opened his eyes he would be underwater, would be staring up not at the ceiling of the annex but at the dark sky and the loveless moon receding away through black waters, and he—he—

"You're doing fine," Summer soothed softly. "You're okay, Fox. You're okay."

He wasn't okay.

And with a strangled sound he ripped his hands free from Summer's, turning to claw away.

That had been a mistake, letting Summer go.

Because without those hands to ground him, he was free-floating, surrounded by water and nothing else, his arms sweeping out and hitting nothing but frigid wetness that pushed and pulled at him with the force of his own movements, reflecting it back at him.

He snapped his eyes open.

The railing, the steps, were right there.

And a thousand yards away, when he lurched forward and only went down hard, feet slipping out from beneath him.

The water rushed up to claim him.

Before strong arms wrapped around his waist, hauling him back, and pulling him against the warmth and strength of Summer's body.

And the cold couldn't compare to the heat of him, the solidity of him, Summer becoming Fox's solid earth as Summer wrapped him up tight, held him, walked with him in quick steps to the edge, up, *up*, and the water was gone and Fox was clinging to Summer, gasping, burying his face against his damp shoulder and struggling to draw in as much air as he could possibly manage in needy heavy gasps.

"You're safe," Summer whispered, steady and warm in his ear. "You're safe, Fox. I've got you."

Fox let out a desperate sound, wrapping his arms around Summer, digging his fingers into his back, holding *fast* when he couldn't stand being ripped away, thrust back into that floating nothingness.

He had spent years insulating himself against feeling this kind of fear.

Against feeling *anything*.

And he couldn't let himself give in to that awful, cracking feeling again.

"I couldn't," he gasped against Summer's skin. "I... I couldn't..."

"That's okay." Long fingers threaded into the hair at the nape of Fox's neck, subtle sweet tension grounding him to earth, nearly tugging loose the knot weighing heavy against his scalp. "You don't have to be ready right now. You just…don't. It's okay to have fears you're not ready to face. It's okay to take your time. You still tried." Low words, murmured against his ear, washing over him in sweet-soft waves of quiet, surrounding him in the warmth and vitality Summer exuded like a scent, slipping down inside him with steadying calm. "When you're ready, Fox… when you're ready."

It felt like Summer was saying so much more.

So very much more.

As if he knew…

The thing that frightened Fox the most was Summer himself.

Summer, and the way he made it so very impossible for Fox to stop himself from *feeling* all these riotous and wondrous and monstrous things—the brightness that made him laugh, the exasperation that masked his affection, the way his entire body drew tight and hot every time Summer stole his daily kiss, sometimes sweet, sometimes searing, sometimes submissive, sometimes so insistently needy.

Because every last one of those feelings whispered that Fox could learn how to be happy again.

But if he dared to claim happiness, to grasp at it with all his heart…

Then it could be torn away from him again in a single crashing instant.

He didn't know if he could face that ever again.

And he couldn't think about it right now, couldn't grapple with the ongoing battle between his yearning…and that dark, ugly thing inside of him that was so convinced he would lose the very thing he reached for with both hands.

As he lifted his head, looking into Summer's eyes, into their softness, the way they shaded toward darker colors at the center like twilight shading up into night.

"Help me," he whispered, capturing Summer's face between his palms, cradling his jaw, leaning into him...and stealing his lips, gasping his plea into that mouth that made him want things no man should want, but that he couldn't deny. "Help me forget."

Chapter Ten

Summer shouldn't have pushed Fox.

That had been the only thing on his mind when he realized Fox was hyperventilating, standing in water up to mid-hip, his boxer-briefs soaking dark against his pale amber skin.

And his chest rising and falling in rapid wheezes, muscles constricting tight against his skin, as he froze in place.

It had taken less than a second for Summer to realize Fox wasn't with him anymore.

Fox was somewhere else, somewhere dark, trapped inside his own head.

And Summer had done the only thing he could do:

Pulled him out of the water the moment he'd started struggling, panicking, and taken him into his arms as if he could somehow lock out whatever black nightmare had crawled into Fox's thoughts, and keep him safe.

Maybe he was young, inexperienced; maybe Fox was so much older, so much stronger, hardened by dealing with things Summer couldn't imagine.

But that was all he wanted, in the end.

To have the strength, the surety, to keep Fox safe.

To make him feel as sheltered, as protected, as Fox made him feel when he pulled Summer close and held him until the panic attacks calmed and he could breathe again.

So Summer held him.

He held him, listened to his breaths calm, stroked his fingers against his scalp, murmured to him—anything he could think of, anything to tell him it was okay.

It was okay to not stare his demons in the face.

Not now, maybe not ever.

Summer...

God, Summer would love him either way, whether he faced his fears or thrust them away forever.

And that was when it hit him, hard as a blow to the solar plexus, punching the breath from him and making his grasp on Fox tighten convulsively.

He...

He loved Fox Iseya.

Not just the idealized figurehead he had made of Fox during his childhood years.

But the very real, very vulnerable, very flawed and yet perfectly beautiful man currently trembling and damp in his arms.

He loved this difficult, strange man of subtle whims

and irascible tempers, this quiet creature who tried to be a statue of graven stone but was instead all steel and sharp edges, and every time Summer's heart bled with the cuts it only filled that much deeper with that slow-growing love he hadn't even realized was creeping up on him with every day, every kiss that made him hope more and more that Fox could ever...

Could ever *feel* something for him.

But then Fox was straightening, looking down at him with those glacial silver eyes that suddenly weren't so cold anymore, weren't so closed, raw and open and driving into him with breathtaking force as their eyes locked.

As Fox's long, agile fingers stroked along Summer's cheeks, cradled his face.

As Fox whispered, "Help me." Those lips descending, parted, heated. "Help me forget."

Summer couldn't be hearing, understanding that right.

But the feeling of Fox's kiss could never be wrong.

And there was no mistaking the fire of Fox's mouth on his own, the heat of his body, the pressure and desire and need building up between them as Summer sank into the wildness of Fox's lips, the plundering desperation that seemed to beg something from him.

Something that he was only too willing to give.

He felt as though he were begging, as he slanted his mouth hotly, eagerly against Fox's—crying *take me, love me, fill me* with every moment that their lips crashed together and Fox reminded him how it felt to surrender entirely; to be caught up, swept into the insistent, hungry throb of sensation that made his entire body pulse in a singular dark rhythm of desire every time Fox so much as looked at him.

Charged, perfect, that kiss rocked through him until his body came alive each time Fox's tongue slid into him in intimate suggestion, stroking deep; each time their bodies moved together as slickly as if they were glazed in wet glistening sugar, caging fire inside. The damp sleekness of Fox's body overwhelmed Summer, steaming against him and jolting him with little erotic rushes of *awareness* each time he felt flesh to flesh. Heat to heat.

Lust to lust, as the tangled pressure of their bodies grew too taut, too hot to bear, arousal undeniable and his cock desperately straining against his swim trunks.

He let himself be pushed back toward one of the lounge chairs on the side of the pool, Fox's hands on his waist, Fox's tongue tracing his lips, Fox's *body* so tight against his with nothing between them but the thinnest layers of cloth, Fox's tall, perfectly sculpted, sinuously elegant body moving hard against Summer's as he tumbled Summer down to the chair.

Then weight—God, he loved Fox's weight atop him, loved those moments when Fox lost control and pinned him to the desk or against a wall, loved *this* moment when his world narrowed down to heat and hardness moving over him with absolute dominance and control, Fox settled between his legs and the wet rasp of cloth to cloth, cock to cock, fire to fire as Summer arched, writhed, surrendered himself to the feeling of Fox crushing him with the caged power writhing under that taut skin, Fox kissing him as though he was the air Fox needed to breathe, desperate and deep and driving hard and hot, mimicking with borderline obscene thrusts of tongue to Summer's tingling lips until he was gasping, sizzling, seared with the need for more than just this momentary kiss that would tease and flirt and taunt and never give quite enough to sate the dark, heady *wanting* inside him.

So he clung while he could—moving with Fox as Fox arched and drove his hips against him, grinding hard, leaving him dizzy with wild shocks of friction-burn pleasure and shocking bursts of need that took his breaths away, Summer clutching at Fox's hips to pull him in deeper, begging with his lips, with needy little bites, asking *please, please*. He'd never wanted anything like he wanted this: Fox pinning him, Fox claiming him, Fox whispering against his lips.

Whispering his name.

"Summer," Fox breathed, tracing his upper lip in an erotic rasp of sensation. "*Summer*."

"*Fox*," Summer answered—then broke off in a moaning, desperate cry as Fox's hand slipped between them, molded over his swim trunks, cupped his cock in knowing, deft fingers that kneaded in perfect rhythm, just enough pressure to make him burn for more and yet never enough to fully satisfy, leaving Summer's toes curling, his head tossing side to side and back, thighs aching and clenching against the bulk of Fox's body as he whimpered, as he pleaded without words, as he thrust himself up into that tormenting hand that was everything he wanted and nothing he needed.

Those silver eyes watched him, fixed, intense, as if Fox

could see nothing else…and he gripped Summer tighter through the fabric, molding to his shape, thumb tracing under the head of his cock as Fox breathed, "Do you want me, Summer? All of me?"

Summer stilled, struggling to process those words through pleasure that bordered on pain as fabric teased against hyper-sensitive flesh, struggling not to just give himself over in a writhing mess as he looked up at Fox dazedly with his legs spread and his hips lifting in involuntary little convulsions. Did…did he mean…?

Summer licked his lips, his mouth aching, hungry, and nodded slowly. "I…fuck, I've…wanted that for so long, Fox…"

"Have you?" Pale eyes lidded, and Fox dipped two fingers downward between Summer's legs, stroking over the swell of his balls against the tight fabric and making Summer jerk, catching a sound in the back of his throat, as his cock bucked and surged in response. "We have a problem, then, since we seem to be without adequate lubricant."

Summer flushed, the heat that roiled through his body seeming to concentrate in his face for a few moments.

And, with shaking fingers, he reached over the side of the chair to where he'd discarded his jeans in a heap, feeling around in the back pocket until he came up with one of several little portable blister packs of lube, holding it up between two fingers sheepishly.

Fox arched a brow, expression going flat. "Have you really been keeping—"

Summer grinned breathlessly. "I always had hope."

Fox rolled his eyes.

Plucked the lube from Summer's fingers.

And stole his grin from him with another kiss, a burning thing that tore at Summer's senses with an onslaught of pleasure—and lifted him up into a near-assault of touch, of taste, of the rush of breath storming between them in urgent swells.

Fox's hands were everywhere. Stroking at him, teasing over his body, tracing every outline of him and stopping to find the spots that made Summer suck his breaths in, from the peaks of his nipples to the dip of his stomach right below his waist, from his inner thighs to the undersides of his knees, searching out and discovering him. He writhed; he begged, gasping out his cries again and again; he curled and arched and twisted his body into every touch as if Fox had some compulsive power over him, pulling the strings of his need until he felt naked even with his swim trunks on, this consumptive and dizzying pleasure completely bared for Fox, his vulnerability on display each time Fox *touched* him and made him whine, made him clutch at him, made him whisper Fox's name, his mouth drying with the rush and sigh of it again and again.

But he nearly lost it when Fox stripped his boxer-briefs down to his thighs, touched his naked cock skin to skin, toyed over it, teased it, stroked it in knowing, feather-light touches that gathered the slick gleam of Summer's own pre-come against his skin and streaked it over him, making his cock tighten and swell with the near-agonizing sensation of that heated wetness cooling against his skin…

…before Fox cracked the little tube of lube open over his fingers, snapping it in a single brutal grip and coating his hand, thick clear runnels dripping down in loops to splash on Summer's skin.

Summer hissed as it landed on his cock, even those little licks of sensation too much, hyper-sensitive shocks that punched into his core like the most delicious pain—but it was nothing compared to those lube-slick fingers probing down between his legs, slipping under him, dipping along the cleft of his ass.

Fox pressed one fingertip against Summer's clenching entrance, the lightest brush of callused skin against tender flesh.

Clamped the other hand against Summer's throat, fingers pressing in just hard enough to whisper of strength, control, *possession*, the most perfect pulse of pain against Summer's skin.

And slid one finger inside him, penetrating him in a slow smooth dip of probing flesh, *opening* him with an intimacy that made him feel so vulnerable he nearly screamed before Iseya's first knuckle had even stretched open his pliant inner walls.

Summer sucked in a shallow breath—only for that dominating palm against his throat to stop it, not quite cutting off his air but only leaving him no doubt that he was in Fox's grasp, at his mercy, writhing underneath him with his thighs spreading so achingly wide of their own volition, baring him while he arched his back and jerked his hips and tossed his head back. Deeper that finger probed, a slow searching glide that touched over every secret place inside Summer with excruciating slowness and attentive strokes of pleasure, while Summer whimpered shamelessly and flinched from every too-raw burst of touch; it was too *good*, too fucking good to care about pride, and all that much better because it was *Fox*.

Fox sliding that long finger into him, searching ever deeper. Fox adding a second finger, stretching him, twisting them, plunging in and out in a rhythm that made Summer keen with the unbearable pleasure of it; with the borderline invasive feeling of being filled, his flesh played in malleable caresses, his entire body responding with quivers so deep he felt them vibrating in his gut.

Fox watching Summer with devouring eyes that seemed to see nothing else.

Fox stroking over and gripping his throat with a grasp that made a delicious thrill tighten in the pit of Summer's stomach—sending ripples throughout him that only clenched his inner muscles against Fox's fingers, imprinting the shapes of Fox's knuckles from within in little bursts of pleasure, holding on as if Summer could pull him deeper inside his body to touch every forbidden heat inside him.

Fox wanting him.

And that was all Summer needed.

Yet he craved more, *more*…and Fox gave him more. A third finger. A fourth. And then…

God.

The head of his cock pressing against Summer, thick, hot, seeming to jerk and buck and twitch with a life of its own, promising searing pleasure, every sharp detail of its flared shape teasing against him until an emptiness pulsed inside him in the outline of that hard, surging flesh, a craving that demanded to *feel* that heat sliding inside him, teaching him what it meant to be so *full* with someone else he thought it could destroy him.

Fox hovered over Summer, looking down at him with those consuming eyes that seemed to cut into Summer's very soul.

Tumbling hair falling down around them in half-loosed wisps.

That strong, honed body captured in a moment of perfect grace, taut-rippling sinew, arched over Summer in that last moment.

And that rumbling voice, breathing, commanding when there could be no other possible answer, "...say yes."

"*Yes*," Summer whispered without hesitation, wrapping his arms around Fox's neck.

And with that one word, Fox gave him his every desire.

Thickness split him open, parted his flesh to force him to mold around the shape of Fox's cock, sliding into him in a slick slow glide that thrust his voice up from inside his chest to pour out his throat, his lips, in gasping, broken cries as he opened his body for Fox and rose up to meet him, locking his thighs around his hips, pulling him *in*, struggling to make himself more and more open for Fox if only because he wanted to feel him *everywhere* inside, desperate for it with a wanton and shameless need. Fox's cock was a heady burn inside him, a weight that flowed so hard, remaking Summer in the image of his own desperate pleasure.

God, Summer was in so deep, his heart on fire...

And he needed Fox to be in deep, too.

Needed to feel flesh become desire, needed to feel the

two of them moving together, and as he crashed into Fox and Fox sank into him, their mouths met once more and hot breaths traded between, rushed and yet completely in synch, completely *together* in the urgency that made them thrust and writhe, shudder and grasp, moving together. Slow at first—so slow, Fox's breaths wet against his neck, his back arching in serpentine flexes of musculature under Summer's fingers, the grasping and relaxing pressure on Summer's throat seeming to guide the tempo driving them as Fox thrust into him again and again with a sort of controlled animalism, power and strength held in perfect rein as if he wanted to torture Summer with every suffering moment when Fox withdrew—until there was a void inside Summer that left his heart breaking for Fox, the only point of connection left that shivering feeling where the flared head of Fox's cock spread Summer open so wide at the most tender, sensitive point of his entrance.

And as if he wanted to reward Summer with that pleasure of fulfillment again, of flesh kissing to flesh inside him and making sweet sensation ripple down his inner thighs and course over his body like a crashing flood, points of pleasure igniting in the pit of his stomach, in the flutter of his pulse against Fox's palm, in the tingling ache of lips that begged for another taste…

…in the wondrously tight pain of his body *stretching*, wrapping around Fox's cock, *needing* it when he was so burnt up inside, this feeling almost *wrong* when every time Fox sank deep it was like he was piercing some inner vulnerability that Summer had never allowed anyone else to touch.

Anyone else but Fox.

Fox made him wild, as those thrusts came faster—that strength slowly slipping its leash until their bodies came together hard, bruising force slamming rough sounds from both their throats, trading them in hot, grasping kisses. Every time Fox sank into him harder, *harder*, Summer nearly screamed, clutching his thighs against Fox's waist, inner muscles twitching, jerking, gripping as he rose up to meet him. Again and again, every moment more fragile, more unbearable, rising to a fevered and quivering pitch, moving in racing tandem to tumble ever closer and closer to that unbearable edge of pleasure.

Tumble closer...

And spill over, breaking to the point of shattering.

Summer wrapped his fingers around his cock. He was so fucking hot, so *wet* with pre dripping over his flesh in burning runnels, its scent part of this simmering smoky miasma of lust enveloping them. He squeezed his cock and cried out against Fox's lips, his entire body answering with a hard clench that made him lock tighter still around Fox, tearing a wicked, rough growl from Fox's throat—and earning Summer a deeper, harsher thrust that tore over him in a battering rush. Again and again, matching his stroking rhythm to Fox's gasping, growling, searing thrusts, tightening deeper inside, loving every suffering moment when he made Fox snarl and punish him again and again until they fought each other to slam their bodies together, to meet with every driving thrust.

Hotter, building hotter still, tightening up inside, tension winding deeper and deeper—until he was locking around Fox's cock. Until Fox was snarling out his name. Until his back shuddered under Summer's fingers, and his hips jerked, his cock writhing hotly inside Summer, and Summer was stroking just a little harder, a little faster, and then—

Cracking. Splitting. Crumbling. Ripping apart. As if the burst of his climax was a thing of sheer destruction that shredded him apart from the inside out, savaging him with claws of pleasure, every hard-knotting spurt from his cock making him clench even more convulsively around Fox in little spasms of pleasure-pain, giving him the satisfaction of Fox's strained, harsh cries. Then Summer was wet inside, wet and warm and dripping with a sudden feeling of heavy, liquid fullness...and Fox's face was so fucking beautiful and perfect and *right* as he lost himself, and somehow they were coming down together in a tangled sweaty heap, breathing hard, sprawled against the lounge chair in a mess.

Sated. Sore. Breathless, grasping on to each other, nuzzled together in a mess of lax limbs while they both sank hard into the chair. So content, Summer thought fuzzily, a lovely feeling of slow lassitude sweeping through him to leave him boneless.

And almost completely naked, tangled up in each other.

In the pool house.

In public.

It was like they realized it in the same moment, the afterglow fading to a wide-eyed stare, before Fox peered slooowly over his shoulder.

Nothing there.

But, "Hold on," he murmured, gripping Summer's hips,

parting them in a burning rush of friction, before he was tumbling to his feet and reaching for Summer's hand with far more agility than he deserved to have after he had just fucked Summer's legs out from underneath him.

"Your room or mine?" Fox asked, and Summer grinned.

"Yours. Do you really want to see Dr. Liu like this?"

"No," Fox said dryly…then laughed. A laugh that lit up his face; a laugh like none Summer had ever heard from him before, and if Summer hadn't been in love… he would be now, looking into those sparkling gray eyes as Fox tugged him toward his clothing. "Now get your things…and *run.*"

Chapter Eleven

Summer never thought he would be falling asleep in Fox Iseya's bed.

Yet here he was—fresh out of the shower, still warm from the steaming spray, tying the drawstring on a pair of Fox's borrowed pajama pants; pants that dragged on the ground with Summer's every step as he shyly ventured from the bathroom and into the bedroom, watching as Fox turned down the sheets on the bed.

And paused, as Summer stopped in the doorway, unable to help drinking his fill of the sight of him.

Of that tall, hard-tapered body that had arched over him, driven into him, pale amber skin flexing and flowing like silk pulled tight over some great machine. He was still so sore, not even the shower easing it, but it was a soreness he wanted to hold on to, to savor, to feel again and again and again until his body was branded in it and he forgot how it felt to walk without the lingering perfect pain of Fox Iseya inside him.

While Fox halted mid-motion, arrested in silence, one hand still gripping a pillow covered in a subtly textured, dark gray pillowcase... Summer ducked his head, unable to stop from smiling no matter how he bit his lip to contain it, his cheeks warming.

He could still see it, from the corner of his eye.

The marks of his nails down Fox's back, red faint lines he'd left when he'd clutched at him and grasped so hard, dug so deep, begging without words *don't let me go.*

He felt like he was going to explode everywhere, in showers of light.

Especially when Fox made a soft, amused sound, his voice relaxed and low and almost coaxing. "Planning to sleep in the doorway?"

"No, I...uh..." Summer raked a hand through his hair, laughing helplessly. "I just... I realized I kind of assumed you'd let me stay, after...*that.*"

"Ah. Yes. *That.*" The mattress creaked faintly. "We should probably discuss *that*, but perhaps that discussion would be easier if you were *here.*"

Summer peeked back over his upraised arm. Fox sat on one side of the bed, one leg propped up, the other hanging over the edge, his body slouched like grace and ennui gathered up and crafted into the essence of a man, his disarrayed hair falling in loops from its twist to pour over his shoulders. He'd taken his glasses off, leaving them on the nightstand...and every inch of him glimmered in faint gilt edges of moonlight, pouring in silver arcs over his hair, running pale along the line of his jaw and the slope of his throat, slipping in soft-light touches over the defined ridges of his pectorals, the narrow, toned taper of his abdomen, the length of legs draped in loose black cotton.

Summer's mouth dried, as he tried not to stare.

God, Fox was beautiful.

And sitting there waiting for *him*, inviting Summer into his bed as if…as if…

As if Summer had a *chance*.

Summer licked his lips, then took a tentative step closer into the room, then another, before sliding his knee onto the bed and settling gingerly on the other side, leaning against the headboard but very carefully not touching Fox.

He didn't know why everything felt so much more tentative, now.

But…

Sex was sex.

It didn't mean anything, no matter how much he wanted it to, and he didn't want to jump to conclusions.

"So," he said, fidgeting his fingers, plucking at the leg of his pajama pants. "That…happened, didn't it?"

"If you're not certain if it did or not, perhaps I need to reconsider if I adequately satisfied you," Fox said dryly, and Summer spluttered, his ears burning—God, it felt like his *nose* was even on fire, his flush rolling through him fast enough to make him dizzy.

"N-no!" he sputtered. "I mean—you did, it was—you were good, it was good, it was *everything*, I just—I don't—"

Fox's cool expression didn't change, save for a subtle twitch of his lips.

A glimmer in his eyes.

And Summer realized Fox was, in fact, quite pointedly fucking with him.

Summer scowled, glowering at him. "I liked you better when you didn't have a sense of humor."

"No, you did not," Fox said, but relaxed into a smile, tilting his head back against the bank of pillows propped against the headboard behind him. "I suppose we should discuss what it means that it happened, though."

"I...it...it doesn't have to mean anything if you don't want it to," Summer said quickly, even as his quick-skip heartbeat smashed its fists against his rib cage in protest. "I don't...want to pressure you."

"But you want me." Husky, enthralling in that deep rolling voice, that voice that Summer had slowly started to pick up on the tiny nuances in, from the hint of an accent that had almost disappeared into precise American English to the fine peaks and valleys of emotion—and there was a question in that rumble now, a curiosity. "And you want to know what *I* want. If I want you...or if this was just a momentary lapse."

Summer nodded slowly, and braced himself.

Braced himself for this to hurt more than he was ready for.

Fox... Fox didn't want this.

He knew that already.

Knew Fox was determined to isolate himself one way

or another, as long as he never had to hurt again. Indulging Summer was just a momentary thing.

But even if he'd steeled himself for it to sting, to ache, to lash him hard...

Still he wasn't ready for the clutching jolt of pain that went through him as Fox looked away, his eyes shuttering, his voice neutral as he said, "I'm still retiring after this school year, Summer. And once I do, there'll be no place for me at Albin Academy. No reason for me to stay in Omen."

Couldn't I be? Summer wanted to plead, but held himself back—clutching his fingers together and pressing them against his chest as if he could physically restrain himself from leaning toward Fox, reaching toward him. *Couldn't I be enough of a reason?*

But instead he only asked carefully, "What does that mean, then?"

He was almost impressed with himself that his voice didn't waver, didn't fall.

But it was a bittersweet victory, when inside he felt like he was breaking apart.

Fox said nothing, at first, and the silence dug its hooks into Summer's heart as he searched that impassive face for something.

For anything that might tell him Fox felt even the tiniest thing for him.

Finally, Fox exhaled, seeming resigned. "Could you live with it? With being with me for the rest of the school year, knowing I'll leave you in the end?"

"Are you so sure of that?" Summer asked, voice cracking. "That you'll leave me. That you'll even want to leave me."

With a small smile, so bitter, dark with something turned inward, turned on himself, Fox let his head fall toward Summer, watching him through the messy spill of hair looping across his brow. "Are you so sure you'll even want me by then?" he asked, brittle words that came out slow, his red mouth shaping them as if he was bleeding them out. "You'll grow tired of me, Summer. I'm still the same weary old man. I'm still quite dull, quite proper, quite stiff...and quite incapable of knowing how to be with someone like you."

Summer closed his eyes—if only so Fox wouldn't see.

Wouldn't see the wetness springing to his eyes unbidden, so quick he couldn't stop it, the burn deep and prickling in his nostrils.

"You've been doing a pretty good job so far," he whispered.

Warmth covered his hand, then, trapping it against his thigh. Fox's fingers, curling over his, gripping tight. Summer sucked in a broken breath, lifting his head, sniffling back hard as he opened his eyes, scrubbing his free hand against his nose and staring at Fox miserably. At that smile that seemed the vessel for every pain he'd ever seen, ever known, awful and dark and heavy.

"I'm sorry," Fox said. "Maybe if I'd known you in another life...known you as someone else. Before...everything. But I can give you these few months, Summer... and I hope it will be enough."

No—no, it's never enough!

Nothing is enough...not until I can call you mine, and you call me yours.

It was almost cruel of Fox—cruel of him to let Summer know how it could feel to be with him, to be loved by him, to be wrapped up in his passion and the full unfettered force of the emotions Fox tried so hard to repress.

What had happened back there...

That hadn't been just lust.

Not the way Fox had kissed him, not the way Fox had touched him, whispered his name like a prayer, nearly worshipped him with every touch and every crash of their bodies. Fox had given him so much, and God, when he'd *laughed*, when Summer had seen that brightness transform his face until he came alive...

It only left him that much more cold when Fox withdrew once more behind a wall of quiet melancholy more stubborn and impenetrable than the harshest rejections, so determined to believe he was nothing else.

Summer wanted to shake him, wanted to beg...

But he couldn't.

His heart was too sore and heavy, right now.

He was too raw with all the emotions that Fox had touched, stroking the exposed nerves of his heart to leave them too quivering and sensitive.

He couldn't take this tonight.

But he wouldn't give up, he told himself, even as he turned his hand to press palm to palm with Fox's, lacing their fingers together, blinking back the blurring in his vision and forcing himself to smile.

"If that's what you want," he said thickly. "A few months is more than I ever thought would happen."

Fox's gaze flickered back and forth over Summer's face,

searching—before he tugged on their clasped hands, drawing Summer in.

"Come here, you ridiculous boy," he sighed. "Just… come here."

Then Fox's arms were around him, enfolding him like an apology, drawing him in close against Fox's chest, his warmth, the strength of him.

Summer told himself he wouldn't break.

Wouldn't cry.

But he clutched tight at Fox, buried his face in his chest, and breathed in deep wet gasps until that feeling of desperation passed, until he no longer felt like…like…

Like he was losing something before he even had a chance to grasp it tight.

Fox's heat and bulk curled around him, fingers stroking against his back—before one hand pulled away.

And a moment later, something cool fell over Summer like rain, lashing and licking against his skin in silken washes.

He opened his eyes, sucking in a soft breath, watching as the spill of Fox's hair cascaded down in threads of black diamond, fine and wispy and floating like feathers in looping arcs to spill over Fox, over the bed, over Summer. It was longer than he'd ever imagined, pouring in a river over the dark gray sheets, shining like thin threads of starlight shooting through a black night sky, liquid as water and silken-fine and wreathing Fox in a cloak that made him look ethereal, unreal, almost inhuman.

Summer's heart thumped harder still, as he looked up

into gray eyes that seemed to whisper a sorrow older than even Fox himself, older than the sky, older than the moon.

"Sleep, Summer," Fox breathed, and bent over him, pressing his lips to Summer's brow like a blessing. "Sleep... and this will all look different in the morning."

Fox felt as though he had committed a crime.

A desecration. A sin. A defilement against everything he held dear.

A betrayal.

Not against Michiko; not against the memory that still perched on his shoulder like a silent thing, whispering in his ear endlessly in a constant stream of sounds he couldn't understand but that would never give him peace.

Against Summer.

Fox curled on his side with his head pillowed on one arm, his other arm draped around Summer, gathering him close against his chest. Summer slept tucked tight into him, resting in the crook of Fox's arm and burrowing his face into his shoulder, the mess of his hair spilling in black arcs over Fox's chest and mixing with his own until they were just a sea of ink together, and all that tanned, taut skin pressed up against his in dark contrast, Summer's body heat as tangled with him as the young man's long, agile legs.

He looked so peaceful, in his sleep. So relaxed.

So young.

But even this, right now...

This was *hurting* him, and Fox was only making it worse by letting Summer's attachment grow deeper.

That moment of impulse, that burst of passion, of desire, had been wrong—so wrong. No matter how good it had felt, no matter that for a few minutes he had no longer been a grieving widower or a frozen shadow locked away with his ghosts, but simply a man entwined with another man and completely lost in the rapture of him, the passion of him, the wildness and so much dizzying, spinning emotion and pleasure building up into a thing of crashing, interlocked beauty...

In the end, he could only hurt Summer.

And he'd just...just callously made certain that when it came, that hurt would be ten times worse.

All because he was selfish.

He was selfish, and wanted to hold on to this for a few months longer before he...

Before he gave up, he thought.

He didn't know what he would do once he left Albin Academy.

He just knew that he was tired, and had no reason to stay...and he thought, perhaps, once he left he would give up on trying to be a man at all, and simply find somewhere to *be* until time finally did its work and ended this haunting when he'd been a ghost for so very long already.

His body just hadn't figured that out yet.

Summer shifted against him, letting out a soft sigh in his sleep, a murmur, one that blended into a tired call of "...Fox..."

Fox tightened his hold, smoothing his hand down that strong, sloping back. "I'm here, Summer," he whispered, even if that felt like a lie, a false promise. "I'm here. Sleep."

Summer settled against him with a low sound of contentment, and Fox closed his eyes, pain reverberating through him like the echoes of a struck bell.

What am I doing?

What can I offer him, while I continuously take and take and take as if I can feel alive again on his vitality alone?

He found no answer inside himself.

No answer in the beat of Summer's heart against his chest, strong and vibrant and seeming as if it would beat for the both of them, until the dead thing inside Fox's chest remembered how.

And so he only told himself to sleep, to let go, to rest, to forget.

Only to lie awake well into the night, his only companion the sound of Summer's sleeping breaths.

Chapter Twelve

Summer was alone when he woke in the morning.

At first he didn't quite realize where he was, when he rolled over and his arm sprawled across a bed that...wasn't his.

His bed was piled high with pillows, and if he was waking up he should be smelling *something* burning as Dr. Liu torched whatever he made for breakfast.

But instead he was alone against cool sheets, and as he fumbled out groggily his fingers brushed against something dry that crinkled like paper.

He creaked one eye open on gray sheets.

Only to slam awake as if he'd been struck, awareness rocking through him with an earthquake's force as his senses started to filter in. The scent of honeysuckles that seemed burnt into the sheets beneath his cheek; the sensation of a body that had been pressed against his own; the deep, sore ache inside himself where Fox had filled him and teased him and made him burn for that deep-stroking sensation coursing wildly through him.

That…that had really happened last night, hadn't it?

Right there at the pool, where *anyone* could have caught them.

Summer let out a breathless laugh, burying himself into the pillows and breathing in deep of Fox's scent. Of Fox *himself*.

And remembering the bittersweet ache of watching Fox take his hair down, something that had' felt so painfully intimate and yet somehow not *enough* when Fox had told Summer in no uncertain terms…

This was temporary.

But it was *something*.

And Summer had been telling the truth, when he'd said he'd always had *hope*.

Hope that maybe, just maybe, he could change Fox's mind.

…maybe, just maybe, he could…he could make Fox understand that Summer *loved* him.

Not the terrifying idealization he'd known as a boy.

Cranky, stubborn Fox *himself*, who didn't seem to know what to do with himself when someone asked him to just be a *person* instead of an authority figure.

He was so much more than that, to Summer.

He was sweet, in his own quiet ways. Much more easily flustered than he let on. Awkward, but he hid it behind an intellect that could be terrifying in its incisiveness, used to create a defensive barrier that protected him from others. Quiet. Thoughtful. Sometimes so absorbed in whatever was going through his mind that he was as bad as Dr. Liu, if not as destructive—forgetting his papers in the classroom, forgetting to charge his phone.

And he made Summer feel...

Like he could *be* something more than this frightened thing he was.

Knowing that Fox had come to the States and felt like he hadn't fit in, and yet still had managed to survive and become someone others respected, admired, even if they also feared him a little...

It told Summer he could do it, too.

That he could find a place for himself.

That place right now, though, should probably be in Fox's office, reviewing homework assignments to get ahead of schedule.

He had a feeling that no matter how deeply, how hotly Fox had loved his body last night...

There was no way in hell he'd go easy on Summer in the office.

Grinning to himself, practically bouncing to the beat of his heart, he rolled over and caught up the scrap of neatly folded paper left on Fox's side of the bed, flicking it open with his thumb.

Faculty meeting this morning. Nothing interesting.
Sleep in.
I left breakfast in the oven for you.

Terse words in Fox's sharp, slashing handwriting, but with a subtle touch of...*something*, something that made Summer's heart beat faster still.

If he didn't calm down before class, the boys were going to give him hell.

He rolled out of bed, nearly tripped over the over-long hems of his borrowed pajama pants, and padded into the kitchen to peer into the oven—where a thickly piled panini oozing with cheese and bits of egg waited, left to keep warm on low heat. Grinning to himself, he pulled on a pair of oven mitts and tugged it out, transferring it to a plate and settling in to enjoy his breakfast with that hope inside him burning brighter than ever.

It was one thing for Fox to feel enough attraction to fuck him.

But if he actually liked him enough to *feed* him, Summer just might have a real chance.

Fox wasn't sure what he was expecting, when he escaped another interminably dull staff meeting and returned to his office.

He had expected to find Summer waiting.

He hadn't expected to find Summer sitting in Fox's chair, rather than the chair he usually claimed opposite the desk.

When Fox opened the door, for a moment he halted on the threshold; Summer stopped moving in quiet freeze-frame, not even breathing, his gaze darting up.

They stared at each other for several frozen seconds, Fox's heart an odd and light thing in his chest.

Before Summer smiled, breaking the silence and shifting to rise out of the seat.

"Sorry," he said, soft and almost embarrassed, as he edged to one side. "I... I wanted to..."

"Don't," Fox said dryly, rounding the desk and settling into his chair. "If you say something ridiculously sentimental, you're working out in the hall today."

"...I'm still going to think it."

"I can't control your thoughts," Fox pointed out, settling his satchel on the desk next to a stack of papers. "But I can ask you not to embarrass yourse—"

He broke off.

Because he suddenly had a lap full of young man, Summer's body settling warm across his thighs, weight quite pleasingly heavy and body heat washing over him in a liquid wave. Summer's arms slipped around his neck, and the tip of Summer's nose brushed Fox's as that shy, almost coy smile returned.

"Not saying anything," Summer whispered. "Is this still embarrassing?"

"Quite," Fox grumbled...and settled his hands on Summer's waist, soaking that warmth into his palms. "We cannot possibly work like this."

"Sure we can."

Summer shifted against him—and Fox found himself entirely and suddenly far too distracted, as trim hips and the taut muscle of his bottom dragged against Fox's lap. He still felt...*raw*. Sensitive, as if the nerves controlling arousal had temporarily died only to flare to life in shocking intensity, far too *real* after years without...and he sucked in a breath through clenched teeth, dropping his hands to grip at the arms of the chair as Summer wriggled his way between Fox's thighs and settled perched on the chair between his legs, leaning his back against Fox's chest.

"There," Summer said, looking over his shoulder at Fox with his eyes glittering, his cheeks faintly flushed. "Now we can both use the desk."

Fox eyed him. "...how, exactly, are we supposed to work on simultaneous tasks like *this*?"

He lifted his hips, rocking them rather pointedly into Summer, letting him feel *exactly* the damnable effect he had on Fox—and Summer caught a quiet breath, before exhaling in a soft moan.

"Ah... F-Fox, I..." He took a deep breath. "Maybe I didn't...quite think this through..."

"That seems to be a hallmark of many of your life decisions, yes."

"*Ouch.*" But Summer was still smiling, still flushed, even as he leaned away from Fox with ginger, careful movements that still couldn't stop how their bodies slid together, nestled as they were. He dragged over the open course gradebook he'd been reviewing, before snuggling back into Fox. "But I actually needed your help with this...so we can look at it together?"

The soft note of entreaty in Summer's voice made Fox sigh.

Because he already knew damned well that he would do whatever Summer asked, even if it meant working in this *highly* compromising position.

"What were you looking at?" he asked, ignoring the

tight, pulling sensation in his cock and instead settling his arms around Summer's waist, resting his chin to his shoulder. "Show me."

He couldn't miss the pleased tinge to Summer's smile, as Summer turned his head and kissed Fox's cheek, before bowing his head to look down at the gradebook.

"I've been talking to some of the students," he said. "The ones who get bullied the most. Asking when it started… I'm not clueless enough to ask *who*, or they'd clam up. No one wants to be the snitch. But based on the conversations…" He sighed, his body going a bit heavier in Fox's arms. "The slow decline in their grades almost exactly matches up with when their bullying started."

Fox kept his smile to himself, if only because the urge to smile unbidden was so strange he naturally suppressed it.

Of course Summer cared about that, to the point of going far beyond his duties.

Of course.

He pressed his mouth against the back of Summer's shoulder, watching one tanned fingertip skim down the lines, stopping on specific names. As expected, Jay Corey and Eli Schumaker were on the list…but several others, as well.

"You know the Assistant Principal won't like this," he murmured. "He's still worried about risk of liability, when you're only a TA."

"I know," Summer said. "There's not much I can do, but…" He bit his lip. "A teacher, an actual tenured teacher, could call parent-teacher conferences, couldn't they?"

With a groan, Fox rested his brow against Summer's back, tightening his hold around his waist. "Did you seduce me simply so you could use your wiles to convince me to call their parents in so you might intervene?"

Summer made a strangled noise. "I... I didn't *seduce* you at all! I...i-it...it just *happened*, you were there and I was there and then you kissed me and...and..."

"Breathe, Summer." Fox smoothed his hand against the tight planes of Summer's stomach, feeling the shallowness of his inhalations. "I suppose my utter lack of tone makes attempts at humor fall short."

"*Dick*," Summer said, but laughed, reaching back to lightly thump Fox's thigh. "Will...will you help, then?"

Fox wrinkled his nose. "I suppose they cannot fire me if I already intend to quit. But are you certain you know what you're getting into? You *do* recall who the parents of these students are, don't you? It will likely take two weeks simply to wrangle them into showing their faces."

"And they'll probably be assholes, I know." Summer sighed. "But I have to *try*, Fox. What's the worst that could happen if I try? That those boys know *someone* cares about them, even if their parents threw them away like trash?"

Fox just...*looked* at Summer.

He didn't know how anyone could be so very terrified of the world at large, and yet still open his heart so freely and invite the very world that frightened him into its inner chambers.

Summer was a strange beast, indeed.

And, with a deep exhalation, Fox offered a smile. "You did not have to convince me," he said. "I already knew I would say yes the moment you asked."

In a flurry, he had his arms full of Summer—as the

gradebook landed messily on the desk, and Summer landed messily across Fox's lap again, that soft sweet mouth finding his with a quiet urgency, a need that was almost clumsy in its eagerness, only making it that much more alluring for its guilelessness.

"Thank you," Summer breathed against his lips. "You won't regret it."

Fox had his doubts about that.

But he had other things on his mind, right now, as he pushed Summer back against the desk, leaning into him, leaning into that enticing, wetly stroking mouth, sliding his fingers over the buttons of Summer's shirt.

"If that was all you wanted," he rumbled, "I suggest we find a reason to make better use of our office hours."

And better use they made, indeed.

As Summer arched beneath him, and the desk shook and rattled while Summer twisted his gloriously golden body against it, making a mess of the papers and books, making a mess of *himself*. The door was unlocked, Summer's voice a rush of gasps and cries stifled against the back of his hand, but in this moment...

Fox didn't *care*.

Because sweet thighs were around his hips, sweet flesh tight around his cock...

And a sweet voice called his name on slick, needy lips, and he couldn't stop even if he wanted to.

If he had only months...

Then for those months while he gave himself to Summer without thinking of the consequences of the future, he might as well *live*.

★ ★ ★

Summer thought he might just have to get used to being sore.

Not that he minded it.

Especially when it gave Fox another reason to use those long, devious fingers on him, slipping them inside Summer coated with a soothing, specially handmade herbal cream that at once eased the pain and made it burn that much deeper as the warming salve soaked into his abused, battered, swollen flesh.

He just…hadn't been particularly sexually active before, save for a few one-night stands while he was figuring out himself and what he liked, and he hadn't really built up any stamina for the perpetual feeling of being stretched open and filled until he thought he would burst, then left throbbing with the perfect empty ache of it that wouldn't let him forget Fox even when they weren't in the same room.

But it sure as hell made *sitting* an interesting prospect.

And he'd thought, over the past few days of quiet mornings working over assignments and lesson plans, quieter evenings taking work back to Fox's suite over dinners they made together with a sort of familiar comfort that shouldn't have come so easily but that *did*…

He'd thought for all his stoic expressionlessness, Fox had *enjoyed* watching Summer squirm to get comfortable on the sofa, in the easy chairs, in the office chairs, on the little café stools where they'd gone out for lunch yesterday, just a simple thing and yet it had brought Summer such pleasure to be out under the midday sun with Fox's eyes always on him, trailing him with so many things left unsaid.

Things that made Summer's heart seize up tight.

Things that told him by the time they got back to the bedroom every night...

Fox would give him even more reasons to be so deliciously, wonderfully uncomfortable.

But Summer was struggling with the desk chair now, as he tried to squirm his way into a comfortable position on the thin padded seat and keep his concentration on digging up phone numbers, names. He'd already tried sending emails to the parents of several of the boys he wanted to speak to, and only gotten four responses when he'd contacted over a dozen.

This was going to be like herding cats, he could tell.

But he had to *try*.

Even if a backwoods like Omen was somewhere people sent their kids to forget about them, somewhere so hidden that they couldn't embarrass their wealthy, prestigious parents in the public eye or be easily scoped by the paparazzi...

Summer had to believe at least some of those parents cared.

And wouldn't want their boys to be as unhappy as they were.

He glanced up, though, as a little alarm on Fox's laptop went off, chiming the signal for ten minutes to the day's block of afternoon classes.

And Fox wasn't back.

He'd gone off to dig up something for class at the town library, some obscure older book on Fechner, and he'd be late and Summer...

Summer still wasn't sure he'd be ready to lead the class on his own, not after almost two weeks.

He'd try, if he had to.

But he was starting to think, more and more, that his place wasn't at the front of the class.

He dug his phone out, though, and tapped out a quick text message. *Ten minutes to class and the clock is ticking. Did you want to do something for dinner tonight? Maybe in town?*

He waited three minutes, watching the clock, and hoped Fox just didn't answer because he was driving. Though Summer knew the real reason, and he sighed fondly.

Fox had probably let his phone die yet again.

He wasn't a technophobe, but God, he never remembered to charge the thing unless Summer stole it from him and put it on the charger himself.

Smiling to himself, he gathered up his class materials, stacked them in his arms, and headed out to find the man he only wished he was brave enough to call his boyfriend.

Chapter Thirteen

Fox had come seconds away from never coming back, today.

And he didn't think the gorgeous, artlessly sprawled young man stretched out in the bed next to him had any idea.

He'd slipped by the library hoping to find a copy of Gustav Fechner's *Elemente der Psychophysik* for a class presentation, because *someone* had stolen the school library copy Fox had donated, one of many from his personal collection that had gone on the shelves only to disappear into one student's hands or another's over the years.

He'd checked out both the German and English versions, as well as a few other books he'd thought might be useful for a more organic approach to teaching. Something that might be more Summer's style than his own, but just from watching Summer work with the students Fox had started to think perhaps, just perhaps, he could relax his more rigid teaching methods to try something that might work better with young, malleable, and easily distracted brains.

Then he'd sat behind the wheel of his car, books stacked high in the passenger's seat, and asked himself...

Why.

Why was he making plans to adapt his teaching methods, when he was leaving in a year?

Why was he thinking about a future here at Albin as if...

As if something could *change* somehow, could make everything new and different and bright?

Nothing had changed.

Nothing, he told himself.

And yet everything had changed, from the moment Summer had kissed him and Fox had kissed him back and some rusted-shut door inside him had opened, a tiny voice whispering *please, come in, it's dark and lonely here, please... please.*

While the rest of him had screamed *what's the point?*

What was the point of any of this?

Why was he doing this, letting Summer believe there could ever be anything between them when Fox just... just...

He'd wanted to lie down and just...quit, he realized.

In that nebulous grayness of his plans after he left Albin... it had just been this open-ended desire to do *nothing.* As if he could blank out and simply cease to be.

But now images were forming in that haunting grayness, that darkness, that shadow of an undefined future, and those images didn't promise nothing. They promised something, *everything*, this idea of a *life* again, this idea that he could care about things again and actually wake up every day *not* terrified that caring would just mean he would lose them all over again.

He watched Summer sleep, following the way the moonlight fell in soft outlines over his bare shoulders, his neck, his jaw, his hair, as if he was an illustration of a beautiful man traced in lines of silver ink. He was so *young*, and yet somehow years had transformed him from a nervous boy into a quiet, sweet, still *entirely* nervous man who somehow had found some sort of serenity and strength nonetheless. It was as though he calmed himself by terrifying himself.

As if Summer was more afraid of not trying…

Than he was of trying, and failing.

Of trying, and *losing*.

He'd been willing to risk losing Fox completely, losing his job, just for the thin chance at having him for just a little while.

And Fox was letting himself get sucked into that idealism, when he knew better.

He knew better, when unlike Summer…

He knew how it felt to believe in forever, only to have it cut short.

And just thinking about the idea of forever with someone like Summer, thinking about letting himself get tangled that deep and giving in to this quiet feeling of longing that kept pulling him into the vibrant young man as if they were tethered by unbreakable strands of fragile, glittering spider's silk…

It had terrified him.

It had terrified him, and he'd almost driven away from

the library, out of Omen, and out of Massachusetts without ever looking back.

Summer would never know the struggle of will it had taken Fox to turn his car around, drive back to the school, and show up just in time for his class blocks with some murmured excuse about not being able to find the books he'd wanted and losing track of time.

And Fox didn't want him to know.

He was already going to hurt Summer by leaving him, by leaving Omen, once this charade was over.

While they were here, while they were together…

He could at least keep his fears, his hesitations, to himself—and not use them as blunt objects to hurt Summer even more.

Right now, though…

He suddenly couldn't stand to be idle, in this moment.

Couldn't stand to lie here playing at domestic bliss, with Summer's body heating the bed.

And so, gently disentangling his hair from the snares of Summer's limbs, he slipped out of bed and into the living room, drifting to the window.

The plants along the windowsill were hardy succulents, and he ran his fingers over their dry, waxy leaves, stopping on an aloe plant. He hadn't made anything, from the simplest aloe salve to herbal pain relievers, in so very long; even the salve that helped Summer not be quite so obvious about why his nethers were smarting was from older stock that Fox had tinned and set aside ages ago.

And he smiled faintly, bitterly, to himself as he tested the jagged edge of another thick leaf with his fingertip, then let go, lifting his head to stare down at the spindly trees below and the way the mist crawled and rolled through the nighttime forest like a strange, smoky thing.

He used to *create* things. To take pleasure in making things simply for the sake of building something useful with his hands; simply because that was one of the things that made him feel alive.

He would say he didn't know why he stopped, but he knew.

The same moment when he'd stopped doing anything that wasn't the bare necessity to function, and to fulfill the duties that were expected of him.

He drifted his hands along the shelf beneath the windowsill, stopped when he found the familiar gritty shapes of an old, pecked stone mortar and pestle, an antique piece he'd picked up on his last visit to Japan, when wandering shops in Sapporo. He didn't know why he felt so hollow, right now. So pointless, so devoid of purpose, his hands aching for something to do, but…

Gathering his hair up behind his head, tucking it into a knot, he dragged a chair over and pulled over the aloe plant, the mortar, the little carved wooden box he kept on the shelf full of various dried herbs and ingredients.

He didn't know what he'd do, not just yet.

All that mattered was that he was doing *something*.

Instead of continuing years and years of doing absolutely nothing at all.

Summer wasn't sure what woke him.

Maybe the emptiness of the bed, the sheets cooling

around him when he was getting used to the warmth and weight of Fox against his back, heavy arm over his waist.

Maybe it was the chill of the night air, prickling at his skin.

Or maybe it was the overwhelming scent of peppermint, drifting through the suite and powerful enough to sting his nostrils.

He creaked one eye open, sniffling and rubbing at his nose, then pushed himself up and squinted drowsily around the room. No sign of Fox, but that smell was overpowering. Had something spilled in the essential oils in the bathroom...?

Yawning, rolling the stiffness out of his shoulders, Summer stood, rubbing the back of his neck and padding out to the living room—only to stop at the threshold of the doorway, as he saw Fox.

Silent, his posture gracefully taut, Fox sat at the windowsill, using the shelf beneath it as a table. He was surrounded by many of the potted plants scattered through the apartment, different herbs, some of them delicate, some thick and succulent. A carved wooden box with multiple compartments sat open next to him, and he worked over a mortar and pestle, grinding something green and strong-smelling into a waxy, oily paste against the carved stone basin.

And his expression was...

Summer didn't think he'd ever seen Fox with his expression so relaxed, so gentle, calm and at peace.

Completely transfixed on what he was doing, Fox worked his hands with a quiet, knowing deftness, a delicate touch, constant rhythm stopped only by a pause to add a leaf plucked here, a sprinkle of something dried there. His lips were subtly curled in a soft, thoughtful smile, his eyes half-lidded, gleaming like captured moonlight, the shadows and light from the window falling over him in soft gray shades to make him a misty, ghostly thing, ethereal and silent.

And Summer had never seen him more beautiful.

Not even when he arched over Summer in a moment of captured pleasure did he look so serene, so...*content.*

And it hurt, in the strangest way. Lovely and odd and hollow all at once, when Summer loved to see Fox like this—open, unguarded, and doing something that clearly made him happy when he'd seemed so determined to punish himself with misery for so very long.

It just ached that...

That Fox had never looked at *him* that way.

That Summer couldn't make him happy that way, and instead just seemed to bring Fox more and more trouble, more and more heartache.

He shouldn't look at it that way. It was selfish—but then Summer himself was so very selfish, for clinging so tight to what he craved so desperately with a man who clearly only tolerated him because it was easier not to argue; easier to indulge him.

It felt like a knot lived in the back of Summer's throat lately, one he couldn't ignore every time he stopped letting himself believe in hope and remembered just what their situation was. A casual arrangement. A dalliance. A way to pass the time until Fox could escape Albin...

Escape *him*.

And that knot in Summer's throat grew to the size of a fist, as he stepped backward soundlessly, slipping from the room to return to bed.

And leaving Fox to his peace, without Summer there to intrude.

Fox still hadn't returned to bed by the time Summer woke on his own without an alarm the next morning.

He had a moment of panic—until he remembered it was Saturday.

But he curled up on his side for long minutes, just staring at the empty half of the bed, and wondered if Fox had even come back last night and Summer had just slept through it, or...

Or if Fox was avoiding him.

He was starting to think the latter, when he dragged himself up to shower and there was no sign of Fox anywhere; the scent of mint still lingered, though not as strong or overpowering, but his tools and herbs had been put away.

But there were several fresh muffins left warming in the oven for Summer.

No note this time, but...

This was starting to become routine.

And he smiled to himself as he settled in to read the news on his phone over breakfast, before ducking himself into the shower and then dressing and heading out into town. He'd promised his mother he'd stop in today, both to help with the yard and just to visit; considering she was half the reason he'd moved back, she'd been remarkably adamant about insisting she didn't need anything, no no, get settled in, don't worry about her.

But she was all smiles, as Summer parked outside her house and stepped out—and she came tumbling out to meet him again. That was just how Lily Hemlock was; why wait for guests to arrive when she could be so very *happy* to see anyone who came to her door that she just went rushing out to greet them?

"*Summer.*" She grasped him in a tight hug, nearly squeezing the life out of him, then laughed when he grunted, wiggling his fingers, arms trapped against his sides. "I missed you."

"You kept telling me not to come," he protested with a laugh.

"Oh, you know, I know you're getting settled in, and so much work to get used to—I didn't want to be a bother." She swatted his chest lightly, then caught his hand and nearly dragged him inside. "It doesn't mean I didn't miss you."

Summer just smiled down at her fondly, letting himself be ushered into the house. "I missed you too, Mom. And I'm here all day, if you need me."

"Don't say that or I'll put you to work in the garden." Her eyes glittered as she glanced at him, then pushed him toward one of the kitchen chairs. "Let me feed you first. I've still got some pancakes left over. You just missed Fox, by the way. By fifteen minutes."

Summer nearly missed the edge of his chair, and went plunking half toward the floor before he caught himself on the edge of the kitchen table and dragged himself up, set-tling clumsily on the seat and staring at his mother.

"Fox...was here...?" he asked, mouth dry.

"Oh, yes." Bustling about busily, his mother piled a plate high with pancakes, even though Summer had no appetite—but no heart to tell her that, either. "Showed up quite out of the blue. I haven't seen him in months, and I...well." She clucked her tongue. "He was *smiling*. And actually stayed for tea. He always says no, but he's...well. Something's different. Whatever do you think has gotten into that man?"

It's more like who he's gotten into, Summer thought, but clamped down on his tongue hard.

He didn't want to think it was because of him, anyway.

But he could hope.

"I, um... I really wouldn't know," he said, fumbling around his teeth, his tongue. "He's pretty hard to read sometimes."

"Is he?" She slid the stack of pancakes in front of him, the bottle of syrup following almost like a challenge. "I've always thought he was quite painfully simple."

"Really?" Reluctantly, Summer picked up his fork. He loved his mother's cooking, just...he'd already eaten at Fox's, but he didn't want the hangdog, sad look that would come if he turned her down. "Maybe you could explain to me, then, because he's driving me sideways just trying to understand what he *wants*."

"Fox wants what anyone wants, dear." Lily settled in the chair adjacent to his, and rested her warm, thin hand to his wrist, watching him with her eyes clear and soft and sympathetic. "To never hurt again. The problem is...even as old as he is, he's never realized that that's not possible. Not unless you shut yourself away completely, so that you can't feel anything at all. And that's no way to live."

Summer bit his lip, poking at his pancakes, leaving little rows of four holes in the stack. "I want to tell him hurting is just a part of life," he murmured. "But I... I can't imagine what he feels to even say that. It feels disrespectful. I was so young when Dad died... I don't even remember how it hurt."

"I do," Lily said softly. "Your father was the love of my life, and there'll never be another. Losing him shattered me, but that doesn't mean I would let myself stop feeling everything just to avoid that pain." She smiled, then, and offered her hand to Summer. "If I had, I'd never have been able to love you...and I couldn't live without that, my precious boy."

Summer set his fork down and slipped his hand into his mother's, clasping tight. It ached to think how old she was; that one day she'd be gone, too, and he'd learn what that pain felt like all too deeply.

But he had her now.

That warm, soft hand in his, so very real and here and *now*.

Sometimes that was all that mattered was having *now*, instead of worrying about what might come later, or when *now* would inevitably end.

Everything ended.

Just because things ended was no reason to avoid beginning them at all.

He smiled, running his thumb over his mother's knuckles. "Love you too, Mom. I just…wish it was as easy to say that to Fox."

His mother arched a sly brow that said she knew far more than she let on. "Oh, I think he knows how you feel. Considering the way he nearly spilled his tea all over himself when I asked how well you were performing at the school."

Summer choked, inhaled, wheezed, then stared at her, the tips of his ears going vividly hot. "*Mom!*"

Lily only smiled that innocent smile of hers. "Well. I hadn't been one hundred percent certain, but that reaction certainly confirmed it. I do hope you're being safe, darling. And using plenty of lubricant."

"I—you—*I cannot have this conversation with you!*" he garbled out, every word twisting and tripping over his tongue horribly; he just stared at her in horror, fingers rigid in hers. "You—you *knew?*"

"I do now." With a pleased smile, Lily pulled her hand from his and patted his knuckles, then rose to her feet, briskly dusting her dress off. "Eat your pancakes, dear. I'll get you some milk."

Summer just…stared after his mother, as she bustled to the fridge.

And Fox wondered why sometimes, Summer just bit the bullet and dove in, no matter what outrageous things were in his head.

Summer had learned from the best.

But even on his worst day…

He'd never be as incorrigible and wonderful as Lily Hemlock.

★ ★ ★

The fact that Summer wasn't back yet shouldn't make Fox so restless.

Fox shouldn't be so…so *needy*.

Shouldn't want to be *around* Summer so much.

He was the one who had set the time limit on this.

Even if he was greedy to want to make the most of it, to enjoy what he could while they had *something*…

If he wanted too much?

He wouldn't want to leave, when the time came.

But he still didn't think he could stand to stay.

Nor could he stand to sit still. He'd been staring at the stack of homework assignments in his lap for nearly an hour, since Summer had texted and said he was staying late at Lily's to do some work on the house, and to eat without him.

No—more, he'd been staring at the coffee table, fixed on a spot just past the tip of his pen.

Hellfire.

What was this agitation eating at him?

With a frustrated sound, Fox tossed his pen onto the coffee table with a clatter, sending it spinning against the dark lacquer, then dropped the stack of pages next to it, stood, and stalked into the kitchen. His fingers fumbled clumsily with the apron strings as he strapped it on over his shirt and slacks, before ducking into the refrigerator to see what was left when he had been too wrapped up in work, in life, in *Summer* to remember the grocery store this week.

Except rather than empty shelves…

He found the refrigerator nearly overflowing.

Summer must have gone shopping while Fox was visiting Lily to stock his herb cabinet, this morning.

Fresh mushroom caps in a little plastic-wrapped foam bin—Fox hated the stems. A crisper full of iceberg lettuce and cherry tomatoes and baby carrots; real baby carrots, instead of adult carrots shaved down to nubs, something Fox fussed over because the taste was different and he was something of a picky eater. Even bell peppers...but the yellow ones.

Fox liked the yellow ones.

He didn't care that they were the same vegetables as the green ones, the red ones; he'd swear they tasted different.

Two percent milk, instead of one percent or skim. Cups of Greek yogurt in every flavor Fox liked. Eggs, but the brown ones, because that, too, was another thing Fox fussed about with food.

Summer had paid attention to every little thing over these short days, and remembered.

Something so small shouldn't hit Fox so hard, but it made him realize exactly why he was so restless.

He was *lonely*.

And rather than cooking dinner alone as he had for twenty years before Summer had come tearing into his life like a summer storm...

He wanted to be where Summer was.

Helping him fix up Lily's tidy little house. Laughing with him over how his mother did so enjoy embarrassing him. Staying to help them make dinner. Creating something not just with his hands, but with other people that he cared about. Being *part* of something, with both his old friend and the man he was starting to think of not as a casual, temporary fling, but as...but as...

As his lover.

How long had they been doing this?

A week? More?

Time had no meaning, not when he drifted in a haze of Summer from waking until sleeping, until even those moments in class when they had to separate as Professor Iseya and Mr. Hemlock were only a bristling haze of tension waiting until they were alone again, slamming each other against the desk, devouring each other in kisses that were beginning to feel as if they could never sate the hungry void inside Fox.

A void that had only seemed to grow larger, since he'd opened himself to this.

He closed his eyes, leaning his forehead against the icy freezer door.

Was he trying to make up for so many lost years all at once?

He couldn't do this.

Couldn't fall so fast, so hard.

He wouldn't *let* himself.

And he forced all thoughts of Summer from his mind, as he pulled the bell peppers out and dragged a cutting board off its wall hook, before turning the sink on and beginning to scrub one of the firm yellow peppers under the warm spray. He'd make a simple stir-fry, he thought; peppers, onions, mushrooms, perhaps the beef tips he'd glimpsed in one of the cooler compartments. He—

Fox almost hated himself for the delicious, horrible,

sweet, painful shock that went through his heart at the
sound of the front latch clicking.

He told himself not to look up, but he couldn't stop
himself.

As Summer stepped inside—a dirty mess, his T-shirt
stained with grass and dirt and rust and who knew what
else, his hair sweaty and raked back from his face in a tangle
of black fluff, smudges on his cheeks, his arms grimed with
sweat and dirt that outlined the hardened shapes of toned
musculature. His shirt clung to him in a film of sweat, and
his old, ragged jeans hung temptingly low on his hips, as
if trying to remind Fox of the way those hips moved and
twisted and undulated when Summer straddled Fox's body
and completely lost himself moving in such hungry, wanton rhythm on Fox's cock.

Summer froze just inside the door as their gazes met,
Summer's eyes widening briefly as he made a startled
sound, before smiling shyly. "Oh—hi."

Don't smile at me that way.

Fox looked away sharply, lowering his gaze to his hands,
and realized he was practically crushing the bell pepper between his palms. He set it aside on the cutting board and
picked up another, plunging it under the stream of water
and only hoping the cold water would cool the flush of
aching, longing need building up inside him.

Don't make me want you like this.

"I wasn't expecting you back," he said neutrally. "Should
I make dinner for two, then?"

"Oh, um… I…"

Even not looking at him, Fox could hear the blush in

Summer's voice. The sweet hesitation, that way he had of being so guileless, so open with his feelings, with his warmth, with a neediness that seemed to sit so much more comfortably on him than it did on Fox.

"I finished at Mom's early," Summer said. "And I wanted to have dinner with you. I can have dinner with Mom any time."

…don't remind me that I'm just going to leave you.

Even if Summer hadn't meant it that way…

It hit hard.

Their time together was short.

And it was all because Fox was too afraid to let it be anything else.

So it would seem Summer, too, was making the most of what they had, while they could.

Fox closed his eyes, his fingers stilling against the slightly rubbery skin of the bell pepper clasped between his hands, no sound between them but the rush of the water pouring from the faucet, the sound of the spray striking the metal sink with hollow drumming noises like rain.

He took a deep breath, trying to center himself, trying to just…

Detach.

Somehow.

Because if he didn't now, it would be that much harder later.

"Go wash up," he made himself say, as he set the second pepper down and opened the refrigerator to pull out a third and fourth, since he was now doubling portions. "I won't have you at dinner looking like you've been rolling in the dirt like the overeager puppy you are."

Summer's laughter was soft, startled…so very sweet.

As sweet as the feeling of his lips, as he slipped into the kitchenette and brushed his mouth to Fox's cheek. "Sure," he said. "I'll try to be fast so I can help you finish up."

Then he stepped away, leaving behind only the scents of earth, of grass, of Summer himself.

While Fox stared into the refrigerator without breathing, without moving, save for the drift of his fingers, rising to touch his cheek.

Summer made this look so simple, so easy.

While for Fox, the idea of having this and then losing it…

Suddenly didn't feel so easy at all.

Summer didn't know how he managed to smile, as he finished toweling off his shower-wet hair, dragged on a clean pair of jeans, and stepped out of the bathroom to join Fox in the kitchen.

When he'd walked in the door and Fox had gone so stiff, looked at him so strangely, then turned away as if nothing was wrong…

Maybe Summer was reading into things.

But he'd felt like he'd run face-first into those stone walls again, the cracks in them sealing over to shut him out.

He lingered in the bathroom doorway, propping his shoulder against the frame and watching Fox chop vegetables as swiftly, efficiently, and methodically as he did everything else. He seemed calm, relaxed, that initial tension gone as if it had never happened, and Summer tried to tell himself he was imagining things. He was tired, and he'd probably just startled Fox when he'd come back unexpectedly.

This was still such a new thing, after all.

But it felt like a knife slid between his third and fourth rib and *twisted*, every time he remembered he'd never get the chance to make it an old thing, a familiar thing, a thing steady and forever and true.

Damn it.

He couldn't do this to himself right now.

So he pushed the thoughts down, held on to his smile, and pushed away from the door to join Fox, stepping into the kitchen and pulling the refrigerator door open.

"All clean," he said. "What do you want me to start with?"

"For starters," Fox said tartly, "you can finish dressing yourself, you heathen. Then you can put some rice on, if you actually want to be helpful."

Summer grinned, closing the fridge and pulling open the pantry cabinet instead, but not without stopping to briefly lean his bare shoulder against Fox's arm. "I don't need a shirt to cook rice."

"You don't need a shirt to end up with oil burns when I put the stir-fry on, either," Fox retorted. "Dress yourself, you unruly, uncivilized monster."

"Am I a monster now?" Summer turned his head and bit down lightly on Fox's shoulder, tugging at his shirt in his teeth. "*Grawr.*"

"You absolutely insufferable—" With a strangled sound,

Fox lightly smacked Summer on the nose with a cold, wet-beaded stalk of celery, glaring at him with narrowed eyes and twitching lips. "Shirt. *Now.*"

Summer just laughed, pulling away and heading into the bedroom to find one of the button-down shirts that had somehow ended up staying here instead of in his own suite.

But there was a raspy ache in the back of his throat.

Because he hadn't missed the slightest pause, the faintest moment of hesitation before each of Fox's reactions, as if he was choosing what to do, holding himself back behind something careful that created just enough distance for Summer to feel it.

And Summer didn't have the heart to push him about it.

Not right now.

Not when pushing might mean losing what little time he had.

Having something was better than having nothing at all, wasn't it?

...wasn't it?

He asked himself that again and again, as he slid into his shirt and worked his fingers up the row of buttons.

But he didn't have an answer.

So he only told himself to smile, and smile, and smile again...

And stepped back out to join Fox for dinner.

Chapter Fourteen

Summer's palms were slimed with sweat.

He could do this. He *knew* he could do this, he just…

He was about to face down the very wealthy parents of six different boys—the only ones who had responded to the summons, out of a dozen. People who were annoyed at having to waste their Sunday traveling for this. People who felt they were too important for parent-teacher conferences; people who didn't even bother coming to get their boys for holidays, from the things Summer had heard from the other teachers, even if he spent less time talking to the other faculty and staff than he should considering how completely wrapped up he often was in Fox.

Fuck.

Fox.

He should be so happy, right now.

But he felt like he was wearing a mask of a relationship, versus the real thing.

They'd fallen into the last two uneventful weeks so easily that it had felt almost mechanical, these comfortable days and nights together, evenings of passionate, heady sex that left him wrung out and sore, wordless and clinging to Fox and afraid to say anything into the silence in case he crossed some line that would make Fox just...

Not want to do this anymore.

But it felt like Fox had already checked out, and was going through the motions.

And it felt like Summer had forgotten how to be brave, because suddenly every time he thought to challenge Fox's silence, the way he withdrew into himself, the way his very blandness just built those walls thicker around him when for just a moment, Summer had been allowed a glimpse inside...

The words crumbled on his tongue, and he couldn't say anything.

But he was starting to wonder if sleeping with Fox had made things *worse*, somehow. That threshold had been a turning point, perhaps.

Yet the path it had turned them down only gave Summer access to Fox's body and a physical facsimile of his affection.

While pushing him further away from Fox's heart.

He just wanted to know if Fox felt something for him. Anything other than the tired affection one felt for an overly gregarious puppy.

But he was still so hard to read.

So hard to understand, and he always seemed to have

a way of glossing over and retreating somewhere distant every time Summer looked at him with his heart in his eyes and kissed him with his love on his lips.

Fox looked almost bored now, though, as he leaned back in his desk chair and tapped a pen against his knee, watching Summer with arched brows.

"Do stop pacing," he said. "They're rich. They're not gods."

"I don't care about their *money*," Summer said, doing another circuit from side to side of the office, swallowing and yet he couldn't loosen the clotting in his throat. "I just... what if they don't care? What if they tell me I wasted their time? What if—"

As he pivoted on his heel for another stalk across the office, he stopped as he slammed right up against the wall of Fox's chest.

And suddenly he couldn't move at all, as Fox's arms wrapped around him and stopped him in his tracks.

"Enough *what if*," Fox said, a deep rumble that washed over Summer in soothing vibrations, while strong hands curled against his back. "They are here. It is done. This is what you wanted, so you have to follow through. If they don't care, if they feel you wasted their time...you didn't waste your own time, because you *tried*. And is that not what you said matters? That these boys know *someone* is trying for them."

"That's...that's what I'm telling myself." Summer curled his fingers in Fox's crisply starched shirt-sleeves, resting his head to his shoulder, turning his face into his throat. "But I'm scared to just...jump into this with both feet, and fuck it up."

"Ah." Soft, warm, understanding, and Fox's arms tightened around him. "I do know that feeling quite well."

God, there it was.

Those ambiguous statements in that low, thrumming voice, that made Summer wish, hope, wonder...

Wonder if Fox really did feel something for him.

Deeper than just tolerant affection.

Deep enough to hold him like this, comfort him like this, because he *mattered* to Fox—and Summer clung just a little tighter, the question on his tongue.

The question, and the soft words he'd been holding inside, keeping them in his heart while they grew and grew and grew until they wouldn't fit anymore and he was going to burst with them.

I love you.

He wanted to say it.

He wanted to say it so much, but if he did...

Fox might go completely cold on him, and then Summer wouldn't have even the quiet moments of intimacy he stole with every touch, needing to feel Fox's heartbeat against his own just so he knew that heart still ran hot somewhere behind that cold façade.

So instead of those words, he swallowed, whispered, "You'll stay, right?"

"I will stay," Fox promised softly. "This is your endeavor, but I will be here. You will not be alone."

"Thank you." Summer pushed himself up to kiss Fox's chin, smiling weakly. "Seriously, thank you. I don't think I could do this without you."

"You could," Fox said, something odd in his voice, in his

gaze. "That is what makes you strong, Summer. Stronger than you realize." He brushed his knuckles against Summer's cheek, a rough graze of sensation—then lifted his head at an imperious knock on his office door, two silhouettes moving restlessly outside the clouded glass. "And you will need that strength. Here they are."

"Oh, God." Summer wet his lips, then breathed in deep, filling his chest so fast his head went dizzy and light. "I can do this. I can do this. I can do this," he told himself, then strode forward to open the door with the best smile he could manage, squaring his shoulders and reminding himself...

If Fox believed he was strong, then he had to be.

He *had* to be.

So here we go.

Maybe this hadn't been the most miserable Sunday of Summer's life.

But it had come close.

And the only reason he hadn't broken down completely and utterly in front of these boys' parents was out of sheer disgust, overwhelming his nervousness as he realized everything he was saying was falling on deaf ears.

If Jay's grades were slipping, it was a failure of the school, and not anything his parents could do to support him while he tried to survive ostracization and bullying; not anything they even cared to discuss as far as giving Summer permission to step in as a secondary parental figure beyond the strictures allowed by the school and the boarding arrangement. They didn't want to be bothered, things were fine as they were.

Eli's parents were even worse, haughtily annoyed that this wasn't a *real* problem, but just some adjunct who seemed to think he had any say in who Eli chose to be friends with.

The same for the parents of three other boys whose grades in all subjects had been slipping for months, and who had been showing signs of social isolation and victimization to some of the more aggressive boys in the student body.

Summer had kept his backbone stiff, had been firm about the necessity of parental intervention when supporting the boys through a difficult developmental period, but even with Fox a watchful and almost menacing presence at his back, they just…

Hadn't wanted to listen.

He had one more pair to get through.

Theodore Rothfuss's parents.

And considering that Theodore was the heart of the problem…

He had a feeling they wouldn't want to hear it, either.

They'd just be interested in getting in and out as fast as possible, before they got caught in the building storm threatening outside, leaving the day as gray and cloudy and ominously dark as Summer's mood.

He leaned against Fox's desk, closing his eyes, pressing his fingers to his throbbing temples. "So," he said. "If you're waiting to say 'I told you so,' I'm waiting to hear it."

"I am not, because I did not tell you so. And you are not done yet." Fox settled next to him, shoulder to shoulder, weight leaning subtly against him in a comforting pressure. "Headache?"

"The *worst*. Got any Advil?"

"No, but I may have something else that could help."

Fox's warmth pulled away. Summer lifted his head, opening his eyes and watching as Fox bent over to pull open the small side drawer in his desk, feeling inside before he came up with a small vial of thick golden liquid, with a cork stoppering it.

The mint scent when he thumbed it open was unmistakable, albeit much less overpowering than that night in the living room—subtle, and tinted with other things such as vanilla, maybe even a hint of clove, mixing together into something sharp-edged but somehow creamy and soft.

"Here." Fox pressed his fingertip to the mouth of the vial and tipped it, dabbing the oil onto one finger, then set the vial down on the desk and spread the oil between the fingertips of both hands, making them glisten. "Close your eyes and just relax."

Brows knitting, Summer did, already bracing himself for the contact—but he was still surprised by the warmth of it, that slick oily feeling seeming to absorb and amplify Fox's body heat until it was like being touched by gentle sparks, as Fox pressed his fingertips to either side of Summer's forehead and began to rub in slow, soothing circles.

"Breathe deep," Fox murmured, his voice seeming to roll to the cadence of his touch. "It doesn't work if you don't take in the scent, as well."

Summer started to nod, then caught himself and held still as that gentle touch massaged a quiet, relaxing sensation into his temples, the oil's warmth seeming to penetrate deep down to slowly melt away the tension and pain throbbing in his skull. He tried to time his breaths, counting in and out so he would hold them long enough to enjoy the scent, tingling his nostrils and flowing through him until each breath felt as though it spread relaxation from his lungs out to the very tips of his fingers.

"S'nice," he murmured. "Helping. Thank you."

"You seemed as if you needed something before you spontaneously combusted." Gentle amusement, turning Fox's voice husky. "You are not wasting your time, Summer. Even if they were not willing to listen today, they will still remember and may come around later. You have let them *know* their sons need them, when they may not have been aware before. That is no small thing."

"I know. I do." Summer stopped that massaging touch by capturing Fox's wrist, turning his head to press his lips to its underside. "I guess I'd just...wanted to see something more helpful happen *today*."

"Change takes time. Change involving people, even more so." Fox's fingers curled against Summer's cheek, just a warm trace of oil and then rough knuckles. "Few things terrify people more than feeling challenged in their preconceived notions of themselves and others, and being forced to take action in the face of knowledge they do not want to absorb into their worldview when it might shake the foundations of their egos."

Summer opened his eyes, looking into that silvered, reflective gaze so close to his own, that face that even in this gentle moment of comfort was so inscrutable, so strange.

Is that you? he wondered. *Are you afraid of changing this path you've set yourself on, because you can't face looking at who you'll be if that happens?*

But he couldn't say it.

He only smiled, squeezing Fox's wrist before letting go. "We should get through the Rothfusses before they get annoyed and leave. But thank you. I feel better now."

Fox said nothing, yet the look that lingered on Summer seemed oddly meaningful, as he withdrew to cap the vial and tuck it away in his desk once more.

Summer rolled his shoulders, breathed in with that delicate scent still hovering around him and calming his senses, then leaned out into the hall and beckoned to the Rothfuss couple with a smile.

"Sorry for the wait," he said. "But it's good to meet you. I'm Summer Hemlock, one of the instructors in the psychology elective track."

He'd found that was better than introducing himself as a TA or adjunct.

Because if there was anything that would get people to ignore him, it was admitting he didn't have any real authority.

The Rothfuss duo were a stately-looking couple just past late middle age and entering into their older years, hair still touched with hints of color, clothing quietly understated and yet clearly quite expensive without being overly flashy or ostentatious. They carried themselves with a sort of unconscious dignity that said they were used to being the most important people in the room, their authority acknowledged without necessarily requiring deference, and they offered Summer polite, not unfriendly nods as they each shook his hand quite formally before stepping into the office.

Summer settled to sit against the desk once more, ges-

turing to the two empty chairs; both Mr. and Mrs. Rothfuss settled with perfect posture, he folding his hands in
his lap, she crossing her legs with her hands settled against
her purse.

But before Summer could say anything, Mrs. Rothfuss
spoke, her voice curdled at the edges with worry. "You
said this was about Theo's performance and behavior? But
you're in the psychology program?" She pressed gloved fingertips to her lips. "Has he done something that will affect
his qualification for AP college credits?" She exchanged a
worried glance with her husband. "He needs those so desperately for university."

"Theo's grades are holding fairly well," Summer said
carefully. "I've been reviewing his performance scores and
it looks like he's only had a few lapses since his freshman
year. But while his grades are fine… I'm worried about his
social integration with the other students."

Mr. Rothfuss's brows knit; for such a thin man, he had
a very thick moustache, and it twitched rapidly as he repeated, "Social integration? Is he being bullied?"

"No," Summer said. "I'm afraid he's the bully."

Both parents gasped, glancing at each other almost guilt-
ily, before Mrs. Rothfuss turned her wide eyes back to
Summer. "Are you quite certain? Our Theo?"

"I'm afraid so." Summer clasped his hands together
against his thighs so he wouldn't have to really focus on how
sweaty they were; he was all right now, just these two with
Fox at his back, a silent protector…but his nerves were still
exhausted, shredded, and it was taking everything in him
to keep his voice steady and calm and pleasant when he was

just waiting for another haughty dismissal. "I won't name names, but we have reports from several students of Theo taking extremely aggressive action against them, from causing them physical injury to desecrating or destroying their personal property, as well as socially manipulating them with threats and causing schisms between other students."

Both Mr. and Mrs. Rothfuss went stiff.

Summer braced himself.

Here it came.

Mr. Rothfuss turned on his wife, scowling. "I told you sending him here was a mistake. We should have home schooled him where we could keep an eye on him."

"It absolutely was not a mistake," Mrs. Rothfuss shot back. "Theo needs to learn how to function in the larger world instead of having his every need catered to. Home schooling would have just pampered and isolated him more. He's too used to getting his own way."

"And he's repeating the same patterns here, only now we can't rein him in!" Mr. Rothfuss countered. "If keeping him at home doesn't help and sending him away doesn't help, then what are we supposed to do?"

Summer just watched with wide eyes.

Not…what he was expecting.

Not what he was expecting at all.

But Fox cleared his throat softly behind him, reminding Summer…

Right.

This was his rodeo, and he had to keep things moving productively.

He raised his voice slightly, just enough to cut off another volley between them. "I think Albin Academy can still be a good, nurturing environment for Theodore," he said. "But we aren't his parents. In order to help Theo acclimate and stop his antisocial behavior, we need you to be more present for a while. Set boundaries for him. Structure. There's only so much we can do, legally. But we can help you know what *you* need to do. And I think that if we can get Theodore on a better path, that will go a long way to helping several other boys whose grades have been slipping because of his bullying."

Mr. Rothfuss's shoulders slumped. Mrs. Rothfuss fussed at her purse, looking at Summer in consternation. "He's been affecting the other boys' grades?" She bit her lip. "I'm sorry. This is our responsibility, and clearly we failed."

Mr. Rothfuss smiled bitterly. "Somehow, even after all these years, we aren't quite ready to be parents. But you mentioned being more present?" He glanced at his wife. "I could afford to take a few weeks off of work."

"I'm sure I could swing it as well," she said, frowning, tapping her lower lip. "Theo won't like it, but..."

"Sometimes we have to give our children what they need, not what they want," Summer said—but inside, God, he was jumping, buzzing, *shouting*, the air in his lungs suddenly seeming to go a mile further when...maybe, just maybe, this might go somewhere. "There's a lovely bed and breakfast down the hill that usually has rooms open year-round, if you'd like to book a stay."

"Y...es," Mr. Rothfuss said thoughtfully, his moustache *and* his brows twitching quite firmly as he stretched the single syllable out into two halting sounds with a long breath in between. "Yes, I think we shall. Thank you for informing us of this, Mr.... What was your name again?"

"Hemlock," Summer said, offering a smile. "Summer Hemlock."

Mrs. Rothfuss blinked. "Oh, my," she said. "What an unusual name." But she offered a smile as well, rueful, chagrined. "We're so sorry we've not been as attentive as we should be with Theo, but we'll be in touch again soon. Is it all right to visit our son in his room?"

"Of course." Summer stood fully, offering his hand. "Do you need to be escorted?"

"We know the way." Mr. Rothfuss shook his hand firmly, followed by his wife, before Mr. Rothfuss squinted at Summer. "...I say, I do know that name. I'm a graduate from the old school here, you know. And you're the spitting image of your father at your age."

Summer stopped, his breaths catching, before he numbly let go of Mrs. Rothfuss's hand. "Oh, I...thank you," he said, even if he wasn't quite sure if it was a compliment or not.

It was just...

Odd.

To be reminded that even if he barely remembered his father...

Summer had roots here at Albin that went deep.

And maybe he'd always been meant to come home here after all.

But he barely waited until the Rothfuss couple had excused themselves from the office.

Before he turned around and threw himself into Fox's arms, catching the professor just as he was standing and hitting hard enough that for a second they unbalanced, Fox rocking backward.

"Oof!" Fox exclaimed, before steadying them both with firm hands and planted feet—then letting out a soft chuckle. "I take it you're proud of how that went."

"*Yes*," Summer breathed, burying his face in Fox's chest. "They *listened*. They cared, they…oh my God it *worked*."

"Many people are inherently selfish without realizing it," Fox said gently. "But there are those who aren't. We just have to find them, and hope they will listen." His arms came around Summer, holding him steady, holding him tight, gentle approval rumbling against his ear. "But they never would have listened if you had not had the courage to speak."

Summer let out a laugh; he couldn't stop it, bursting up from inside him, and looked up into Fox's eyes. "So does that courage earn me another kiss?"

Fox's lips curled. "If we're still trading kisses as currency, I'm afraid you've spent years' worth of your allotment at this point and are deeply in debt."

"So…" Summer leaned harder into Fox—into the tall, strong breadth of his body. "What do I have to do to earn—"

A soft clearing of someone's throat from the door cut him off.

And instinctively he and Fox sprang back from each other, Summer flushing. Fuck, if one of the boys' parents caught them…

Worse.

Assistant Principal Lachlan Walden stood in the open door of Fox's office, watching him with freezing eyes, and crooked his finger.

"Mr. Hemlock," he said thinly. "A word, if you please."

Ah, *fuck*.

Summer stole a nervous glance at Fox, who only gave him an encouraging nod and brushed a hand to his shoulder before gently nudging him toward the door. Shoulders slumping, Summer followed Walden out into the hall.

Walden fixed him with a critical, blistering gaze as Summer shuffled to a halt in front of him.

"What did you think you were doing?"

"Trying to stop an already bad situation from getting worse," Summer said quickly. He hated how his voice cracked, but he'd already done what was done and wouldn't back down now. "We can only discipline the boys up to a certain point. Once things get beyond that, we have to get their parents involved."

"*We* have to get their parents involved," Lachlan said scathingly. "Not you. You are barely one step above a temp, and it was underhanded of you to make use of Professor Iseya's position to avoid school policies." His lips thinned. "This is still not your job."

"I know it's not," Summer said.

And that was when it hit.

What he wanted.

Why *teaching* felt wrong, but being at Albin…

Being at Albin didn't feel wrong at all.

His heart rose into his throat.

The tiniest flutter of hope went through him, hope and a sense of purpose, elation, lightness.

"But if we could talk…" He scrubbed his sweaty palms against his thighs. "I'd like it to be."

Walden parted his lips to respond.

Only for an angular, strong shoulder to bump into Summer, *hard*, nearly knocking him aside as Fox edged through the doorway past him.

And walked away without a backward glance, his stride swift and tight enough to make the few loose tendrils of his hair lash back and forth sharply in his wake, the set of his shoulders hard and taut.

"Fox…?" Summer called.

But Fox didn't stop.

If anything, his stride only quickened.

Before there came a loud *bang*, echoing down the hall, as Fox disappeared into the stairwell.

Summer's heart plummeted.

What was wrong?

Why was Fox…?

He threw a wide-eyed glance back at Lachlan. "Please. Can we talk later? I—I need to—"

He wasn't expecting the softening of Lachlan's frigid blue gaze, or the understanding in his voice.

"Go," he said. "It would appear you have some things to discuss with your mentor."

Summer took a shaky breath, nodding.

"Thank you," he rasped.

Before he turned and ran, chasing after his elusive fox with the sudden and terrified feeling that he might have lost him for good.

Fox Iseya was…

Was an entirely selfish asshole.

And this was why he was so bad for someone like Summer.

He'd known what was coming the second Summer had said he'd known counseling the students wasn't his job; had looked at Walden with that particular light he got in his eyes when he was terrified but intended to be brave, to take a chance anyway.

Summer wanted the guidance counselor job.

Instead of replacing Fox as the psychology instructor, he wanted the guidance counselor job, which meant... which meant...

Fox couldn't leave.

He *could*, he could walk away and leave Albin without a psych instructor for an elective course that was entirely optional despite the AP college credits attached, but whether or not he morally and ethically *would* was another question.

And that changed everything between himself and Summer, because he had realized, in that moment standing there like a shadow who wasn't supposed to witness what he was seeing...

That Summer had been his excuse.

Summer was both Fox's thing to run from...and the excuse that let him run in the first place. Because as long as Summer was his replacement, Fox wasn't needed here anymore, and he could just...

Go.

Wander into that gray nebulous nothing and disappear. Stop existing. There would be no place for him anymore, and he'd *wanted* that, but with the idea of Summer shifting tracks into the guidance counselor role suddenly Fox would be here, would be bound by his own sense of re-sponsibility to stay, and if he *stayed*...

If he stayed, then he would have to love Summer.

He would have to love Summer in the bright, eager way he threw himself at everything, the way he gave his heart without question and without shame, the way he *cared* so much about other people, the way he fought himself to be brave so often even when it did terrible and terrifying things to him. The sweet way he put up with Fox's can-tankerousness. The way he made Fox want to be bright, too, to remember how it felt to be someone who created things, who helped others, who touched and held and cra-dled others' feelings tenderly instead of cutting them off so cold and living numb.

But if he had all of that, he...

He would just lose it again.

Just like he'd lost Michiko.

And if that happened again...

He wouldn't survive it.

He wouldn't survive that shattering of his heart a sec-ond time.

He sat on the shore of Whitemist Lake, staring into the water as he pulled up flowers, threaded them together, let-ting his hands move out of habit to give himself something to do. Something to keep himself occupied so his thoughts wouldn't run in circles as endless as the loops he formed with delicate flower stems.

These hands...these hands had done so many things in his lifetime. Splashed about the shallows of Joudogahama. Drawn kanji in wet sand. Written line after line of intense studious work, throwing himself into his schooling. Learned herbs by touch and texture, by their scent when they bruised, by the softness on the underside of their leaves. Held slender fingers in his own, caressed hair back from a delicate face.

Slipped a wedding ring onto a slim finger.

Slid a wedding ring off his own, wrenching it away hard enough to rip his knuckles and not even sure, now, where he'd left it in his grief, his denial.

Touched the strong line of a tanned jaw, a muscular throat, the beat of a wild young heart and the powerful lines of a beautiful, lean body.

Stroked the shape of laughing lips.

Yes, these hands had done so much…

…yet they couldn't seem to reach back to the one who was reaching for him so desperately with all his heart.

And that one wouldn't let him run away, he realized.

When he heard the soft scuff of footsteps at his back, that familiar stride, before Summer sank down to sit next to him, close enough to make the blades of grass between them shift and tickle and poke against the undersides of Fox's slacks.

Summer draped his arms over his upraised knees, looking out over the water, expression thoughtful. "Hi," was all he said, quiet and neutral.

"Hi," Fox said, and immediately felt more the clumsy old fool for it.

And rather than say anything else, he just…plucked up more flowers, and threaded them into the slowly thickening crown.

Summer glanced at him, darkened blue eyes on his hands, the work, before he asked, "Making a wish?"

"I don't know yet," Fox whispered, and wove another blossom in. "I just...don't know."

Summer let that lie between them for several long seconds, then looked away again, watching the water, his brows lowering. "I never made wishes here, when I was a boy," he murmured. "With throwing the flower crowns in for the dead girl's wedding so she'll hear my plea. The story of Isabella always made me so sad. That she couldn't be with the girl she loved, and they called her a witch... so she drowned herself. Don't you think it just...hurts her, people asking her for things when she could never have what she wanted?"

"Perhaps that's where the legend came from," Fox answered. "Wanting to believe that someone who lost everything would feel for others' plights enough to want to spare them her suffering."

He almost laughed to himself, then.

If only he could claim such selfless reasons for his own denials.

If only he could say he was trying to spare Summer the pain he'd already known himself...instead of trying to protect his own shriveled heart.

He pushed the thought down, plucked another flower, ran his thumb along its fronded petals. "But Isabella was real. And her story is not at all what the legend says."

Summer's head came up sharply enough to make his tousled hair tumble across his eyes. He stared at Fox, with that wide-eyed curiosity that made him such a bizarre mixture of ingenue and minx. "She was real? What happened to her?"

"She died of old age many, many decades after her supposed suicide," Fox said, tracing his thumb along the flower's stem, then inserting it into the band of the crown, weaving it in and out until it was securely affixed, spacing the heads of the blossoms so they formed an even circlet among the green. "With her lover by her bedside. When the girls were forbidden to be together, they ran away to New York City, and lived long, happy lives as lovers and partners. Neither ever drowned themselves. They chose another path, instead."

Summer inhaled audibly—then let out a soft laugh, pressing his knuckles over his mouth. "I... I like that a lot better. But...if you know the legend's not real, why are you making a crown to make a wish?"

"Because," Fox admitted, the words like spears in his throat, digging deep. "All I ever wanted was what she had. A long, happy life with someone I loved...and that was taken from me." His breaths were barbed, his throat closing, and he clenched his fist against the crown, the stems in his grasp crushing wetly, the petals crumpling against his palm. "It was *taken*, and I don't know how to get it back."

He glared out at the water—but the water was suddenly somehow running together, the reflections of the gray, moody sky in the surface of the pond turning into fuzzy watercolor impressions, and he closed his eyes tightly, struggling to push it down, to ignore it.

But Summer wouldn't let him escape this feeling.

Not when that warmth drew closer, settling shoulder to

shoulder...before Summer's hand pressed hot to the small of his back, and Summer's voice was a close and intimate thing in the dark space behind his eyelids.

"You don't get it back, Fox," he whispered. "What's gone is gone...and instead of trying to get it back, you have to let it go and build something new. Every new thing is its own thing. You can't...turn it into something else."

Fox knew what he was really saying.

You can't turn me *into* her.

And he didn't think he wanted to.

Not when deep down, he was...he was *angry* at her, and he couldn't even understand why.

Or why he'd been taking that anger out on Summer all this time.

Breathing in harshly, Fox lifted his head, glaring at Summer miserably through the wet sheen over his eyes. "I don't know how to make something new," he bit off. "I don't know how to be anything other than cold and selfish and horrible. Do you know what I thought, when I realized you were about to ask Walden for the guidance counselor job?"

Summer watched him with those soft eyes. So *soft*, but soft things were so easily hurt by rough handling, and Fox didn't know how to be delicate right now.

"Tell me," Summer urged gently. "It's okay, Fox."

But it wasn't. Fox smiled bitterly, a brittle and awful thing. "I thought, 'You can't. You can't, because the school will need me to stay and if I stay, then *you'll* need me,' and I can't stand that. You needing me." He let out a harsh bark of laughter. "I don't know how you *can* need me when I'm not... I'm not anything, I'm not anything anyone needs,

I'm just awful when I know damned well that you would be the best guidance counselor this school has seen. Even more, I know *you*. I know it would make you happier than teaching, and yet...my first thought was of *me*."

He expected that handsome, bright face to crumple with hurt.

With betrayal.

Yet instead, Summer only sighed patiently, shaking his head.

Before his arms came around Fox tightly, drawing him in. Drawing him in the way Fox usually drew Summer in with his anxiety attacks, only somehow now it was Summer wrapping around him and resting his chin to the top of Fox's head; Summer enveloping him with the half-crushed flower crown between them, with its broken cloying scent rising up to fill the space around them.

"You know me," Summer murmured, his voice a soft vibration between them, "because you pay attention to me. Because you care what makes me happy and unhappy. And caring that much scares you, because caring means you can be hurt. But I'm going to tell you what my mother told me." Strong arms tightened, an encouraging, gentle squeeze, as if Summer could knead all his bright, effusive emotions into Fox. "You want what anyone wants. To never hurt again. But that's not possible unless we shut ourselves off from feeling at all...and I think you've been shut off long enough, Fox. I think you know that, too... and it frightens you, but it's okay to be scared."

"Just because it's acceptable doesn't mean I *want* it," Fox hissed—but he couldn't pull away from Summer, couldn't seem to break back from that gentle yet sheltering hold. "Something as old and broken as I am...you can't fix, Summer. You can't fix me just by caring enough. You'll never make me someone whole enough to care for you the way you care for me."

"What you don't seem to understand is that I'm not trying to fix you." Here, now, was Summer's strength, his steadiness, how his anxiety seemed to vanish when Fox was the one to break down, leaving Summer the one speaking in calm, soothing tones, giving back that warmth and care he seemed to possess in infinite supply. "I love you just as you are, Fox. Broken bits and all. I don't want to make you someone else. I want *you*, and for you to care for me as *you* would...not as anyone else."

No three words should cut with such knifelike keenness.

The last person who had said them to him had said them idly, an afterthought, on the way out the door to an ordinary day that would turn into a shattering, life-changing night.

Fox jerked back, staring at Summer. Staring at him as if those words would crumble Summer into nothing before his very eyes, but there was only a solemn young man looking at him with his heart written on his face and...and...

Fox was shaking.

He was shaking, everything in him building up to a scream, his lips parting and—

And the sky crashing open in a cracking roar of thunder, as if it was calling out for him, as if it cried in his voice. Heart slamming, he stared up at the sky; so did Summer, as lightning slashed across the darkened clouds and the storm that had been building since morning finally broke.

The rain came down as if a bucket had been tipped over, sluicing down in icy slashes. Summer yelped, covering his head, then stumbled to his feet, reaching for Fox's hand with a laugh, rain soaking his hair to his skull in a black cap, immediately darkening his shirt to a translucent layer of pale blue that let golden skin shine through.

"Come on!" he gasped, and before Fox could protest he found himself hauled up, dragged along, dropping the flower crown from lax fingers to send it flying into the lake, his dress shoes slipping on the wet grass but they were dashing, running, darting inside and he felt like those words were on his heels, chasing him, nipping at his ankles, even if he could never escape them when the one who had spoken them held him so fast.

As if Summer would never let him go.

They didn't stop until they reached Fox's suite, tumbled inside, dripping all over the floor. Summer shook himself like a puppy, then let out a breathless laugh.

"I kind of feel like nature had a little color commentary for my big confession," he said sheepishly. "And she didn't approve."

Fox flinched, pushing loose strands of wet hair back from his face. "You...you..."

You love me, he tried to say.

But he couldn't seem to get the words out.

He didn't need to, because Summer went quiet, bowing his head, but still watching him with that hopeful gaze. "Yeah," he said thickly. "I do. I love you, Fox."

Being loved shouldn't feel like heartbreak.

And Fox knew exactly how broken he was, now, that he couldn't say those words back.

Couldn't say anything to them at all.

Couldn't find his voice past the shattering, cracking feeling inside him, and so...

Rather than speak, Fox kissed him.

Lingering, slow, he kissed him as if this was the first time and would be the last; as if he had to make this kiss count for every kiss he might never know again in the future. He tasted every tiny crease in Summer's lips, pressed his teeth gently against the soft giving flesh of his mouth, suckled softly at his lower lip and stole inside where Summer always seemed filled with some intoxicant that rode his breath and slipped into Fox and took him over until his senses were full of Summer and only Summer.

He didn't have words for these feelings inside him. He couldn't *stand* words for them, when words would make them real. Real enough to hurt. Real enough to be torn away, to become something fragile he could break or crush or ruin the same way he kept ruining those soft feelings Summer dashed against Fox's walls again and again.

No...he couldn't tell Summer what he felt.

So he showed him.

With every kiss, every slow deep exploration of yielding lips, he tried to show him. With every touch, every tracery of Fox's fingertips over Summer's pulse-pounding throat, over his shoulders, the shivering sensitive spots Fox had memorized over his chest and ribs and stomach, with that suntanned skin gliding so hot and firm beneath his fingertips, with Summer shuddering and sighing out his pleasure as their flesh made friction and charged kinetic energy shivered between them like static… Fox tried to say what he couldn't say.

That Summer's love was too good for Fox.

But that Fox was too needy, too greedy to reject it.

He didn't know when he'd become so desperate for this beautiful strange summer child of a man, but somehow Summer had become a compulsion, pulling on him in ways that made him feel like his blood moved to Summer's rhythm, his body drawn to his magnetism. The way Summer sighed and melted for him, so luxuriously pliant as Fox kissed him, one step at a time, into the bedroom…

How could he give himself so sweetly to someone who gave nothing back at all?

And so Fox tried to *give*.

In his own way, he tried to *give*, tumbling Summer back to the bed, stripping him in a fevered rush until that sensuously compact, tightly muscled body lay bare beneath him, touching every inch of him until he knew how Summer tasted in the hollow of his throat, the peak of his collarbone, the flat round circle of his nipple, the tight skin of his inner thigh, the sensitive underside of his wrist. Fox tasted him *everywhere*, mapped his body with his tongue, savored when Summer whispered his name, when he dug his fingers into Fox's hair, when he spread his thighs until he was a portrait of beautifully luscious obscenity, when he betrayed an erogenous zone with an arch of his back and a shudder of his hips and his hard, straining cock leaking clear, tart-scented wetness from the tip, splattering against the fluxing ridges of his toned belly.

Irresistible.

Enthralling.

And Fox only hoped Summer could feel how beautiful Fox found him in every touch of lips, of hands…of desperate fingers that sought out Summer's heat from within, that touched him just to feel how *tight* he gripped as Fox plunged and twisted and sought inside Summer's body with wet-slicked fingers; he was so *hot* inside, like he was trying to melt Fox into him, and the way he threw his head back, the way he twined his arms together over his head and rocked his hips up into every slow thrust, the way he made those needy keening sounds when Fox slowed down to deny him then thrust hard to give him satisfaction the moment he seemed on the verge of breaking…lovely. So lovely the way Summer gave himself up with such *bliss*, such abandon, putting himself so wholly in Fox's hands that Fox could have done anything to him, he thought, and Summer would welcome it no matter what.

When all Fox wanted…

All Fox wanted was to love him without feeling like he was too broken to even try without leaving Summer as empty and hollow and shattered as himself.

Please, he thought as he gathered Summer's thighs around his hips, as he kissed his name from Summer's honeysuckle-dripping lips, as he lifted that receptive body into his own, as he found that perfect point of heat and buried himself, melted himself, sank himself into the tight-slick fire of Summer's flesh. Pleasure was more than pleasure, his flesh almost an afterthought of building, coiling tension when his heart was tearing itself apart, ripping itself open, destroying itself in violent shredding beats that rushed in rhythm with their flowing bodies.

As if the only way he knew how to give himself to Summer was to break himself.

And put those fragile, shattered, jagged-edged pieces into those tender hands.

Again and again, losing himself in the sheer drugging immersion that was Summer, drowning himself in the pleasure of his cries, of his grasping hands, of his rushing breaths, of his needy flesh that tried to devour Fox whole and sucked him in deeper, deeper, until his thighs turned weak and his knees shook with the sheer erotic intensity of it and Fox hardly recognized his own voice, calling out desperately as he arched over Summer and buried his face in his throat and tried to find his way to that deep place inside Summer where all of his brightness, his beauty was born. *Please.*

Please don't let me ruin this.

…please don't let me ruin him.

Chapter Fifteen

Fox, Summer thought to himself, didn't look very well.

Maybe he was coming down with something from the few minutes they'd been out in the rain yesterday, but...he looked grayer, somehow. Sunken. Ashen, even, in the dim light filtering through the curtains, the storm still raging outside and leaving the day swallowed in gloom.

Summer tucked closer to Fox, watching his half-asleep face, his half-open eyes. "Hey," he murmured, and pressed his palm to Fox's brow. He felt cooler than usual, but at least not feverish. "Are you okay? Do you feel sick?"

"Tired," Fox murmured drowsily, then turned his face into the pillows, leaving nothing but a tangle of hair flowing everywhere in dark rivers of silver-streaked black. "Not sick...just sleepy."

Summer frowned. Fox, despite being so quiet, was such

a high-energy man, always alert and ready to do what was necessary, but ever since last night...

He'd just seemed drained.

Like something vital had been sucked out of him, and Summer couldn't help that flush of guilt that he'd...he'd just *told* Fox he loved him when those words were probably so damned hard to hear.

He hadn't known what he'd expected, when Fox had already said he was so afraid to have to stay here. That Summer wasn't reason enough to *want* to stay, but instead a trap when Summer's decisions might hold him here.

That fucking hurt.

He understood. He understood in a lot of ways it wasn't about him, but about Fox needing to run from a place that had become as much of a prison as his own self-isolation.

That didn't change that it had hit Summer hard enough to make him reckless, make him say something he shouldn't have, as if somehow those three words would change Fox's mind and give him a reason to stay.

Things like that only worked in fairy tales and romcoms.

Not in real life.

He didn't know what to do.

Not when Fox was motionless and silent, burrowed into the bed.

So Summer only bent to kiss his shoulder blade, stroking the veil of his hair away to find pale amber-ivory skin.

"I can handle class prep this morning on my own," he said, murmuring against Fox's skin. "If you're tired, stay in bed a while longer and I'll see you in class, okay?"

Fox only made a low sound of affirmative, muted against

the pillow, before he lifted his head enough to look at Summer with dull gray eyes.

"Breakfast," he said listlessly. "Don't forget to eat. Sometimes I think you wouldn't if I didn't feed you."

It was a shallow attempt at his usual barbed tone, but an attempt nonetheless. Summer smiled, though he felt like crumbling inside. Something was wrong.

Something was deeply wrong, and he didn't want to leave Fox like this, but...

Maybe space was what they both needed.

Yesterday had been strange and painful, even if they'd fallen into bed together and Fox had kissed him, loved him with such *intensity*, held him tight deep into the night...

They'd stabbed each other rather deep, before that.

So maybe if Summer just...took care of work this morning, let Fox have space to settle himself, then they could talk things through tonight once they'd gotten through classes and didn't have anything else to worry about.

So he only smiled, and leaned down to press his lips to Fox's brow. "I won't forget," he said, before pulling away to roll out of bed. "And this time, it's my turn to leave something in the oven for you. Get some rest, Fox. I'll check in on you during lunch."

Fox's only answer was another muted sound.

Summer lingered, watching him, but Fox only turned his face away, closing his eyes, pulling the covers up around his shoulders.

Fuck.

Eyes stinging, nostrils flaring, Summer made himself turn away and made himself walk out of the bedroom.

Even if it was the last thing he wanted to do.

★ ★ ★

Fox lay in bed for nearly an hour after Summer left, wishing he…wishing he…

Wishing he had had the courage to at least kiss him goodbye.

He wasn't sure when he'd decided, concretely. When he'd realized what he meant to do. Some time in the middle of a long, sleepless night, listening to the rain fall.

She'd died on a night like this day, rain-washed and dreary, as if the world was already dead.

Perhaps it was fitting that he should leave on a day like this, too.

He needed to start over.

And he couldn't do it here.

Couldn't do it where all he would do was drag Summer down.

The school didn't need him. They'd find someone else, or abolish the psychology elective. He'd been lying to himself that he was needed at all, as if that could somehow give him an excuse to stay and enjoy this short stolen season of summer in his heart before winter came, gray and terrible, once more.

Excuses.

Always the excuses.

Excuses to stay. Excuses to leave.

No—it was best that he go.

Maybe one day, one year, he might come back as someone better, someone brighter, someone who still knew how to live, someone who knew how to be with a man as lovely as Summer. And maybe Summer would still be here, holding that vulnerable heart, and if he hadn't given it to someone else…

Yes.

Maybe then.

But for now… Fox was no good for anyone.

And, his body feeling heavy as stone…

He dragged himself up to pack, flinging the walk-in closet doors open and stepping inside.

Summer couldn't concentrate.

He tried. Words on the page blurred together into marching ants; he couldn't even keep half a thought focused in his mind, forgetting whose paper he was reading halfway down the page and having to start over at the *name*, let alone processing the content.

He sat in Fox's office, surrounded by the sound of rain on the windows and the dripping of honeysuckle scent, and just…

Wished he was back in that room.

Back in that bed with Fox, kissing him and touching him and begging him to *talk* to Summer until they sorted everything out and made this better.

Fuck.

He couldn't *think*, like this.

And he couldn't leave things open-ended this way with Fox, everything festering in silence until class was over. He shouldn't have walked away this morning at all.

Summer marked off a few more things, then stood, locked up Fox's office, and headed back to their floor.

But he stopped the moment he crested the stairs.

Fox's door was just down from the stairwell, the first thing Summer saw every time he came up or down the steps and spilled into the hallway.

And his door stood open, right now.

Just by a marginal inch, but still unlatched.

Summer hadn't left it that way.

Sick fear lodged in his throat. A million nightmare scenarios ran through his mind. Fox more sick than he let on, struggling to get to the door and almost collapsing. Someone breaking into the room to hurt him for some obscure reason. Fox getting an emergency call and dashing out carelessly. A million other thoughts about why that door could be open, none of them good.

Summer didn't want to look.

But he *had* to, when…when…

What if Fox was inside, hurt?

What if Fox needed him?

He forced himself across the hallway, his heartbeat timing his steps in thunderous roars, his head spinning as his anxiety tried to steal his breath and weave terrible things from it out of whole cloth. Tentatively, he pushed the door open with just his fingertips, sending it swinging easily inward.

No sign of Fox.

But many of the books were missing from the shelves.

The box of herbs, the mortar and pestle, gone.

Summer rushed inside, into the bedroom, where the closet stood open. Empty. No clothing, no shoes. He stumbled backward, fumbling back into the living room. No—no, he didn't want to believe it, *couldn't* believe it, but as his gaze fell on the cabinet mounted against the wall, that shrine...

He had no choice.

The Buddha, the photo, the scrap of framed kanji inside...

Gone.

Summer's vision blurred, his knees weakening as he sank down on the sofa and buried his face in his hands.

Fox had left him.

Fox was *gone*.

And Summer only let himself cry about it for five minutes.

No.

No, goddammit, he was not going to let Fox Iseya do this.

Just...just...*leave* like this, without even giving Summer the chance to talk to him about it, to ask, to say *please, please let me try. Let* us *try*.

He tried his phone first, tried calling, tried...but there was nothing. One ring, voicemail, and Summer closed his eyes and pressed his forehead to his screen, blinking back the wetness in his eyes, sniffling, breathing deep.

"Goddammit, Fox," he whispered. "You never charge your fucking phone."

He sent a text anyway—*Please don't leave like this, please*—before he was out the door, pelting down the stairs again, one more quick text fired to Walden—*cancel psych classes, personal emergency*—and he only stopped on the last step to let disappointment crush him that the terse, buzzing response wasn't Iseya before Summer was spilling out into the rain, into the parking lot, staring through the drizzle.

Fox's Camry was gone, too.

Like the final nail in the coffin.

That didn't stop Summer from sliding behind the wheel of his car and sending it down the hill, into town. He didn't know what he was looking for. As if he hoped he would catch Fox parked somewhere, just casually waiting right where Summer needed him to be, but there was nothing. Nothing as he scanned the streets through the windshield wipers, nothing as he struggled to breathe when every fear inside him was trying to crush him, choke off his air, cloud his head into a foggy mess.

Maybe that fog was how he somehow ended up at his mother's without even realizing he'd driven there.

He stared over the steering wheel at her bright little house, turned gray and drab by the rain.

If he went inside she would comfort him, hug him, tell him to move on, it was okay to let go, because he'd never really had Fox in the first place.

That was what hurt so much, wasn't it?

That he had never really had Fox in the first place, but somehow he'd still lost him and Fox had kept him at such careful arm's length that Summer didn't even know the first place to look.

He didn't know how long he sat there, clutching the steering wheel with his mouth twisted up in this crumpled thing that was struggling not to become a sob...but he stiffened as his mother's voice floated distantly across the lawn, filtered through the pattering rain and the exterior of the car.

"Summer…?" she called. "Are you coming in…?"

He lifted his head, watching her miserably. She stood under the porch overhang, her arms wrapped around herself against the spray-drizzled breeze, her expression dark with concern.

She would stay like that, getting herself soaked when she was too old and frail for this sort of thing, until Summer came in.

Swallowing back the taste of tears, he shut the engine off, pulled his shirt up in a useless shield over his head, and ducked out into the rain to trot to her door.

She stepped back, making room to let him in, fussing and fluttering her hands at him. "Look at you, you're soaked, you'll catch your death!" She clucked her tongue, pulling at him, but he stayed on the mat, biting his lip.

"I'll get everything wet," he said faintly, and she scowled.

"As if I care about that. Come in, sit down, get warm."

That was how he found himself bundled up, settled on the sofa, wrapped up in a blanket and his shirt and undershirt replaced by one of his old T-shirts from his childhood bedroom, while his mother pressed a hot mug of tea on him and dropped a towel on top of his head.

"Now get yourself dry," she said briskly, "and tell me what happened."

Summer half-heartedly scrubbed at his hair, managed a sip of his tea—but at that question the horrid feeling inside him nearly broke, threatening to rip past his numb, dazed quiet, his mouth doing that quivering *thing* that he hated again while he tried to clamp his lips together and make it stop.

But he couldn't stop how choked, how wretched he both sounded and felt as he fumbled out, "...Fox left me. Without...without even saying anything, he just...went behind my back and *left*..."

Lily Hemlock regarded him gravely, settling on the couch next to him and patting his knee. "What makes you so sure he's gone for good?"

"He packed. He took...he took that shrine to his wife. After everything, he couldn't even say *goodbye*, I tried so hard and I just... I just wasn't enough, and now he's *gone*..."

"Summer..." His mother squeezed his knee. "What makes you think you have to be *enough* to convince someone to stay? That's not love. That's trying to buy someone's love."

"I wasn't," Summer protested. "I just... I hoped he'd just..."

"Open his eyes, if you did everything right?" She sighed. "Darling, someone who doesn't want to change won't change until they're ready to. Fox will open his eyes when he's ready, but you can't make him do that. Just as he couldn't make you open yours, either."

Summer flinched. "What...do you mean, I'm not..."

Sometimes, his mother saw too much. And she seemed to see right through Summer as she studied him with a sad yet gentle smile, then reached up to tuck his hair back.

"Did you really love Fox Iseya?" she asked. "Or did you just need his approval to feel like you'd finally found yourself?"

Fuck.

That hit like a sledgehammer, smashing the breath out of Summer's lungs. He stared at her, fingers clutching tight at his tea mug.

"I...oh, fuck."

"Language," she said mildly, and he groaned.

"Now is not the time, Mom." Closing his eyes, he set the mug aside on the end table, then pulled the blankets closer around him. "I... I love him. I do. I just..."

"You just...?" she prompted gently.

"I... I think... I made myself believe I needed his approval to be confident...and then I got addicted to it, when... I should be able to find that confidence myself. I *need* to find that confidence myself, because...because..." He swallowed. "I do love him. I do. And I know why he's scared...and if he's scared, I need to be brave enough for both of us. Because I don't want to let him go unless he really, truly wants to go."

His mother's eyes creased thoughtfully, smile softening as she cocked her head. "You think he would leave even though he didn't really want to?"

Summer let out a brittle laugh. "The sad thing about loving him is knowing...he's made an art out of running away while staying in place. I guess this time he just didn't stay... but God knows the more he wants something, the faster he'll run because he's afraid of wanting anything at all."

"It sounds like you *do* know him." She brushed her knuckles to his cheek. "And it sounds like you do love him. Which explains why he was here not an hour ago, telling me goodbye and being *entirely* evasive about it." She arched a brow. "He was headed north toward the interstate, when he left. I would be careful driving in this rain, though."

Summer was going to die of a heart attack if his heart kept stopping like this every few minutes, slamming so hard it just shuddered itself to a halt.

He stared at his mother. "He...was here?" he croaked. "He was here and you didn't *tell* me?"

"Well he didn't come here to see *you*, now did he?" she tutted, then flapped her hands at him. "Go. Shoo. Go pull that stubborn old fox out of his hole."

Summer didn't need to be told twice.

He was already on his feet, darting toward the door, shedding the blanket in his wake.

"Stay dry!" his mother called after him, and he waved a hand back before flinging the door open and bolting out into the rain.

He might just catch his fox after all.

And all he needed was just...

One minute with him, to plead for one last chance.

Fox could hardly see the road ahead of him.

The storm came down in heavy sheets, wind billowing until it made curtain-like patterns in the silver droplets striking down and splashing in waves against his wind-shield. He was moving at a crawl, keeping a far distance from the dim red spots of the tail lights yards in front of him, barely covering any ground as he took the highway toward the interstate, following the winding roads between the trees.

If it got any worse, he'd have to pull over and wait it out.

When all he wanted was to put Omen behind him and be somewhere, anywhere else.

He squinted through the windshield, though, as the car ahead of him—a silver SUV—slowed, then stopped...then plowed forward, sheets of water pluming up to either side. Fox couldn't quite make out what they were doing until he drew closer, though.

And stopped at the foot of one of the highway bridges spanning the Mystic river.

A bridge that was currently barely visible under the rising floodswell of the river in spate, the water moving slow and lazy but pouring over the rails.

The SUV had managed to power through, making it to the other side with water sheeting in its wake like some kind of strange boat.

If the SUV had made it, Fox could too.

Don't, a small inner voice of reason whispered to him. *Wait. Turn back. Go back to Omen, go back to Summer, look at why you're so desperate to run away that you have to leave now and you're about to do something...to do something...*

Dangerous.

Beyond dangerous.

Just because she died in this river doesn't mean you have to, as well.

But even if that voice spoke so clearly, it was still so quiet. So much more quiet than the roar of his beating heart, the blood in his veins, the sense of desperation that said to get out. To run. To put as much distance between himself and the thing that frightened him as he could, because if he didn't...

He might run back to Summer.

And he was more afraid of Summer than he was of the washed-out bridge.

Wasn't that bitter irony.

That soft, sweet puppy of a man...

Terrified Fox beyond all reason.

He closed his eyes, resting his brow to the steering wheel.

Then breathed in deep, slowly pressed his foot down on the gas, and inched forward.

The strength of the current hit him as the Camry edged onto the bridge; the water might *look* slow, but he could feel it rocking against the car and pushing with a terrible force. Gritting his teeth, he picked up speed, forcing the Camry forward; it was barely more than a hundred yards, just a short hop to the other side, he could make it, he could *make* it, he just had to remember he was safe inside a two thousand pound vehicle and the water wasn't touching him and he wouldn't hyperventilate, black out, lose control...

He had one bad moment as he hit a bump in the concrete on the bridge—and for a moment it felt like the car was about to lift off and float away, pitched over the side and sinking down, down, as water under the wheels left him drifting, skewing. Barely breathing, his lungs caving in, he wrenched the steering wheel, floored the gas, lurched forward. He *heard* the water sucking up into the engine, heard it coughing, sputtering, but he kept his foot on that gas pedal and made the Camry *move*, spraying up water to either side of him as he went tumbling in a clumsy skew of tires off the foot of the bridge and onto the highway on the other side.

Right as the engine started choking, grinding, wheezing.

And he barely managed to get free of the waters spilling over the riverbank, hauling the steering wheel to one side, and swerving himself off the road onto the shoulder before the engine died.

Fox just...sat there, staring through the windshield blankly, his heart hammering. For half an instant he thought to check his phone to call for roadside assistance or 911, but of course it was dead. Of *course*. He let it drop into the cup holder.

Before he let out a broken, raspy "*Fuck!*" and thudded his forehead against the wheel.

What was he *doing?*

He could have just...just damned well killed himself, being reckless, acting like some melodramatic asshole because he just...because he just...

Fucking hell.

His eyes were leaking.

And they wouldn't stop, no matter how he tried, searing past his tight-closed eyelids while he tried to breathe past the adrenaline closing his throat and the rage clotting up inside him.

Rage.

At himself, at...at *her.*

"*Why did you do this to me?*" he demanded, gasping out wet, hoarse breaths, clawing his fingers against the wheel. "Why...why is it so hard...why did you get to *leave* and I had to stay here with this and I can't even let myself *feel* anything or I'm terrified I'll fall apart, and I just... I'm so...

I'm so *tired* of grieving and you *left* me and now I'm leaving him when I want... I want..."

He didn't know what he wanted.

That was the worst part.

He didn't know what he wanted, and he didn't know how to reach for what he didn't know.

He just knew he didn't want to be stuck here on the side of the road in a washed-out car, choking on his own tears after he'd done possibly the most reckless, ill-considered, childish thing of his life.

No...he knew.

He wanted to be back in Omen.

He wanted to be back at Albin Academy.

He wanted to be curled up in bed with Summer, watching the rain fall and listening to him talk about whatever troubles the boys laid at his feet *today*.

But instead he was alone.

Shaking.

Sobbing.

And only hoping the headlights glowing hot in his rear-view mirror from across the river were someone with a truck powerful enough to drag him out of this mess of his own creating, and take him back to Summer.

Take him home.

Summer couldn't believe he'd found him.

And there were over a hundred yards of rushing water standing between them, the Mystic completely overrunning its banks and washing out the bridge.

With Fox's car on the other side, the tail lights glowing red.

He must have stalled out, but...but...

Fuck.

He was *right there*, and so far out of Summer's reach.

And if Summer waited, waited until the bridge was passable again, waited until he could cross over to the other side...

Fox would be gone.

Summer just...just *knew it*.

He stared through the windshield at those tail lights, pressing his lips together, asking himself. Asking himself if he could really risk it. If the Acura would make it through the flooding waters over the bridge without getting swept over the side, or stalling in the middle and leaving him stranded.

He didn't know what to do, was about to do something so goddamned risky...

When the Camry's driver's side door opened, and Fox stepped out into the drenching rain.

He stood there for long, silent moments, and even if he was so far away Summer couldn't see his expression...

Everything in his body language, miserable and stiff, said he knew.

He recognized Summer's car.

And he gestured broadly, arms cutting through the rain, his mouth moving, a dark O against his pale face.

Summer couldn't hear him. And he bolted out of the Acura, stepping out into wind that whistled over him, snapped through his hair, drove the rain into him like needles of ice.

Fox was shouting something.

Shouting across the river, over the storm, and Summer couldn't quite make out what it was...

But he thought it just might be *go back*.

No. No, he couldn't. He *wouldn't*. His heart beat sick at the very thought, lurching and colder than the rain sluicing over him could ever be, dark and heavy with dread certainty.

If he turned back now...

He would never know where Fox ran to.

And he knew—

He could call and call and call again, beg, plead, but that phone would never answer, voicemail picking up and then going dead without even a recording, just a *click* and empty air that might hear him, but Fox never would.

Because Fox was afraid, Summer thought.

Not of dying, not of death, not of anything that might harm his flesh...

...but of anything that could touch a heart that had been shut away so long it had turned as thin and fragile as flower petals shut from the light, translucent and pale and ready to shatter at the slightest touch.

If Fox wanted to run so much, if he really couldn't stand to let Summer need him, want him, love him...

Summer would let him go.

But not until Fox gave him the chance to at least, first...

Ask.

Ask, beg, *plead*.

And hope deep down…

That Fox truly wanted to stay at Albin, and stay with *him*.

There was only one thing for Summer to do.

Hell, the only thing he'd gotten good at when he'd left Omen for Baltimore.

Pushing through the rain, cold sluicing heavily over him, he stripped out of his shirt; it would only weigh him down, and he tossed it by the side of the road as he stepped onto the foot of the bridge, into the first few inches of floodwater.

His stomach constricted, his heart turning over.

He took a deep breath.

And, with Fox's voice echoing over the storm, calling to him, warding him away, it didn't matter when that voice was Summer's siren-song and he couldn't turn away…

He kicked his shoes off, and dove in.

Fox was going to kill Summer.

If Summer didn't kill himself.

What was he *doing?*

Fox's heart had nearly jumped out of his chest when he'd recognized Summer's rental Acura.

Then plummeted as he'd stepped out and tried to warn Summer away from the bridge…

Only for Summer to strip his shirt and shoes off, and go diving right into the water.

Every nightmare Fox had ever had rose up to swamp him, locking his legs in place as ice shot through his veins and in his mind's eye he saw Summer, beautiful bright

Summer, sinking into black water and disappearing for-ever, no one to hold his hand, to reach for him, no one to save him, no one to—

Stop.

He was breathing in shallow, hyperventilating gasps, but he could still see Summer, and…and…

Summer was still on the bridge.

Holding fast to the railing, forging through with one hand sweeping through the water to drag him along, half-walking, half-swimming but with the railing of the bridge holding him steady to keep the overflow from sweeping him away, powerful movements practiced and sleek and smooth and so very fierce with determination.

Fox tried to find his voice. Tried to cry "*Go back!*" again before Summer was too far, before it was too late, before he couldn't turn back—but he could barely manage a croak, standing there in the rain with it dripping down him in waves, frozen in place, his entire body numb as he help-lessly watched the man he loved do only the second most reckless thing he had seen in his life.

Please, he begged silently, even if he didn't know who he was begging at all. He knew Summer was a strong swimmer, had experience, but this was a river in full spate and if Summer was swept away right in front of him, Fox would…would…

…*please*.

One agonizing second after another… Summer forged on, gasping as harder surges splashed and threatened to swamp over his head, pushing himself up to keep his head above water. But as a particularly hard swell hit, the water slammed into him and lifted him off his feet, jerking his entire body to one side and leaving him holding on fiercely to the bridge rail, while the surge of water tossed him up and down.

And Fox broke.

Mindless, thoughtless, he knew only one thing:

He had to get to Summer before Summer was torn away from him.

And without hesitation, he dove into the icy water on the other side of the bridge, finally finding his voice as he grasped on to the railing.

"*Summer!*"

Summer's head jerked up, as he managed to drag his other hand over to tighten his grip on the railing; the surge subsided, his body settling back down through the water to touch down with both feet, and he stared at Fox, before crying out, "Don't move—Fox, I'm coming!"

He thrashed through the water harder, faster, pushing himself toward Fox, but Fox refused to go back, he had to get to Summer, to see him safe to the other side, even as the water was rising up around him—his thighs, his hips, his waist, his chest, and suddenly he was back in every nightmare, struggling to breathe as the water slapped and frothed around his shoulders, and he couldn't let go of the railing but he couldn't move forward either, and he was going to drown, going to—

"*Fox.*"

One of Summer's arms wrapped hard around him— and suddenly his heated, wet body pressed against Fox, grounding him, holding him fast with one arm while the other hand stayed tight to the railing, and Fox clutched at him, sucked in several panicky breaths, buried his face in his shoulder.

"Summer, *Summer*..."

"I've got you," Summer soothed, voice steady despite his panting, walking them forward, their combined weight a bulwark against the water; Fox could barely make his stiff legs move, but somehow he crawled along with Summer, refusing to let go. "It's all right, Fox. I'm here."

The waves lashed them, battered them...yet Summer held strong. Strong enough for both of them, Fox realized dimly, as, shaking, they spilled off the bridge onto the other side near his Camry, stumbling out of the water and nearly falling before they caught each other with gripping hands.

Fox wasn't crying.

He *wasn't*.

It was just the rain, he told himself.

Just the rain.

Summer clasped his shoulders, then his face, staring at him. "Fox—Fox, why did you do that? I was coming to you—"

"Why did *you* do that?" Fox flared, clutching at Summer's wrists, his chest feeling like it would explode with the rush of fear suddenly built up and bursting out. "I couldn't let you...what if you'd been...what if you'd..."

Then Summer's arms were around him again—strong enough to block out the driving rain, warm enough to erase the sucking, icy sensation of waterlogged clothing, while Summer buried his face in Fox's shoulder.

"I wasn't. I didn't," he whispered, voice trembling. "I'm

safe, Fox. I'm here. I'm here with you…if you'll just…if you'll just stop running from me."

"I *had* to run," Fox gulped out—and yet somehow his arms moved of their own volition, creeping around Summer, clutching at his back, and suddenly that free-floating feeling was gone, that black drowning sensation, as long as Summer was in his arms. "I can't… I can't figure out what I'm doing, I need to just… I've been stuck here for so long, stagnating, and if I left I could…"

"Nothing," Summer said softly. "Leaving Omen didn't change me, Fox. I didn't find what I was looking for out there because where you are doesn't matter. It's *who* you are…and you're not going to find who you are by running. I learned that the hard way. I didn't find who I wanted to be until I found *you*…right back in the town I ran away from for all these years."

Fox lifted his head, stricken, staring at Summer.

He had changed, Fox thought.

Because he was so steady now, so strong, so calm, so certain of himself.

And Fox had changed, too.

Because now he was the one uncertain, fragile, frightened, when before he had tried to make himself so untouchable, so unshakeable.

And he would have to learn to be open to that, to flow with it, to just…*reach* for something with no certainty that he would ever be able to hold it forever, if he wanted to be with Summer.

"What if I don't know who I want to be yet?" he whis-

pered. "What if you hate who I become while I try to figure this out?"

"I don't think that will happen, but there's only one way
to find out." Summer half-smiled, and still that light of
hope burned so bright in him, and Fox didn't understand
how his own thoughtless cruelty hadn't snuffed it out. "Or
you can run, but if you run… I'll go with you. That's all
I ask. If you have to find yourself somewhere else…let me
go with you, so I don't have to find myself without you."

"But I…" He shook his head desperately. "I don't know
how to *do* this, Summer. I don't know how to live for you."

"Oh… Fox. You don't." Summer's smile turned so sweet,
and he curled a hand against the back of Fox's neck, drawing him in, their brows resting together, a quiet temple between them creating a warm space free of the rain; a warm
space filled with blue eyes that captured and held Fox so
deeply. "You live for yourself, and you let me live with
you. And it's hard. I know it's hard. I know it's hard, but
Fox… Fox, all you have to do is *try*." Summer swallowed
hard, his voice so thick, so tight, but surely that, too, was
just the rain, making wet tracks down his handsome, gentle
face. "And if you fail, it's okay. I'll fail too. But we'll fail
and fall and help each other back up, and it'll be okay." His
voice broke on a hitching sound that tore at Fox's heart.
"I just need you to say that you're willing to try. Try for
me." Tentatively, he brushed rain-slick lips to Fox's, a feeling like lightning striking. "Try…and *stay*."

If only he could make Summer feel the twisting and
spiking and shuddering inside him, the earthquakes that
went through his heart.

If only Summer knew what he was asking.

But…he did, Fox thought as he met those eyes that made him tremble with the fear of this, the fear of the unknown…

…the fear of never knowing what could be.

The fear of losing Summer, which spoke so much louder than the tiny nattering fears of his tired and cracked heart.

Fox darted his tongue over his lips. He'd never been at a loss for words when he chose to speak, and yet this quiet, brave young man who was asking Fox to be brave with him, to risk his heart, managed to somehow leave him fumbling, lost.

"You terrify me, Summer," he whispered. "And I think…"

Say it, he told himself.

Say those words he'd said to no one in years.

Say those words that could break the chains he'd bound himself in.

He was twisting a knife in his own heart, and begging Summer not to make him bleed.

And, "I think that is why I love you," he said, a rush, choked and hot and he couldn't breathe, but he'd *said* it and now that those words were out he couldn't stop even when Summer's eyes widened, even when Summer stared at him with his expression alight. "You break me until I can't be cold anymore…you make me feel *so much*, and that frightens me so terribly." But he couldn't let go, either, grasping on to Summer with all his strength. "But what frightens me even more is that I trust you. I trust you to take that fear…and make it something *better*."

Summer let out one of those soft, sweet laughs of his,

those quiet things full of light that seemed as though he couldn't keep his emotions inside, always letting them out everywhere as if he was putting stars in the heavens, each bright glow made of feelings he couldn't help but share to illuminate someone else's way.

"You frighten me too, Fox," he admitted. "Half of love is fear." But those strong, warm hands held Fox so close, fingers weaving into the heavy, waterlogged knot of his hair. "The other half is knowing that person cares for you enough to never use that fear against you. You wouldn't fear me at all if you hadn't given me the power to hurt your heart." He smiled shyly. "So all I can do is make sure I never do."

"You know that's impossible," Fox whispered.

"It doesn't mean I won't try. As long as you try for me, I'll try for you." Summer's lips pressed to his brow, the bridge of his nose...hovered over his mouth, entreating, waiting. "Because I love you, Fox Iseya...and wherever you run, I'll follow."

I love you, Fox Iseya.

Maybe Fox was breaking, right now.

But maybe he needed to break, to shed what was binding him, holding him locked in place, keeping him numb.

Maybe he needed to break to become stronger.

To become who he needed to be, now that he was ready to leave his grief behind.

Ready to start again.

Ready to *try*.

And he felt as though his next heartbeat was a fresh new thing, a different rhythm, a different timbre as he leaned into Summer, captured his mouth, whispered, "…I love you, Summer. I *do*. And I'll try for you. I'll *try*…and I'll stay. So that you don't have to go anywhere."

Summer grinned, his mouth moving in a warm curve against Fox's. "I don't think we could go anywhere anyway, since I think you killed your car and I'm not crossing that river again to get to mine. So we're kind of stuck, but maybe we could get out of the rain…?"

Fox pulled back, looking at him flatly. "I just admitted that I love you after I nearly drowned myself to get away from you, then drowned myself to get *to* you, and you ruin the moment with *that?*"

"Well, yeah." Summer shrugged merrily. "I have to give you a reason to be mad at me to save your pride, after that."

Fox narrowed his eyes, glaring at Summer through the water dripping off his lashes. "I take it back. I hate you."

"No, you don't," Summer said, and tugged him toward the Camry, lacing their fingers together, sweetly intertwined. "You love me just as much as I love you…and I'm never going to let you forget it."

"Hate you," Fox muttered again as Summer pulled the back seat door open, and sank down inside the car, tugging Fox after him.

"Uh-huh."

"As soon as we're back at the school, you are in every bit of trouble," Fox grumbled, as he tucked himself into the dry warmth of the car and pulled the door shut, locking out the lashing winds and rain.

"Sure I am."

Fox narrowed his eyes, squinting at the very sodden

young man currently dripping all over his back seat, his
entire body glistening with sweet-wet runnels of water.
"Are you taking me at *all* seriously right now?"

"Absolutely seriously," Summer said, with a sly smile that
made a liar out of him; he leaned in, nipped Fox's upper lip,
drew him in tight and close with a heat that felt less like lust
and more like joy, building between them into something
too bright to be denied. "Now c'mere...*beloved*. Because
we've got a lot of time to kill before someone comes to
save us...and I need to remind you exactly *why* you stayed."

Epilogue

Summer had never seen anything quite so amazing as the sight of his name on an office door.

GUIDANCE COUNSELOR in all caps in bronze embossing, right above the name *Summer Hemlock*.

And right next to the door whose plaque read *Professor Fox Iseya*.

He almost hadn't wanted his own office, but when he'd protested, his fiancé had very pointedly threatened murder if Summer was always underfoot and stopping him from getting his own work done.

Considering you're no longer my assistant, Fox had said tartly over dinner prep, even while feeding him shreds of grated gruyere plucked from the mixing bowls, *you are more of a hindrance than a help, and an entirely annoying distraction.*

Summer had grinned, leaning over to steal a taste of

Fox's fingertips, and to hell with the cheese. *I don't think you find my distractions annoying at all.*

I find everything about you annoying, Fox had said with a prim, haughty sniff. *The way you leave your socks tangled in the sheets when you kick them off every night. The amount of closet space you take up. The fact that you vacuum the floor every morning even when I want to sleep in. You are an irritating intrusion.*

And Summer had only laughed, nipping at Fox's fingertip. *And you love me.*

Instant scowl. Every time. It was so predictable it made Summer laugh, while Fox had yanked his hand back, glaring at him. *So what if I do?*

That's all, Summer had answered sunnily, and dumped the shredded cheese over the bowl of tossed salad before pressing a kiss to Fox's cheek and sailing out of arm's reach to take the salad to the dinner table. *I just like reminding you that you love me as much as I love you.*

For now, Fox had called after him. *I'll likely hate you tomorrow.*

Sure he would.

Just as he'd likely come to hate Summer every day before that in the months since Summer had transitioned into training for the guidance counselor job.

Yet somehow, despite that supposed *hate,* Fox had invited Summer to move in with him, had fallen into a domestic routine with him, had tumbled him into bed every night to make Summer cry his name again and again.

Maybe he'd figure that hate thing out after a few more tries.

For now, though, Fox emerged from his office, brushing his half-loosed hair back with both hands before deftly twisting and knotting it up. He moved to stand next to Summer outside Summer's office door, broad shoulder bumping Summer's, then cocked his head to one side.

"I don't see the point," Fox said blandly. "You'll only have to change the name in a few months anyway."

Summer snorted, flicking his fingers against Fox's side—his heavy platinum engagement ring warm on his finger, twin to the one glinting against Fox's finger and his hair as he finished binding it up. "Who says I'm even taking your name?"

Something dark glinted in Fox's eyes as he turned a sidelong look on Summer. Something possessive. Something *hungry*, as he swept an arm around Summer's waist and drew him in close and tight, right there in the hallway where anyone could see if they looked out a classroom door or when the bell let out between classes in the next few minutes.

"*I* say," Fox growled. "And I rather like the sound of 'Summer Iseya.'"

Mm.

Summer shouldn't like that so much.

And yet after so much denial, so much heaviness, after Fox had pushed him away so much...

It ached so brightly inside, for Fox to so openly want to claim Summer as *his*.

And with a laugh, Summer leaned into him, resting his hands against Fox's chest. "Fox Hemlock might just mean I'm not the one with the weirdest name here anymore. But since when are you territorial?"

"Since the moment you walked back into my life," Fox answered, then leaned down to seize Summer's lips in a kiss.

Suddenly they were tumbling through the door of Summer's new office—and slamming it behind them, before Fox had him pinned up against it, arms over his head, wrists clasped. Fox always seemed to need that—some measure of control, something to leave Summer whimpering and writhing and completely submitting of his own free will, and *God* did Summer melt now as Fox skimmed his free hand down his body, flicked over his nipple through his shirt, nipped along his jaw in hard biting lines.

"I think," Fox whispered against his skin, "that we need to christen your desk."

Summer let out a breathless laugh. "We've christened half the rest of the school grounds. Might as well."

As if he didn't need it just as much.

As if he and Fox hadn't been nearly ravenous for each other, from the moment a tow truck had dragged them back to Albin to the day, last week, when Fox had taken Summer out to dinner and quietly slipped that ring across the table without a word, the shining platinum itself a question that didn't need to be asked but that Summer answered with an enthusiastic *yes*.

As enthusiastic as his moans, as his spread legs, as Fox pulled him away from the door and pushed him down over the desk, bent and spread for his beloved, slacks dragged down around his ankles—though he caught them before they fell, at first, fishing in his pocket until he found another one of those conveniently portable little tubules of lube, flicking it over his shoulder between two fingers.

And earning a sharp, deliciously stinging smack across the ass for it, hips lifting in a rough jerk as he groaned with the pleasure of the burn.

"*Again?*" Fox asked with a touch of exasperation, plucking the tube from Summer's fingers, while Summer rocked forward with a gasp, grinding his already-hard cock against the desk, trailing into a moan.

"Like I said," he whispered, curling his fingers against the desk, bracing himself for the onslaught—of fingers, of pleasure, of Fox's cock, of Fox's love. "I never give up on hope."

And he would never give up on Fox.

Not through this pleasure, as their bodies crashed together and Fox filled him in that way that only Fox could, leaving Summer clawing at the desk, begging for more, spreading himself and so willingly open and vulnerable to the man he loved.

And not through whatever pains may come.

He and Fox Iseya had taught each other how to be brave.

And no matter what…

Summer would always, *always* fight to love and be loved, exactly as he was and exactly as Fox was—no more, no less. Love that accepted each other in all their foibles and follies and fears and fantasies.

Love that settled inside them, found its home, made *them* home…

…just like that.

★ ★ ★ ★ ★

Acknowledgments

The first people I told about The Call for this book were the group of author friends I call the Fight Club. They were the first to be happy for me; the first to encourage me when I had doubts; the first to shower me with unreserved excitement because we always believe in celebrating each others' successes.

It's been that way for years now, and it's strange to realize that as I write this. That for years we've been holding each other together, lifting each other up, keeping each other on track, motivating each other through the down moments, celebrating our successes.

No matter where we go, we never leave each other behind.

And I hope we never do.

I <3 y'all.

And I'm grateful for you.

*Jude rides a motorcycle, kisses hard and gives Iris
the perfect distraction from her mess of a life. But come
September, Iris is still determined to get out of this
zero-stoplight town—unless Jude can give her a reason to stay.*

Keep reading for an excerpt from Girl Next Door
by New York Times *bestselling author Chelsea M. Cameron.*

Chapter One

Iris

I smelled the ocean before I saw it. I took the long way back; the scenic route. Anything to prolong the inevitable. Turning my car onto a back road, I sighed as I rounded a corner and drank in the view of blue waves crashing over the rocky shore, coating the rocks and turning them dark. This was my home, whether I wanted to admit it or not. I'd started my life here in Salty Cove, and now I was back.

All too soon, I reached the turn for my parents' road. *My* road now. It took everything in me not to start crying when I pulled into the driveway and shut off the car. Time to face my new reality.

"We're here," I said to the snoring gray lump in a crate

in the backseat. "Can you please wake up and comfort me right now?"

With that, my Weimaraner, Dolly Parton, raised her head and blinked her sweet blue eyes at me.

"Thank you."

I got out of the car and went into the back to let her out of the crate. She jumped out and shook herself before sniffing the air.

"I know, you can actually smell the ocean here. It's not covered up by city smell. At least one of us will be happy with this situation."

Dolly started snuffling the ground and then found a spot to pee while I looked up at the house. Why did it look smaller? I hadn't been here for months and in that time, it had shrunk. The white paint peeled in places, and the flower boxes on the wraparound porch needed watering. I hoped the garden out back wasn't in as bad a shape.

The side door opened and out came my mother carrying a chain saw. She didn't look at me immediately, but then she did and her face broke out into the most brilliant smile that made her look years younger.

"Hey, Mom," I said.

She put the chain saw down on the porch before opening her arms. "Welcome home, baby girl."

I forced myself not to cringe at the nickname. I was twenty-two, hardly a baby at this point.

Still, I let myself be folded into her arms, and I drank in the familiar scent of fresh-baked bread and fresh-cut wood. She rubbed my back up and down and then leaned down to pet Dolly, who lost her shit and lapped up the attention.

"A tree came down last week, so I've been cutting it up. Come on in and see your father. You can bring your stuff in later. He's been antsy to see you all day."

I looked back at my car, which was packed to the roof with all the shit that I had left after I'd sold most of everything in a last-ditch attempt to cover my rent.

Mom put her arm around me and started filling me in on town gossip, but a loud rumbling distracted me. I turned my head in time to watch a sleek black motorcycle pull into the driveway next door.

"Is that—" I started to say, but then the rider got off the bike and pulled off their helmet, shaking out their short dark hair.

"Oh, yes, that's Jude. Her parents moved down to Florida and left her the house."

Jude Wicks. I hadn't seen her since she graduated four years ahead of me in school.

Jude didn't glance in my direction as she covered the bike, jogged up the steps, and slammed the front door of the house. I jumped at the sound.

Dolly whined and I looked down at her.

"Her parents left her the house?" I asked as Mom and I walked up the steps and into the house. We didn't have air-conditioning, so fans were doing all the work, just blowing around the semi-moist sea air.

Mom was distracted from answering by Dad yelling at her from his recliner. He'd hurt his back working for the power company for thirty-five years and was retired. They relied on Mom's income as a real estate agent and substitute teacher.

"Iris is here," Mom called to him.

"Baby girl!" he yelled when I came around the corner.

"Hi, Dad."

I went over to give him a huge hug. Dolly immediately put her chin in his lap and whined for attention.

"Hello, Dolly," Dad said with a chuckle, setting his coffee down next to a stack of library books beside his chair.

"What are you reading now?" I asked.

He held up the book he'd rested on the arm of the chair to keep his place. "Started reading these young adult books. This one's about these kids who are planning a heist to steal this magic stuff. You can have it when I'm done."

Mom poked her head in and asked me if I wanted some coffee. "Sure, thanks."

I sat down on the couch as Dolly curled up at his feet and closed her eyes.

Mom brought me a cup of black coffee and some creamer. I added enough so that the coffee turned from black to khaki. Perfect.

"How was your drive?" Mom asked.

We caught up on my trip, the fact that she'd cleared out my room for me, and what else was happening in town. Mostly it was about who my parents knew that had died, what they had died from, and talking shit about a few while simultaneously hoping they rested in peace.

Less than an hour at home and I already wanted to escape, but I was stuck here, at least for now.

I had to unpack my car, find a place for Dolly's food and water bowls, and settle into my room. Luckily for me, my brother, who was ten years older, had vacated it a long time ago to go to college.

My bed was small, but Mom had bought me a new mattress recently, so there was that. Still, it was a twin bed, when I'd been sleeping in a queen in my apartment. That had been left on the street. No one wanted someone else's mattress. The bed frame had been taken by Natalie, one of my former coworkers. I missed her already, and needed to text her that I'd made it home safe. She was so worried about me moving back to Maine that she'd literally bought me bear spray. I told her that the likelihood that I would die from a bear attack was slim to none, but she wouldn't listen.

The walls started to close on me as I looked at the tiny bed. Sure, I'd had to share my old apartment with someone I didn't like, but my bedroom had been twice this size, and I'd had two big, beautiful windows that looked out on a courtyard filled with flowers and butterflies and twittering birds. Maine had all those things, but it wasn't the same.

To add insult to injury, none of my sheets or blankets were going to fit the bed. I added that to the list of things I needed to get with money I didn't have.

Dolly followed me into the room and climbed up on the bed. She took up most of it.

"I'm going to end up on the floor," I said to her. She closed her eyes and huffed out a sigh.

I sat on the edge of the bed and looked around. At least the posters I'd had on the walls in high school were gone, and the room was freshly painted white. My window looked out toward the ocean, which sparkled at me beyond a row of trees. At least I could see the ocean every day here.

My phone buzzed with yet another text. Natalie. I sent her a quick message that I'd arrived safe and had not been mauled by a bear. I ignored the message from Anna, my old roommate, about some dishes I'd apparently left behind and if it was okay for her to have them. Whatever. She could knock herself out. She'd stolen a bunch of my other shit, so I wasn't sure why she was contacting me about this. I considered blocking her number so I'd never have to speak to her again.

I reached out and stroked Dolly's velvet head. She leaned into my touch. "What are we gonna do?" I asked. She didn't answer.

Later that night, after I unpacked my car and had dinner that consisted of meatloaf, mashed potatoes, and a fiddlehead salad, I sat on the couch as Mom watched a reality talent show and Dad read.

This was my life now.

"What are your plans for tomorrow?" Mom asked during a commercial break.

"I'm not sure."

I hadn't thought any further than today. Everything else was a blank. I was always the girl with the plan, but now, I was adrift. An unmoored boat, lost at sea with no hope of rescue.

"I was talking to Cindy Malone the other day and they're hiring for summer help at The Lobster Pot," Mom said. "You did that in high school. I know she'd hire you. At least it would give you something during the summer until you can find something more permanent if you need to."

I tried not to make a face and instead grabbed one of the

books on Dad's "to be returned to the library" pile. Another young adult book; this time a Cinderella retelling. I read the blurb on the back and if I wasn't mistaken, it was a romance between two girls. I was surprised that my dad would want to read that. I wasn't going to comment, though. I cracked open the book and started to read. Mom still stood waiting for an answer.

"Oh, uh, sure. I'll call her tomorrow," I said.

I mean, what else was I going to do? Go down to the local bar and take up day drinking? Hang out at the gas station with the local teens? Sit on the beach with the tourists and get a horrible sunburn? I tried not to think about what I could be doing right now, if I was in Boston. Maybe dinner and drinks or pizza with my friends, a hot yoga class at my favorite studio, or even just taking a book to a coffee shop to read for a while and watch people pass on the street. If I wanted to have a professionally made cup here? I'd have to drive at least ten minutes and they definitely didn't have nondairy milk or know what a macchiato was.

Not that I could even afford a macchiato since I was fucking broke, and I needed money sooner rather than later. Working at The Lobster Pot was my best option.

"Sounds good, baby girl," Mom said with a smile. Her shoulders relaxed and she sat back in her chair. I realized she'd been worried. She seemed to be relieved I'd agreed to her plan so easily.

My parents and I hadn't really talked about what happened and why I was back, mostly because it wasn't for just one reason. There were many reasons, all culminating with me packing my shit in my car, loading up my dog, abandoning my friends, and driving back here.

I asked Mom if there was any ice cream in the freezer and she said that there was. While I was getting a spoon, I glanced out the window, which happened to look right into our neighbor's living room.

Jude.

The lights were on and she stood in the living room wearing nothing but a sports bra and some athletic shorts. The spoon I'd just grabbed clattered on the floor. As I stood up from retrieving the spoon, I found her staring directly at me. Instead of looking away like a normal person, I stared back.

Her hair had been long in high school and her arms hadn't been so...sculpted back then. At least not that I remembered. My mouth went dry and I held on to the spoon for dear life.

"What are you looking at?" a voice said behind me and I shrieked and dropped the spoon again. I turned around and found my mom leaning over my shoulder to see what I'd been staring at.

"Oh, nothing, just staring off into space." I rushed with my spoon and the ice cream back into the living room. My parents kept the room dark and the only light was from my dad's lamp and the TV, so I could hide in a corner with my lobster-red face.

What had come over me? I'd just stood there leering like a fucking creeper. Part of me expected a knock at the door and for her to storm in and ask what I'd been staring at.

That didn't happen, but it didn't stop me from looking up from my book every few minutes to check and make sure.

Before bed, I took Dolly out to do her business and my eyes kept flicking over to the house. The lights were still on, but I wasn't going to stare this time. I hadn't asked for more information from my mom about Jude, but I did wonder what she was doing back here. She'd hated this town, from what I remembered, so it couldn't just be because of her parents' house.

High school in a small town in Maine was brutal for anyone who didn't conform, and Jude had been adamant about not conforming. I'd done my best to get through, and the drama club had been my safe haven. I'd never thought seriously about acting after high school, since that was way out of my league, but I still thought about it every now and then. There was a community theater group a few towns away. Could I put myself out there and get into it again?

Dolly was taking her sweet time, sniffing the bushes at the edge of the porch to find the right one to pee near. I jumped as I heard a door slam, the door to the neighbor's house.

I froze with my back to the house, pretending I wasn't completely aware of what was happening. Was she leaving again on that motorcycle? Where would she go tonight? The only bar in town closed in less than an hour, and there was nothing else open. Unless she might be going to a friend's house for a party?

Or perhaps she was going to the beach for a midnight swim. I shivered at the thought of Jude slipping beneath the waves like a mermaid.

My ears perked for the rumble of the motorcycle starting up, but I didn't hear it. Dolly finally found her perfect spot and did her thing. She seemed content to sniff around the yard, so I let her, wrapping my arms around myself and breathing the sharp sea air. I'd missed this smell, even if I hadn't missed much else. Maybe I'd go for a midnight swim. The only danger of doing that in the height of the summer was encountering drunken teenagers, out having a bonfire on the beach and smoking a lot of weed.

I closed my eyes and took a few deep breaths before turning around. I told myself not to look at the porch next door, but my eyes had other ideas.

She was there, sitting on the porch on an Adirondack chair and staring out toward the ocean, just like I'd been doing. An open beer rested on the porch railing.

I swiveled my head away so she wouldn't catch me looking again, and at that moment Dolly decided that she'd make a mad dash for Jude's yard.

"Dolly!" I yelled as she bounded up the porch and went right for Jude. Well, shit. "Dolly, come back!"

She completely ignored me. I was going to have to go get her.

Groaning inside, I dragged myself over to the house, preparing for anything. What I found was Jude petting Dolly's head and Dolly closing her eyes in bliss and then trying to climb in Jude's lap.

"Dolly," I said, but she acted as if I wasn't even there. "I'm sorry. I should have kept her on the leash." I couldn't look up at Jude, so I watched her hands stroke Dolly's head.

The air around the porch seemed thicker somehow, or maybe it was just harder to breathe near Jude.

"It's okay," she said, and I felt like I'd never heard her voice before. I wasn't sure if I had. "I don't mind."

Dolly finally stopped trying to climb into the chair and settled for putting her paws and her head in Jude's lap.

"Sorry," I said again. I needed to take Dolly and get the hell out of here, but I couldn't move. My feet were glued to her porch.

"Haven't seen you in a while, Iris," she said. Her voice had a rough quality that made me think of bar smoke and darkness. There was a hard quality about her that made my stomach flip over a few times.

"Yeah, I moved back today." My gaze finally crept its way up to her face only to find her watching me with fathomless brown eyes. Her face was all sharp angles, along with her haircut. A fluttering in my stomach erupted, and I forgot what we were talking about until she blinked again.

"When did you get back?" My voice trembled, and I hoped she didn't hear it.

Her fingers danced back and forth on Dolly's head. "Last year," she said, but didn't elaborate. Chatty.

"I should probably go," I said, stating the obvious.

"Stay if you like," she said, picking up her beer and gesturing to the empty chair next to her.

"Okay?" I collapsed into the chair and tried to calm my galloping heart.

"Do you want a beer?" she asked after a few seconds of silence.

"No, thank you." What was I doing here? I should have

grabbed Dolly and run back into the house. Was Jude doing this so she could confront me about staring at her earlier?

I had no idea how to have a conversation with her so I stopped trying to think of things to say and just sat there, my insides twisting around like pissed-off snakes. At least Dolly was enjoying herself.

Jude didn't seem eager to say anything either, so there we were. I kept expecting my mom to open the door and yell for me to come back. At least that would give me an escape route.

Out of the corner of my eye, I watched Jude. She petted Dolly with one hand and the other lifted the beer to her lips periodically. She wore a T-shirt and the same shorts as earlier.

I needed to stop thinking about that earlier non-outfit. I blushed hard and hoped she couldn't see in the dark.

If I strained my ears, I could just barely hear the crash of the waves. Somewhere nearby, a soft boom followed by another let me know someone was setting off fireworks.

"That's a cool motorcycle," I blurted out, and wished I could walk into the ocean and disappear.

"Thank you. It's not very useful in the winter, but it's good for getting around in the summer." She pressed her lips together as if she'd said too much.

"I've never been on a bike. I'm scared I'd fly off or something." This kept getting worse and worse.

"I'm sure you'd be fine, once you tried it. Do you always let fear dictate your life?"

I sat up, shocked. "*No*," I said, but it didn't sound convincing. "You don't even know me." I didn't know her either, but I was the one being called out.

"True. Just something to think about." She moved Dolly's head and stood up. "See you later," she said, and went into the house, leaving me and Dolly wondering what the hell had just happened.

Dolly came over to me and whined.

"Let's go home," I said and she seemed to understand me. I got up with shaking legs and made my way back to the house. The lights were still on next door when I glanced back one more time.

Chapter Two

Jude

I tried to remember her, but since there had been four years between us in high school, the memories were hazy. She'd had friends, from what I'd seen, and seemed to do okay in that fishbowl environment. Not always fighting against the current like me.

I didn't know what she was doing back here, and I was trying not to care, but this was one of the first interesting things to happen in Salty Cove in a while. I also hadn't missed the way she'd looked at me earlier. Might be my imagination, but I was pretty sure I'd seen interest there, which was interesting on its own. She'd definitely been interested in guys, last I knew. I'd known that I liked girls, and girls only, from a young age. I'd refused to hide who I was and had come out at an age where kids were the most vicious. Still, I'd gotten through it but bore the hidden scars.

Not that I was going to pursue anything with her, even if she was interested. No, I wasn't ready, even now. It had been more than two years but not much had changed. Living in Salty Cove and fishing for lobster was like living in a space where time barely passed, where it moved so slow that you didn't notice and suddenly you were old and still living the same life you'd had for dozens of years, even though you swore you wouldn't. This town locked you in, made you forget that there was anything or anyone outside it.

I should probably get out more, but look what getting out of Maine had gotten me. I was back to the place I never wanted to be and I didn't have any plans about leaving. Where would I go? I'd lost everything. I was lucky to have parents who were thrilled that they could stop paying a property manager and get free labor from their daughter. Now they could spend their time soaking up the sun and drinking cocktails every afternoon in Florida. If I could stand to be with them, I might have joined them.

No, I don't think I could handle living in Florida. I wasn't really handling living here, but it was easier to float through my life in a familiar environment, even if that environment was so homogenous that everyone was related to everyone else. Except for me.

My thoughts drifted from my life here back to Iris. She'd clearly gone off to college and now she was back. I knew her father had retired with some injuries, so maybe that was why. Or maybe it was something else and she'd needed a soft place to land. This town was a safety net for so many people. She seemed a little frenetic, or maybe that was her personality. Nervousness radiated from her in waves. It didn't bother me, though, which was surprising. I normally gravitated toward people who were like me, reserved and quiet, but if she was going to be next door for a while, maybe we could hang out. I definitely needed more friends, since I didn't have anyone close, just acquaintances.

I'd touched on a nerve when I'd told her not to live in fear, but I'd done that on purpose to see what would happen. Chalk it up to boredom.

She was cute too, I'd have to give her that much. Wide-set blue eyes that had untold stories behind them underneath light brown curls. Her curves were generous and lush. No, I wasn't going to think about her body. Completely inappropriate. I hadn't thought about anyone's body *that* way since...

Everything always came back to that. To *her.* I couldn't even think her name without a stab to my heart.

If Iris was cute was irrelevant because I wasn't going to love anyone ever again. I'd done it once and once was enough. I'd gambled and lost, big time. Iris probably wasn't going to come back anyway, because I'd been rude and had just left her on the porch with her dog. I'd been afraid that she was going to start asking me personal questions, or try to talk to me, and I was out of practice talking to other people. That was the best part of my job: the no talking to anyone. Sure, there was the stink of bait and the hard physical labor, but every day when I went out, I got to be alone. I preferred being alone these days. It hadn't always been like that, and I still had friends who tried to get in touch every now and then. Some were persistent and kept trying, even when I gave them nothing. I guess there was something to be said for that. Too bad I was such a shitty friend. Maybe I could practice with Iris.

I finished my beer inside and put the TV on so the house wasn't so silent. I didn't really watch it, but the noise and color distracted my brain for a little while. Due to my job, I'd adjusted to a different sleep schedule, so after I put the bottle in the recycling, I stripped off my clothes and headed to bed. I slept with the windows open and the sound of the ocean doing its best to lull me to sleep.

My eyes closed and I felt myself float toward sleep on a soft current. It only lasted for a minute as my brain conjured her face and then I was wide-awake and trying not to cry. They weren't nightmares, exactly, but they did keep me from ever getting a good night's sleep. Most of the time my job exhausted me so much that my body would sort of shut down anyway and I'd take a nap or two in the afternoon, but for the most part, I didn't sleep.

After trying about six different sleeping positions, I got up and grabbed a blanket to sit with on the couch. I was learning how to crochet, which kept my hands busy and my mind thinking about stitches and counting and making sure I didn't leave a hole. I was testing out different techniques on squares, and eventually I'd put them all together as a blanket. At least, that was the plan. I was only on the second square, and my squares didn't exactly look like the pictures, but at least I was doing something. I'd burned through so many hobbies in the last two years, including puzzles, wire jewelry, baking bread, and raising succulents, to keep myself sane. Barely.

I curled up on the couch for a few hours of rest before my alarm went off. It was still dark when I got up and got dressed. I kept my regular wardrobe separate from my work wardrobe. I had to. You could never get the stink of bait out of jeans, let me tell you. I actually kept my work clothes on the porch so they didn't funk up the house. I tossed my extra jacket, boots, and oil pants in a bag on the back of my bike, packed up some protein bars and a sandwich, coffee, and water for the day, sucked down a protein shake, and I was ready for work. My bag was already packed with the other essentials: sunblock, a hat, gloves, a portable charger for my phone, and a few tampons. Just in case.

I spared one glance for the house next door, but the lights were all off, since most normal people weren't awake at this hour. At first, it had been horrible, waking before the sun. Now I relished this quiet. I often spent entire days where I only had to communicate in a few words or grunts. That probably wasn't healthy, but it was working for me right now.

I headed down to the wharf to grab my dinghy and row out toward my boat. I wasn't alone, and shared a few nods and waves and grunts with my fellow cohorts. There weren't a whole lot of women on the water, but the guys had never really said much to me. I was sure they had talked behind my back, but no one said anything to my face. Not that I would have put up with any bullshit from them. I'd been telling men off my entire life and needed more practice.

My shoulders popped and cracked as I rowed out to my boat, named the *June Marie*. I'd bought it from a man who had named it for his wife and daughter, as many did, and I hadn't been able to come up with a better name, so I kept it. Maybe one of these days I'd change it to something like the *Salty Bitch*, but then that would mean I was staying here and the boat was mine and this was my life now. I didn't want this to be my life. I used to picture my life in so many different ways, and now it was a blank. I was stuck, but I couldn't find the way forward. I wanted to dream again. I just didn't know how. Back in the day, I'd planned on getting my MBA and then opening a coffee shop or a greenhouse or a bar. I didn't know what my business would be. I just knew that I wanted to work for myself, and that seemed like the way to do it. I'd been young and naïve then.

The *June Marie* roared to life and I steered it out of the harbor. The first few days like this on the water had been spent acclimating to the waves and the up-and-down motion of the boat, but somehow, my body had stopped fighting it and I wasn't puking over the side while trying not to hit a buoy or a seal.

I always played music on the boat, so I turned on my favorite playlist. Lizzo blasted from the small speakers I'd rigged up in the cabin. It was cold as fuck today, so I wrapped myself up and sucked down half of my thermos of coffee as the sun rose. The forecast was for temps in the eighties later, a rarity for Maine. Right now the air was downright frosty. That wasn't something I had bargained on when I started. I'd learned a lot since then. A bunch of the guys I'd hung out with in high school had worked for their dads, and I'd helped out once or twice, so I wasn't completely new to fishing. I'd still had to fumble my way through at first.

I reached my first buoy, which was painted white with a black stripe around the middle. I hadn't been very creative there, I had to admit. I set about the nasty job of throwing bait into bags to re-bait the trap, and then the business of hauling the trap up from the ocean floor. If I wasn't such a small operation (only fifty traps), I might have had help in the form of a sternman, but then I would have had to talk to someone, and that would have been the worst. I'd rather curse and struggle and take longer doing things on my own than hire someone else. Plus, I'd have to pay them and I was barely making it work as it was. At least I didn't have to pay a mortgage.

I lost myself in the rhythm of my work: bait, haul trap, pull out lobsters, measure, rubber band, re-bait, toss back in ocean.

By the time most people were getting up for work, I was almost halfway through my traps for the day. I had two rotations and alternated them every other day. My body had grown used to the physical work, but I would never get used to the smell of bait and diesel. No amount of showers seemed to remove the smell. Guess that was another bonus of having a sternman: someone else got to do the stinky jobs.

I had a decent haul and headed back to the lobster pound, where they'd buy the lobsters right from the boat, boil them in the restaurant upstairs, and serve them all in the same day. I also threw a few in a cooler on the back of the bike for myself, since it was cheaper than buying organic chicken at the grocery store.

I hosed myself off near the dock and decided to head home instead of hanging out to shoot the shit with the other lobstermen. Sometimes I lurked and they let me hang on the edges of their conversations, listening but not contributing. They didn't seem to mind, since we were all in the trenches together. I could have joined if I wanted to, but I'd never tried and the longer I didn't try, the harder it became.

I stopped quickly to fuel up the bike and grab a fresh-baked croissant and another huge black coffee at the only gas station in town. It was also a variety store, stocking everything from guns to gummies to wedding gowns. Seriously. I didn't know who was buying said gowns, but they had them anyway.

The lobsters went into the fridge out back before I stripped completely and ran for the shower. I honestly didn't care if the neighbors saw me dashing through the house after I abandoned my clothes in the doorway. I didn't used to, anyway. Maybe now I should care a little bit about a certain neighbor seeing me completely naked. No, I wasn't going to think about that. I wasn't going to think anything. I was just going to close my eyes and try and wash off the smell of dead fish guts and also not think about anything at all. Nothing. I wanted to think nothing.

I wanted to *be* nothing.

Don't miss Girl Next Door *by Chelsea M. Cameron,*
out now from Carina Adores.
www.CarinaPress.com

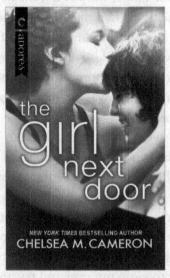